NE:B

WINGS OF RICHES

AL & JOANNA LACY

Multnomah® Publishers
Sisters, Oregon

This is a work of fiction. The characters, incidents, and dialogues are products of the author's imagination and are not to be construed as real. Any resemblance to actual events or persons, living or dead, is entirely coincidental.

WINGS OF RICHES
© 2005 by ALJO PRODUCTIONS, INC.

published by Multnomah Publishers, Inc.
International Standard Book Number: 1-59052-389-X

Cover image by Stephen Gardner, PixelWorks Studio.net

Scripture quotations are from:
The Holy Bible, King James Version

Multnomah is a trademark of Multnomah Publishers, Inc.,
and is registered in the U.S. Patent and Trademark Office.
The colophon is a trademark of Multnomah publishers, Inc.

Printed in the United States of America

ALL RIGHTS RESERVED
No part of this publication may be reproduced, stored in a retrieval system, or transmitted, in any form or by any means—electronic, mechanical, photocopying, recording, or otherwise—without prior written permission.

For information:
Multnomah Publishers, Inc., Post Office Box 1720, Sisters, Oregon 97759

Library of Congress Cataloging-in-Publication Data

Lacy, Al.
    Wings of riches / Al and JoAnna Lacy.
        p. cm. — (Dreams of gold trilogy ; bk. 1)
    ISBN 1-59052-389-X
    1. California—History—1846-1850—Fiction. 2. Gold mines and mining—Fiction. I. Lacy, JoAnna. II. Title.
    PS3562.A256W56 2005
    813'.54—dc22

                                                        2004019828

05 06 07 08 09 10 — 10 9 8 7 6 5 4 3 2 1 0

LAC
343 0528   9/25/06   ▬▬▬
cy, Al.

ings of riches

LNB

This book is dedicated to our dear Christian friends,
Steve and Eunice Ward,
and their precious children,
Amanda, Cori, and Kyle.
We love you!

2 CORINTHIANS 13:14

LeRoy Collins Leon Co.
Public Library System
200 West Park Avenue
Tallahassee, FL 32301

LeRoy Collins Leon Co.
Public Library System
200 West Park Avenue
Tallahassee, FL 32301

PROLOGUE

In this trilogy we call Dreams of Gold, we will tell the stories of three major gold strikes that took place in North America in the nineteenth century and changed this continent forever.

The first is the California gold strike in the late 1840s. The second is the Black Hills gold strike in the mid-1870s. The third is the Yukon gold strike in the late 1890s.

Gold is referred to very early in the Bible:

And a river went out of Eden to water the garden; and from thence it was parted, and became into four heads. The name of the first is Pison: that is it which compasseth the whole land of Havilah, where there is gold; and the gold of that land is good. —Genesis 2:10–12

Many people ask why man has valued gold so highly, practically ever since he has been on the earth. There are several reasons. Gold is good and highly prized because it is warmly beautiful. It is enduring, for it never dissolves away. Under all circumstances it retains its beauty.

Strong acids have no effect on it. Gold is the only metal that is unharmed by fire. In fact, each time gold goes through fire, it comes out more refined than before. It can be melted without harm, and it is marvelously adapted to shaping.

Finally, gold is prized so highly because of its scarcity. Being relatively rare makes it extremely valuable and much sought after. Hence, when gold was discovered in California, the Dakota Black Hills, and in the Klondike region of Yukon Territory in Canada, multitudes of gold seekers rushed to these places to make their fortunes. In this trilogy, we will tell some of their stories.

Gold is also mentioned at the very end of the Bible. In the book of Revelation, the most precious of metals is portrayed as constituting the New Jerusalem, with even its street made of gold so pure that it is transparent as glass. An angel was giving the apostle John a tour of the city in beatific vision, and even used a reed of gold to measure the city and its gates and walls.

> And he that talked with me had a golden reed to measure the city, and the gates thereof, and the wall thereof. And the building of the wall of it was of jasper: and the city was pure gold, like unto clear glass. And the twelve gates were twelve pearls, every several gate was of one pearl: and the street of the city was pure gold, as it were transparent glass. —Revelation 21:15, 18, 21

In between the beginning and the end of the Bible, gold is spoken of so many times that one must use a concordance to find all the references.

So often in the Bible, gold and the less precious metals are linked with money and other possessions that make men rich, and the pursuit of riches is tied to greed and covetousness which destroys lives. Riches are also spoken of in the Bible as often deceptive, unsatisfying, hurtful, and uncertain. Repeatedly in history, many of the superciliously wealthy have lost their fortunes in the blink of an eye.

These truths will be shown in the trilogy, and let each of us take note of what the Spirit of God told Paul to write to his son in the faith, Timothy:

> Charge them that are rich in this world, that they be not highminded, nor trust in uncertain riches, but in the living God, who giveth us richly all things to enjoy.
> —1 Timothy 6:17

INTRODUCTION

Gold in California! When gold was discovered on California's American River in January 1848, the news spread quickly throughout America and the entire world.

People were electrified to learn that on land newly wrested from Mexico, nuggets of gold were lying around on the ground. They heard that a man could quickly take a fortune out of the American River and connecting streams and from the surrounding hills with little more equipment than a shovel, a tin pan, and a contraption called a sluice baffle.

The astonishing news prompted hundreds of thousands of people from around the world to make preparations to travel to California in hopes of finding instant riches. The time to prepare and actually make the trip took many months. Hence, they took the name the *Forty-niners*, from the year the actual rush began—1849.

They sailed from Europe and South America, from China and Australia. Americans on the east coast of this country who were reluctant to travel by land all the way to the west coast chose instead to sail around the tip of South America, through the treacherous waters of Cape Horn and then north to San Francisco.

Americans who chose to travel westward by wagon and horseback made their way slowly and tediously over the land and across the wind-swept plains. Many ventured across the sweltering Great Salt Lake Desert. Others braved California's blistering Death Valley, and eventually they had to cross over the towering peaks of the Sierra Mountain Range.

Expectations were high that sudden wealth was within the grasp of every gold seeker. As our story will reveal, many great fortunes were won…and many were lost.

> Labour not to be rich: cease from thine own wisdom. Wilt thou set thine eyes upon that which is not? for riches certainly make themselves wings; they fly away as an eagle toward heaven. —Proverbs 23:4–5

ONE

It was Wednesday morning, November 10, 1847. A cold wind whipped along the street as hired buggy driver Willie Domire sat in his buggy on Broadway in downtown Manhattan, New York, his coat collar pulled up over his ears and his cap tugged tight on his head. In spite of his heavy coat, Willie felt the freezing wind pierce his joints. He breathed in the frigid air, wincing at the sharp crispness that stung his throat.

The dark brown gelding harnessed to Willie's buggy swished his tail, shook his head, and whinnied softly at the wind as it bit into his eyes and fluffed his mane.

Dark clouds filled with snow hovered over the city. Willie cast a glance above, waiting for the first snowflake to flutter down and ride the wind.

Willie's buggy was third in line in the hired buggy area in front of the tall office buildings on the east side of Broadway, which was near the north corner of the 3800 block. Located on the corner was the large building housing the offices and press rooms of the *New York Tribune.*

Men and women fought the wind, gripping their hats or

scarves and hurrying along the sidewalk, huddled into their coats. Their breath came out in small plumes.

Willie Domire watched them for a few minutes, then lifted his eyes once again overhead. *This is going to be a big storm once it gets started*, he thought. *Our first snowfall is late this year, but when it starts, I'm afraid it's going to be a furious one.*

Abruptly, newsboys pushed their way out the lobby doors of the *Tribune* building, carrying their portions of the morning edition. They tightened their shabby coats around themselves and pulled their colorful stocking caps low on their foreheads, covering their ears against the icy wind. They scurried toward their various corners along Broadway, hoping the papers would sell quickly so they could seek warm shelter.

Soon people were emerging from the nearby buildings and some of them were heading for the hired buggy area.

The two buggies ahead of Willie were quickly hired out, and he moved his buggy to the head of the line. Just as he tugged on the reins to stop his horse, he saw a familiar figure come out of the *Tribune* building and head toward him, signaling with a gloved hand.

The short, stocky thirty-seven-year-old founder and owner of the *New York Tribune* drew up to the buggy, and Willie smiled and said, "Good morning, Mr. Greeley."

Horace Greeley held onto his hat, bent his head against the arctic gale, and started to climb into the buggy. "Good morning to you too, Willie. Looks like we've got a big snowstorm coming in."

Before Willie could comment, a feminine voice pierced the air: "Stop that man! He has my purse!"

Greeley looked down the gravel sidewalk toward the sound of the frantic voice and caught sight of an unkempt young man running his direction with a black purse in his hand. The middle-aged woman who was crying for someone to stop the purse snatcher was scurrying after him. There were other men and women on the sidewalk, but Greeley was closest to the thief. Quickly, he stepped in front of the young man, raised his hands, and shouted, "Hold it right there!"

The thief tried to dodge Greeley, but Greeley met him head-on with a punch that lifted him off his feet and dropped him to the gravel on his back. The purse slipped from his hand.

Greeley's hat flew off and was carried away by the wind. A man on the street ran after it.

The purse snatcher lay on the sidewalk, dazed. Horace Greeley picked up the purse while looking at the frantic woman as she came closer. Several people hurried toward the scene from both directions.

Greeley smiled at the woman as she drew nearer, and at the same time, the purse snatcher rolled onto his knees, blinking and glaring with fire in his eyes at the man who had punched him.

The stout owner of the *New York Tribune* stabbed a stiff forefinger down at him and growled, "Stay right where you are!"

The thief rose to his feet, mumbling vile words. Greeley smashed him on the jaw with his right fist, then followed quickly with a left that caught him flush on the mouth. Without a sound, the thief went down flat on his back, unconscious. Two men pounced on him to hold him securely while another man shouted at a pair of mounted policemen who were just approaching Broadway from the closest intersection. The two officers put their horses to a gallop, making dust clouds on the dirt street.

The middle-aged woman glared down at the purse snatcher, then turned to Horace Greeley, who asked, "Are you all right, ma'am?"

A smile broke across her worn features as she nodded. "Oh,

yes, thank you. I know you! You're Mr. Greeley, the owner of the *Tribune*."

"Yes ma'am," he said as he handed her the purse.

Tears were in the woman's eyes. "Thank you, Mr. Greeley. Thank you so much for what you just did. My name is Helen Simmons."

The man who had chased down Greeley's hat stepped up and handed it to him. Greeley thanked him, and the man smiled, nodded, and slipped into the gathering crowd. There was a cacophony of voices as each person who had witnessed the incident told his or her version of what happened.

Helen Simmons raised her voice above the others and praised Greeley for his heroism. He blushed and said, "Mrs. Simmons, I simply did what needed to be done."

The two policemen drew up, left their saddles, and moved into the crowd. The voices grew louder as the witnesses began telling the officers what had happened.

One of the officers held up both hands, palms forward. "Hold on, now, folks! We can't understand a thing you're saying when you all talk at once! I've picked up that there was a purse snatching, and I see what looks to be the snatcher lying on the ground. Who's the victim, here?"

The petite, silver-haired Helen Simmons moved up to the officer. "I am, sir," she said in a soft, quavering voice. "My name is Helen Simmons." She pointed to the short, stocky man. "That's Mr. Horace Greeley. He's the one who put the thief down and retrieved my purse for me."

The officer smiled at Greeley. "I know him, ma'am. Good work, Mr. Greeley."

Greeley hunched his wide shoulders. "He was running right toward me, Officer O'Brien. Wasn't hard to stop him."

Frank O'Brien grinned, then he and his partner stepped to where the two men held the purse snatcher down. The guilty man was conscious now, though his eyes were glazed and blood was running from the cut on his lips.

The other officer, Clyde Hopper, bent over the thief and regarded him with a steady glare. "Just out of jail two days and you're right back at it, eh, Butch? Well, this time you'll be in a lot longer!"

The thief licked his bleeding lip, gave Officer Hopper a look of scorn, but said nothing.

By this time, a reporter from the *New York Herald,* which was located three blocks away, was on the scene. Clayton Hayman, pencil and paper pad in hand, had already picked up on what had happened. He stepped up beside Officer Frank O'Brien and said, "Seems you and your partner know the purse snatcher."

O'Brien nodded.

"What's his name?"

"Butch Kemper. He's been in trouble with the law time and again for being a thief and a robber. Recently finished a three-year sentence behind bars."

Hayman grinned as he wrote. "Butch Kemper. Mm-hmm. Seems I've heard that name before." He turned to the *Tribune* owner, who had just spotted two of his reporters standing close by. Hayman smiled. "Mr. Greeley, you are to be commended, sir, for single-handedly thwarting this crime."

Greeley made a thin smile, then set his gaze on the two *Tribune* reporters and shook his head as if to say, *Don't put this in the* Tribune.

Clayton Hayman then turned to the middle-aged woman, who was now standing once again at Greeley's side. "Ma'am, it was your purse that was snatched, correct?"

"Yes."

"And your name is…"

"I'm Helen Simmons, young man. My husband is Ralph Simmons, who owns the Simmons Pharmacy two blocks down the street."

Hayman was writing it down when Helen said, "If you're putting this in your paper, be sure to tell that Mr. Greeley is the hero, here."

At that moment the officers lifted Butch Kemper to his feet, cuffed his hands behind his back, and escorted him away. When they reached the horses, Kemper looked back over his shoulder and lanced Horace Greeley with hate-filled eyes.

Greeley met the hateful gaze with cool eyes, then turned and spoke to Hayman in a low voice. "Clayton, please don't put this incident in your paper."

Hayman smiled. "Mr. Greeley, what you did here was a very brave and unselfish thing. The people of New York need to hear about it. I see a couple of your own reporters here, and from what I've observed, you won't want the incident published in the *Tribune*."

"That's right."

"But I work for the *Herald*, and I'm going to see that we put it on the front page of tomorrow's edition."

"Good for you," said Helen. "Mr. Greeley is a hero, and the people of this city need to know it."

"That's right!" shouted a man in the crowd. "Print it!"

The rest of the crowd cheered Hayman and called out their agreement.

Greeley shook his head, smiled, and said, "Clayton…Mrs. Simmons…I must be going." He stepped to his two reporters and said so only they could hear, "Boys, the story is going into the

Herald, and there's nothing I can do about it. But I don't want it in our paper. It would look like I was trying to shower myself with glory. Understand?" Both men nodded and said they understood.

Greeley made his way back to the hired buggy area, where Willie Domire had waited for him. When the *Tribune* owner stepped up to the buggy, Willie said, "Mr. Greeley, that really was a brave thing for you to do. I'm proud of you."

Greeley blushed and stepped into the buggy. "I need to go to the Turley Department Store, Willie. And if you can wait for me while I get fitted for a couple of new suits, I'll make it well worth your while."

Willie pulled his coat collar up around his ears again and smiled. "As you wish, sir."

Willie put the horse in motion, pulled onto Broadway, and headed north. As they moved along with the other traffic, Willie spoke over his shoulder. "Mr. Greeley..."

"Yes?"

"Are you acquainted with Wallace Turley?"

"I am now, Willie. I had seen him at different social functions over the past few years, but actually became personally acquainted with him just a month ago, when I was asked to serve on the board of directors for the Bank of New York. Mr. Turley has been a director there for several years."

Willie guided the buggy around another buggy that was parking at the curb. "Doesn't Mr. Turley own other department stores somewhere?"

"Yes, he does. This store here in Manhattan where he has his main offices is the oldest and largest. His other stores are in Boston, Philadelphia, Providence, and Baltimore."

"Mr. Turley must be quite wealthy."

"That he is, but let me say that his wealth hasn't made him

snobbish and tight like happens to so many people who become rich. He's a fine gentleman. He's also very generous with his money and is a very pleasant person to be around."

Willie Domire thought to himself, *Just like you, Mr. Greeley.*

TWO

Traffic was heavy, and it took more than half an hour to reach Fifty-ninth Street. Just as Willie guided the horse onto Fifty-ninth, making a right turn, heavy flakes of snow began to fall.

Greeley said, "From the looks of those clouds, I'd say we're going to get a foot or more."

Willie nodded, keeping his eyes on the bread wagon just ahead of them. "At least a foot, Mr. Greeley."

Snow stuck to the horses' headgear and coats, coating them white like all of Manhattan. Stirred by what had become only a slight breeze, it drifted onto the walls and balconies of the tall buildings. Along the street, people stood in doorways and looked up at the gray sky and the falling flakes. By the time Willie Domire turned his buggy northward onto Fifth Avenue, the snow was heavy enough that it made a crunching sound beneath the wagon wheels.

At the Turley Department Store, fifty-one-year-old Wallace Turley stood at the large window in his third-floor office overlooking Fifth

Avenue. Gray light filtered into the room from the window as Wallace gazed down at the street, watching people on foot and wagons, carriages, and buggies make their way through the falling snow.

Wallace's thoughts went to his late wife, Edna. He remembered how much she loved the winters in the city, and how excited she always became when the first snowstorm appeared.

A tap on his office door interrupted his reverie. Wallace knew it was his secretary, Charlotte McClain, who was there to take dictation for several letters that needed to go out that day. He called over his shoulder for her to come in, took one more look at the falling snow, then turned around and headed for his desk.

Charlotte was carrying her notepad and pencil. With a smile, she said, "It's coming down pretty heavily, isn't it?"

He smiled in return. "Sure is. Edna would have loved it."

Charlotte sat down in her usual chair beside her boss's desk. "Yes, she sure would, Mr. Turley."

Wallace said, "Okay, Charlotte. The first letter is to Gerald Hyman, president of the Hyman Shoe Company in Chicago. You still have the address, I presume."

"Yes, sir."

Charlotte wrote in her own shorthand as Mr. Turley began what she knew was going to be a long letter. When he had dictated the first page, he left his chair and continued dictating as he ambled his way slowly to the large window. When he had been at the window long enough to dictate another page, he paused, looking down at the snow-laden street below.

After almost a minute of silence, Charlotte coughed softly. "Ah…let me make sure I got that last line right, Mr. Turley. You said—"

"I'm not sure what I said, Charlotte. I was thinking of Edna again."

As he returned to his desk with a sad look clouding his eyes, Charlotte was about to suggest they take up the dictation later when her attention was drawn to a well-dressed young man who appeared in the hallway at the open door of her office. She stood up and looked at her boss. "Please excuse me, Mr. Turley. There's someone at my office door."

"Of course," said Wallace, clearing his throat to ease the tightness that had gripped it.

Charlotte entered her office, smiling at the young man. "Good morning, sir. May I help you?"

The young man smiled. "Yes, ma'am. Could you tell me where I would find Craig Turley's office?"

"Of course. Craig's office is the very next one down the hall."

"Thank you, ma'am. My name is Peter Clark. Craig and I were in college together, and we haven't seen each other for some time."

"Well, I'm sure he'll be glad to see you."

"Not as glad as I will be to see him. Thank you."

As Peter Clark hurried out the door, Charlotte made her way back into her boss's office. He was still looking a bit melancholy. "That young man is a friend of Craig's from his college days. Mr. Turley, would you rather dictate your letters later?"

Wallace shook his head. "They need to go out right away. Sit down, and we'll take up where we left off."

Twenty-four-year-old Craig Turley was at his desk, going over some sales records of certain clothing items when he heard a knock at his door. He looked up and called, "Yes? Please come in."

When the door opened and he saw his old friend, Craig jumped up from his desk. "Peter!"

With a broad grin brightening his face, Peter looked at the lettering on the outside of the door's glass and said, "Wow, first vice president! Already a big shot!"

Craig grasped Peter's right hand and shook it vigorously.

Peter laughed as he said, "You ol' scalawag, it's good to see you."

"Likewise, my friend. The last I knew, you were unhappy with your job in Brooklyn and were trying to get on at that big architectural firm in Jersey City. Did you?"

Peter shook his head. "No, I didn't."

"Well, tell me about it. Close the door and let's sit over here on the sofa."

When they were seated on the small sofa facing each other, Peter said, "Well, after negotiating with the Jersey City firm for a while, I was offered the job and was about to take it when I learned that there was a position open at Bailey, Downing, and Smith here in Manhattan. I don't know if you've heard of them, but they're probably Manhattan's most prominent architectural firm. I applied for the job the third week of September and was hired on the spot. I've been wanting to get over here and see you, but I've been awfully busy. I got a little time off today, so here I am."

"Well, it's sure good to see you, and congratulations on getting the position."

"Thanks. I really like it there."

"Good! So, ah…are you still dating Lucinda Perkins?"

Peter shook his head. "No. Lucinda and I were about to get engaged, but she broke up with me when I started trying to land that job in Jersey City. She didn't want to leave New York."

"Well, if she wasn't willing to go to Jersey City with you, she really wasn't wife material."

"That's the way I look at it."

Craig paused a brief moment, then asked, "So are you seeing someone else now?"

"Not really."

"Well, a handsome, dashing young man like you will soon find another girl."

Peter laughed, then asked, "Have you found a steady girl yet?"

"No. I've got a few that I date now and then, but the right one just hasn't come into my life as yet. I figure Miss Right-for-Craig will come along one of these days, and from what I've been told, I'll know she's the right one when I get acquainted with her."

"That's what they tell me." Then Peter grinned and said, "Remember that weird little gal who had such a big crush on you in college? What was her name—uh—Cleora something."

Craig made a face. "Cleora Wuffel. Let's talk about some of the *good* memories from our college days."

As Willie Domire pulled his buggy up in front of the Turley Department Store, the light breeze scattered glittering snowflakes over the already-packed surface of the street and sidewalk.

Willie hopped out of the buggy and hurried through the falling snow to tie the reins to a hitching post. Horace Greeley stepped out onto the snow and carefully made his way to the sidewalk. Willie moved up to him and said, "I'll wait just inside the front door for you, Mr. Greeley."

Greeley nodded. "Fine, Willie. It's going to take a while, but like I said, I'll make it well worth your while."

Willie smiled and brushed snowflakes from his eyelashes. "You always do, sir. You always do."

crs

Wallace Turley was dictating his ninth letter to Charlotte McClain when she saw one of the clerks from the men's department enter her office from the hallway. "Just a minute, Mr. Turley," she said. "Chester Moore just came into my office."

Wallace looked through the open door and smiled at the young clerk as Charlotte called, "Come in, Chester."

Chester stepped up to Wallace's office door. "May I see you for a moment, sir? It's very important."

Wallace nodded. "Of course. Come on in, Chester."

The clerk moved up to his boss's desk. "Mr. Turley, I just fitted two new suits for Mr. Horace Greeley. He told me that you and he have become acquainted, and he said he'd sure like to see you if you had time."

Wallace Turley rose from his chair. "I sure *do* have time. Charlotte, we'll attend to these last three letters a bit later. I'm going down to see my new friend."

"Mr. Turley," said Chester, "if you'd rather talk to Mr. Greeley here in the office, I'll go down and bring him up."

"I appreciate your offer, Chester, but I'll go down and invite him to come up with me to the office."

"All right, sir."

Wallace smiled at Charlotte. "Take a little break, okay?"

"Yes, sir."

Moments later Wallace Turley and Chester Moore entered the men's clothing department just as Horace Greeley was coming out of one of the dressing rooms, carrying the two new suits on hangers.

Greeley's face lit up. He hurried to them, and Chester took the suits, saying, "We'll have these ready for you by noon tomorrow, Mr. Greeley."

Greeley thanked him, then grasped Wallace Turley's hand. As they shook hands, Turley said, "Come on up to my office, if you have time."

"I'd like that."

When they reached the third floor, Wallace guided Greeley into Charlotte's office and introduced him to her, then took his new friend into his office and closed the door. The two men sat down and were just beginning to chat when there was a tap on the door, and Wallace called for Charlotte to come in.

"Sorry to interrupt, Mr. Turley," she said, "but Craig has someone he wants you to meet. Remember I told you earlier that one of his friends from college was here to see him?"

"Yes."

"Well, his name is Peter Clark, and Craig wants to introduce you to him."

Wallace smiled. "Of course. Send them in."

When the two young men entered, Craig introduced Peter to his father, and then Wallace introduced the young men to Horace Greeley. The young men stayed another couple of minutes, then after they left, Wallace said to Charlotte, "Would you please send someone to the lunch room and have them bring up a pot of coffee and some scones for Mr. Greeley and me?"

"Yes, of course," she said, rising from her chair. "I'll go myself, and have the coffee and scones to you in just a few minutes."

Wallace went back to his office and found Greeley standing at the large window, looking down at the snow-laden street.

"That son of yours is a fine looking young man, Wallace," Greeley said.

"Thank you, Horace. I'm pretty proud of him." Wallace moved up beside Greeley and said, "Looks like this first snowstorm is going to be a good one."

"I'd say so. But I love the snow. It always makes everything look so pure and clean."

A melancholy smile touched Wallace's lips. "You know, that's exactly what my late wife used to say about snowfall. It makes everything look so pure and clean."

Surprise showed in Greeley's eyes. "I didn't know your wife was…gone."

Wallace nodded. "Edna died giving birth to our daughter Madeline—Maddie—ten years ago, when Craig was fourteen."

"Oh. I'm sorry to hear that, Wallace. So you've never remarried?"

"No. I—"

"Here are the scones and the coffee, Mr. Turley." Charlotte entered the office and placed the tray that held coffeepot, cups, and scones on an end table next to the large sofa.

Wallace thanked her, and Charlotte hurried back to her office, closing the door behind her.

While the two men enjoyed their refreshments, Wallace told Horace a bit more about Maddie, then said that he had sent Craig to New York University where he majored in business administration. Upon Craig's graduation, Wallace made him first vice president, replacing his previous first vice president, who had died of heart failure just ten days before Craig's graduation. Wallace said he planned to turn the business over to Craig in another ten to twelve years.

They chatted for a few more minutes, then Greeley stood up and said he needed to get back to his office.

"Thanks for telling my clerk that you wanted to see me," Wallace said. "I'd like to invite you and Mrs. Greeley to dinner at my home sometime soon."

Horace smiled. "Well, my friend, Genevieve and I would love

to come to the Turley house for dinner. She was very pleased when I told her that I had met you."

"I'll check my schedule and get back to you soon."

Craig Turley and Peter Clark were chatting once again in Craig's office. Peter talked excitedly about his new job and his hope that one day, after he had really learned the business, he would step out and start his own architectural firm.

"Well, I commend you for having that goal in your life," Craig said. "I'm sure with the way New York City is growing, you'll be a big success with your own business one day."

Peter smiled. "Thank you, Craig. Now, let's talk about *you*. It must be a thrill to be first vice president in the Turley Department Store at such a young age."

Craig sighed and shook his head. "No, not really."

"What! How can this be?"

"Peter, I have a wonderful father, and I love him dearly, but I don't like living under his shadow. Everyone knows I was born with a silver spoon in my mouth. My father's a multimillionaire. So I'm the 'rich kid' who has it easy in life. And, of course, I was made first vice president in the corporation simply because of who I am. I want to get away from my father and the corporation and become wealthy on my own. I want to make my own way in the world and produce my own success."

Peter frowned. "I won't try to hide that I'm a bit shocked, Craig. Do you have some plan in mind?"

"I can't say that I have any particular plan, no. I'm not sure yet what I'm going to do. But one of these days I'll come up with a solution and strike out on my own."

Peter took a deep breath and let it out slowly. "Well, my

friend, I hope your goal works out the way you envision it. Most young men would give their eyeteeth to be in your position, with most everything handed to them."

Craig pulled at his left ear thoughtfully. "I know. And maybe I'm being foolish, but there's a restlessness inside of me to try my own wings, so to speak, and see where it takes me."

Peter nodded. "Well, I hope it works out for you, Craig. Stay in touch. I'll be interested to hear all about your new adventure."

"I'll do it."

Craig walked Peter to the office door, and they shook hands, agreeing to get together again someday soon.

THREE

In late afternoon, Craig Turley was at his desk in his office when he recognized Charlotte McClain's tap on his door. He called for her to enter.

She opened the door just enough to stick her head in and said, "Your father told me to let you know that he's ready for you to go to the bank."

Craig smiled at her. "Tell him I'll be there in just a minute."

Craig placed a paperweight on the business letter he had been reading and put on his overcoat and hat.

Moments later, he entered Charlotte's office. She looked up from her desk and said, "He's expecting you."

Craig made his way to his father's office door, tapped on it, and called, "Dad, it's me."

"Come in, son," Wallace Turley responded.

When Craig stepped in, his father was moving toward the door, carrying a leather valise. "Here you go, Craig. Charlotte made up the deposit, so it's ready. I realize it's a bit late, so hurry."

"Don't worry, Dad. I'll be back in plenty of time to ride home with you."

Moments later, Craig stepped out into the falling snow, greeted two businessmen he knew, and made his way to the curb. There were hired buggies in the parking places along the side of the street, but he saw a hired buggy drawing near with no passengers aboard, and waved at the driver.

The driver guided the buggy to where Craig stood and said, "Climb aboard, sir."

When Craig was easing onto the rear seat, the driver looked over his shoulder and smiled. "Where to, sir?"

"Bank of New York, please."

"Yes, sir."

As the buggy pulled away from the curb and slipped into traffic, Craig said, "Some snow we're getting, eh?"

"Sure is."

"I don't think I've ever ridden with you before. Are you new here?"

"No, sir. I've driven a buggy for this company right here in Manhattan for nearly five years. I guess in a city this large, some people never see each other. My name's Stuart Rollins. My friends call me Stu."

"Glad to meet you, Stu. My name is Craig Turley."

Stu glanced back at his passenger. "*Turley?* You mean—"

"Yes. I'm first vice president of the Turley Department Store. My father's the president."

Stu nodded, let a slight grin curve his lips, then put his attention back on the traffic ahead.

Some ten minutes later, they were slowly passing the Broadway Tabernacle in the heavy traffic, and a large crowd was gathered on the sidewalk in front. Craig's attention was drawn to a familiar face. Horace Greeley stood on the covered porch of the building, next to a tall, slender, balding man, who was speaking to the crowd.

Craig pulled his coat collar up tighter around his neck and said to the driver, "I wonder what's going on. I recognize Horace Greeley standing there on the porch of the church beside the speaker. For a large crowd like that to stand out there on this cold, snowy day, that man must really have some important message for them."

"That he does," replied Stu. "The man speaking is the pastor of Broadway Tabernacle, Charles G. Finney. I go to church over in Queens, but I have a friend who belongs to Broadway Tabernacle, and I've visited there a few times. My friend told me last week that Pastor Finney is leading a crusade in Manhattan against a new tavern being built on the corner of Broadway and Fifty-second Street. In addition to being a great gospel preacher, Pastor Finney is an unrelenting foe against liquor, as is Horace Greeley."

Craig adjusted his position on the seat. "It doesn't surprise me that Finney and Greeley are crusading against the tavern together. I know from reading Greeley's newspaper that he's an enemy of tobacco and gambling, as well as liquor. I imagine that Finney is also against tobacco and gambling."

Stu glanced over his shoulder and nodded. "He sure is."

Soon the scene in front of the church passed from view, and less than fifteen minutes later, Stu drew the buggy up in front of the Bank of New York, saying, "Here you are, Mr. Turley."

As he was climbing out of the buggy, Craig said, "I won't be in there very long. Can you wait for me?"

"Sure. I'll be right here."

When Craig neared the front door of the bank, his attention was drawn to two newsstands only a few feet apart where teenage boys were selling the afternoon editions of the *New York Tribune* and the *New York Herald*.

The newsboys stomped their feet to help keep them warm as

they held their newspapers aloft, drawing attention from the people passing by.

The boy selling the *Herald* waved a folded copy of it and shouted, "Read all about it! Read all about it! Horace Greeley is a hero! He foiled a purse snatching this morning, and the thief is now in jail!"

Craig stepped up to the young man selling the *Tribune* and looked at him quizzically. "I don't hear you shouting about your boss's heroic deed being in your paper. Is the *Tribune* carrying the story?"

The boy shook his head. "No, sir."

"Well, I would expect Mr. Greeley's paper to tell of his deed."

The boy hunched his shoulders. "One of the reporters told me Mr. Greeley wouldn't let them print the story. He didn't want to appear to be glorifying himself."

Craig nodded. "Well, sure. I hadn't thought about that." He stepped over to the other boy, bought a copy of the *Herald*, and hurried into the bank.

Wallace Turley looked up from his desk when his son came in with the valise in his hand. "Well, you made good time in spite of the storm, Craig."

Craig grinned as he placed the valise on his father's desk. "I told you I'd be back in plenty of time to ride home with you." As he spoke, he unfolded the newspaper he was carrying and flashed the front page at him. "Take a look at this."

Wallace's attention went to the bold headline containing the name "Horace Greeley." He took the paper from Craig's hand and quickly read the article, then grinned and shook his head. "Well, whaddaya know!"

"I imagine Mr. Greeley is quite the hero in that lady's eyes."

"Without a doubt," said Wallace, folding the paper and laying it on his desk on the way to his closet. "Well, son, we'd better be going. Harold is probably down in front by now."

The clouded sky was growing dark when Wallace and Craig stepped out of the building and moved up to the Turley carriage, where their gardener, yard man, general handyman, and carriage driver, Harold Wilkins, was lighting the carriage's two lanterns.

Harold, a sixty-five-year-old widower, greeted both men, then said, "Looks like the snow is letting up some."

"That's fine with me," said Wallace as he climbed into the carriage. "Enough is enough. Especially for the season's first snow."

Craig moved in beside his father. Harold climbed into the driver's seat and put the carriage in motion.

As they headed toward the Turley mansion on Columbus Avenue in the Central Park West section of Manhattan, Wallace held up the newspaper in his hand and said, "Craig, I like what I read here. But I'm not surprised Horace Greeley would do something like that."

Harold glanced over his shoulder and noted the newspaper in Wallace's hand. "Something about Horace Greeley in the paper, Mr. Turley?"

"Mm-hmm. And interestingly enough, it isn't in the *Tribune*, but in the *Herald.*"

"What's it about, sir?"

Wallace and Craig together told Harold the story.

Craig turned to his father. "Dad, I saw Mr. Greeley on my way to the bank this afternoon. He was on the porch of the Broadway Tabernacle with Pastor Charles Finney, who was speaking to a large crowd in an effort to get them to write letters to the mayor in protest of the proposed tavern on the corner of Broadway and Fifty-second Street."

"Well, good for Pastor Finney and good for Mr. Greeley," Wallace said. "I appreciate their efforts. Tell you what, son, one of these Sundays I ought to take you and Maddie to hear Pastor Finney preach. I've never heard him myself, but I'm told he's very good."

When the carriage turned into the Turley's driveway, the mansion's windows were aglow with lamplight, and a small figure could be seen peering out the large parlor window between the draperies.

Father and son smiled at each other. Maddie was always aware of the time each day that her father and big brother should arrive home. In warm weather, she stationed herself on the front porch to greet them.

Inside the mansion, Maddie watched the lantern-lit carriage draw up to the porch and noted that the snow was still falling, but not as heavily as earlier. The trees were bare of leaves now, but the snow gilded the branches.

Maddie headed toward the parlor door and saw her governess, twenty-year-old Kathy Ross, standing in the hall. "Kathy, it looks like a fairyland outside, and here comes the carriage! Papa and Craig are home!"

Kathy smiled as she watched the ten-year-old dash from the parlor and up to the ornate front door. Maddie pulled the handle down, and opened the door just as her father and brother were coming across the large porch.

When Wallace and Craig stepped inside, Maddie dashed to her father and embraced him while Craig closed the door.

Holding his daughter in his arms, Wallace kissed the top of her head and said, "Hello there, Maddie my love. What a nice welcome home!"

Smiling up at him, Maddie said, "Papa, we got lots of snow, didn't we?"

"We sure did, though it's letting up some now."

"Uh-huh. I was worried, though. Snow on the streets can be dangerous. I wanted you and Craig to make it home safely."

"Well, honey, we weren't in any danger. Harold's a good driver, you know, and you needn't have worried."

Maddie backed up a couple of steps, and putting her weight on one foot then the other, said, "I know Harold's a good driver, but you're the only papa I've got, and Craig is the only brother I've got, and I'm glad you're home!"

Craig smiled at his little sister and opened his arms. "Come here, you little squirt, and give me a hug."

With adoration in her big blue eyes, the little blonde rushed into her brother's arms and hugged him tight.

Kathy welcomed both men home and said, "Well, gentlemen, Elizabeth has dinner nearly ready. We'd best move in that direction."

Also in the Turley household were cook Elizabeth Loysen and housekeeper Adelle Brown. Both were spinsters in their mid-fifties. Elizabeth and Adelle's living quarters were at the rear of the mansion on the ground floor, and Harold Wilkins's living quarters were on the second floor of the combination carriage house, horse barn, workshop, and tool shed behind the mansion.

When Wallace, Craig, Maddie, and Kathy entered the kitchen where the cook, housekeeper and handyman were, Wallace showed them the article in the *New York Herald* about Horace Greeley stopping the purse snatcher. He then told them about Craig seeing the crowd in front of the Broadway Tabernacle, Horace Greeley beside the pastor, and what Charles Finney was challenging the crowd to do.

Adelle said, "Good for him! Liquor is a curse on mankind!"

"Tell you what," said Wallace. "I'm going to invite Mr. Greeley and his wife, Genevieve, to dinner very soon. I mentioned it to Mr. Greeley, and he said they would love to come." He turned to the cook. "Elizabeth, you and I will get together and set a date for it, okay?"

"Certainly. I would love to prepare a special meal for the Greeleys." She paused. "And by the way, tonight's dinner is almost ready."

Wallace smiled. "Just give us a few minutes, will you, Elizabeth? I'd like to freshen up, and I think Craig would, too." He sniffed the air. "From the delicious aroma permeating my senses, I can scarcely wait to taste this meal! We'll be back in less than twenty minutes."

"Yes, sir," said Elizabeth, smiling. "But no more than twenty minutes!"

Father and son hurried from the kitchen and made their way up the wide spiral staircase.

Kathy put a tender hand on Maddie's shoulder. "How about you and me going to the parlor for these few minutes? You can practice your piano lesson while we wait."

"Good idea," said Maddie.

Minutes later, the mansion was filled with beautiful music.

On Friday evening November 19, Wallace and Craig Turley welcomed Mr. and Mrs. Horace Greeley at the front door of the mansion. Maddie and her governess waited at the rear of the foyer while Horace and Genevieve chatted with the two men, then Wallace motioned for his daughter and her governess to step up, and introduced them to the Greeleys.

Maddie curtsied politely and told them how happy she was to meet them, and Kathy spoke warm words, welcoming them.

During dinner, Genevieve looked at Wallace with compassion and said, "Mr. Turley, Horace explained to me about your dear wife dying when she gave birth to Maddie. I'm so sorry for your loss."

Wallace set his coffee cup down and gave her a wan smile. "Thank you, ma'am. Even though it's been ten years, I still miss her like she just died yesterday."

"Wallace, I'm quite impressed with your servants, and with Kathy," Horace said. "How long has each one been with you?"

"Well, Elizabeth has been with us the longest. Thirteen years. Harold has been here for eleven years, and Adelle ten years. Adelle had been with us just a month when Edna died. Maddie's previous governess decided to retire a couple of years ago and live with her daughter and son-in-law in Boston. Shortly thereafter, I hired Kathy, who was eighteen at the time. Her parents live in Jersey City. She had just graduated from finishing school, having trained to be a governess. I had an ad in both New York newspapers, seeking a governess. Kathy saw it, contacted me, came here at my invitation to talk about the job, and I hired her on the spot." He grinned and looked at Maddie. "Sure am glad I did. My daughter and her governess love each other very much, and are very close."

A merry twinkle captured Maddie's blue eyes and a bright smile spread over her face as she looked at the Greeleys, then at Kathy.

Kathy reached across the corner of the table and tweaked Maddie's nose.

Maddie giggled, then looked back at the Greeleys. "Kathy is not only my tutor for my schoolwork, she's also giving me piano lessons. She's also teaching me how to conduct myself properly as a young lady."

Genevieve smiled at Kathy. "I haven't heard Maddie play the piano, Miss Ross, but from what I've observed here this evening, I must say that you're doing a wonderful job."

"That she is," Wallace said. He then turned the conversation to Horace's standing by Pastor Charles Finney in his battle against the liquor crowd, and commended him for it.

Greeley smiled. "Thank you, Wallace. I think a great deal of Pastor Finney. I'd like to introduce you to him sometime."

Wallace nodded. "I'd really like to meet him."

Maddie got a foxy look in her eyes and said, "Papa, we could meet Pastor Finney real easy if we visited his church."

Wallace smiled at her. "We'll just do that sometime soon, sweet stuff. I'd really like to see if Pastor Finney is as good a preacher as so many people have told me he is."

When dinner was finished, Kathy looked at Wallace and said, "Maddie and I need to be excused. She has some school lessons she needs to finish."

"Of course," said Wallace. "You may be excused."

Kathy arose from her chair and Maddie followed suit.

Horace Greeley stood up, as did Wallace and Craig.

Kathy ran her gaze between Horace and Genevieve and said, "It was certainly a pleasure to meet you, Mr. and Mrs. Greeley."

Maddie smiled at the couple and said, "I am very happy to have met you, Mr. and Mrs. Greeley."

Horace and Genevieve both spoke of their pleasure in having made the acquaintance of Maddie and Kathy, and the two young ladies passed through the dining room door, holding hands.

Once in the hallway, Maddie let go of Kathy's hand and started skipping toward the spiral staircase. Kathy hurried to catch up to her. She caught her just as Maddie reached the bottom of the stairs, pinched an ear playfully, and said in a hushed voice, "Miss Turley, will you ever learn to just walk instead of skip, hop, and run?"

Maddie giggled. "Oh, maybe when I'm an *old* lady like *you*, Miss Ross!"

Kathy giggled too, and arm in arm, they mounted the stairs together.

FOUR

On Saturday morning, November 20, in Sacramento, California, thirty-six-year-old James Marshall, foreman at Sutter's Mill, walked past his office and the other buildings and made his way toward the bank of the American River some thirty yards away.

The cool air, fragrant with the sweet scent of oak and cypress trees, and some subtle nameless tang, made Marshall glad he lived in that part of northern California. When he reached the bank of the swift-moving river, he put his hands on his hips and breathed slowly and deeply.

The morning sun was just lifting its upper rim above the eastern elevations, sending its bright golden shafts between the towering trees.

Sutter's Mill was positioned at the confluence of two rushing streams—on the east bank of the Sacramento River and the south bank of the American River. Because the mill was closer to the bank of the American River, the mill's boat docks had been built on its bank.

The city of Sacramento was situated in a valley the local

Indians called *Coloma*. The American River entered the valley from the southeast and was the principal tributary to the Sacramento River.

The bottom of the valley was essentially flat, with sandy soil covered by grass and low shrubs. The sides of the valley were dissected by ravines that ran full in rainy weather. Oak trees were scattered about the lower slopes, with cypress trees among them. Higher up the ridges, pine trees dominated the land. The abundant forests provided Sutter's Mill with plenty of timber.

The steepness of the American River's riverbed in the valley was such that the stream moved along at a brisk pace. Averaging fifty yards wide, the American made a forceful, insistent blustering sound that unobtrusively filled the valley day and night. In some wider places it was shallow enough for men and horses to wade across. When fifty yards wide—as at Sutter's Mill—it ran deeper and more powerfully.

Marshall spotted a thirty-foot-long boat coming southward along the American River, then he turned and looked back toward the mill. Three men were arriving for work together in a wagon, and two more employees rode toward the mill on horseback. So far, however, the man he was waiting for was not in sight. He told himself it was early yet.

Marshall heard the sound of the boat's steam engine and turned back to observe it. As it drew nearer, he focused on the man in the boat. It was Carey Slovis, who managed the general store for John Sutter at Sutter's Fort, some forty miles south of the mill on the American River. He obviously had been in Sacramento to load up on groceries and supplies for the store. Carey let go of the steering wheel with one hand and waved, calling out, "James! Hello!"

James lifted his hand and smiled. He was watching Carey pilot the boat on downstream when he saw Tim Benson, his newly hired assistant, coming toward the river from the mill. Tim smiled as they met up and said, "Good morning, boss. I'm ready for school."

"Okay, Tim. Let's head on up the bank here."

As they moved along together with the sound of the rushing river in their ears, James said, "Tim, do you know what a race is?"

"Well…yes, sir. It's when two or more people try to outrun each other."

James chuckled. "Well, that's one kind of race. But the race I'm referring to is a swift current of water, or the channel of such a current. In other words, it's a watercourse made for industrial purposes. When you use the power of fast-flowing channeled water to drive big timber saws, it's much better than using the strength of men like is done in the forest."

"I've heard of using moving water to empower a saw, but I'd never heard of a *race*."

James nodded. "I knew enough about it that when John Sutter hired me to build and oversee the sawmill, I decided to enlist the force of this river to drive the saws."

They were drawing near the narrow channel where water taken from the American River ran swift and strong. As they came to it and stopped, James said, "This is the race, Tim. We call this portion of it above the mill the *headrace*." He pointed back down the channel. "The portion below the mill where the water flows back into the river is called the *tailrace*."

"All right. The *headrace* and the *tailrace*."

"Every morning before starting up the six big saws in the mill house, I come here to the race and make sure the water is flowing as it should. I always start at the headrace and walk along the edge of the channel all the way to the tailrace to make sure no obstruction of any kind has found its way into the water. We need it running at full power for the saws."

"That makes sense."

"It has to look exactly as you see it right now, Tim."

Tim ran his eyes up and down the channel. "Yes, sir."

"When I inspect it, once I know all is clear, I go back into the mill and tell the men to start sawing lumber. You need to know all of this because, as assistant foreman, it'll be your job whenever I have to be away, which happens periodically."

At that moment, they saw a large boat drawing up to the docks.

Leading Tim in that direction along the gurgling channel, James said, "I expect this is someone wanting to buy lumber."

Before they reached the docks, they saw a man leave the boat and enter the mill house. Moments later, when James and Tim stepped inside the mill house, one of the men was talking to the stranger, and pointing at James Marshall.

James said, "Tim, go inform the men at the big saws that they can begin their work. I'll go talk to this customer."

The mill worker who had pointed James out was leading the stranger to him. When they drew up, the mill worker introduced the man as Frank Compton, and hurried away toward the saws. Marshall judged the man to be in his early sixties.

Marshall and Compton shook hands, then Compton told the foreman he was from the Gifford Construction Company in San Francisco, and wanted to purchase a load of lumber.

"All right, sir," said James. "Let's go to my office."

As Compton followed the foreman in that direction, he said, "Tell me about your employer, John Sutter, Mr. Marshall. He has interested me ever since I learned that he owns both Fort Sutter and this mill. I did learn not long ago that Mr. Sutter came to this country from Switzerland. Is he Swiss?"

"No, sir. He was actually born in Germany."

"When did he come to this country?"

"In 1834. But he didn't arrive in California until 1839. Mr. Sutter wanted to establish himself well in California. He persuaded the governor to award him a grant of some fifty thousand acres of land. The governor did so, and the granted land lay in the fertile central valley east of San Francisco Bay along the American River. There, Mr. Sutter built a stockade-type building on the riverbank. He had been a captain in the Swiss army, and liked the military feel of things, so he made it look like a fort and, as you know, even called it a fort."

Compton chuckled. "So that's why it's called a fort."

"Yes," said Marshall as they entered his office. "And you probably know he even calls himself Captain Sutter."

"Mm-hmm. And now I know why."

"Have a seat there in front of my desk, Mr. Compton."

When both men had sat down, Compton said, "Before we talk business, tell me the rest of the story on John Sutter. He established Sutter's Fort in 1839, right?"

"Right."

"And when did he establish this mill? It hasn't been very long ago, has it?"

"No. It was established early this year. In the latter part of 1846, he decided that he also wanted a sawmill to provide lumber for the growing population of northern California. He and I met at a social function in San Francisco in December of last year. When he learned that I was a master carpenter and that I knew something about using swift-moving water to power wood saws, he hired me to find the right spot to build the mill. When I spotted this location, he loved it, and when we were about to finish the mill house and install the equipment, he offered me the job of foreman. I gladly accepted. By early spring, the mill was in business."

Compton rubbed his chin. "Well, it sure looks like Captain John Sutter is doing all right."

"That he is, sir. And I'm plenty glad to be a part of what he's doing."

"I can see why, Mr. Marshall. Well, let's get down to business."

Twenty minutes later, the two men left the office. Marshall took Compton to some of his men and told them to load his boat with a large order of lumber. The two men shook hands, and Marshall went back to his office.

It was almost noon in Sacramento. Marshal Jack Powell was sitting at his desk in his office and looked up to see his pastor, Richard Skiver, coming through the door. He rose to his feet and said, "Howdy, Pastor. Something I can do for you?"

Skiver removed his hat, exposing a thick head of silver hair, and said, "No. I was just passing by and saw you through the window. Decided I'd just come in and say hello."

The marshal shook his hand and said, "Well, Pastor, you're always welcome to stop by anytime. And since you're here, I want to tell you again how much I enjoyed that sermon last Sunday night. I love to hear preaching on the cross, and you brought out a couple of things I'd never realized happened at Calvary."

"Well, it's a feather in my cap when I can teach an intelligent lawman like you something!"

The two men laughed together, then the pastor looked around and said, "Your deputies aren't here?"

"No. There was a burglary at the Yoder ranch east of town last night. I sent Cade out to investigate, and I told Jarrod to go with him so Cade could teach him how to make a burglary investigation."

The pastor nodded. "Deputy Cade Ryer can teach him well, I'm sure." He noted the time on the back wall of the office. "Well, Jack, I'd better head for the parsonage. Rosie will skin me alive if I'm late for lunch."

"I sure wouldn't want that to happen!" As the marshal walked his pastor to the door, he said, "I'll see you and Rosie this evening at our house for dinner."

The preacher put his hat on as Jack opened the door for him. "Rosie and I are looking forward to being there. Your sweet missus is some kind of cook!"

"Don't I know it!"

Marshal Jack Powell returned to his desk and was just getting back to his paperwork when a loud voice from outside penetrated the walls.

"Hey! Jack Powell! Come out here! We wanna talk to you!"

Jack looked through the window and saw three long-haired, unkempt men standing in the dusty street just off the boardwalk. Each one had a low-slung, tied-down holster containing a pearl-handled Colt .45 revolver. They looked a great deal alike, and he figured they had to be brothers.

His mind went back to the day two weeks previously when a lone long-haired man who strongly resembled these three walked up to him on the street when he was about to enter the hardware store...

Jack spotted the demonic look in the man's eyes as he stepped up to block his way from entering the hardware store. He stopped and, meeting his gaze, said, "Pardon me. I'm going into the store, here."

The man took another step toward him, hostility in his eyes. "So you're the hotshot marshal of this town. S'posed to be lightnin' with that gun on your hip," he snarled.

Jack kept his own voice level and held the gunman's wicked gaze. "I don't know who you are, mister, but you smell like trouble to me. Now, I'm going to give you three minutes to clear out of town. If you aren't, I've got an uncomfortable jail cell waiting for you. Wherever your horse is, get on it and ride. Now!"

People on the street were collecting in small groups and looking on. Fear was evident on their faces. They had seen their marshal challenged before.

The gunman pulled his lips tight over his tobacco-stained teeth and spoke with a gravelly voice as he took a few steps backward, lowering his hand over his gun. "I'm challengin' you, Powell. Go for your gun."

"Best you do as I tell you, mister, whoever you are."

"Name's Uben Hacker, Powell." He ran his eyes to the people gathered around. "I want all of you to remember my name: *Uben Hacker!* I'm the one who's gonna put this hotshot lawman down. Tell all your friends…and enemies, for that matter. Uben Hacker outgunned the famous tin star, Jack Powell!"

With that, Hacker's hand went for his gun. He barely had it out of the holster when Powell's gun roared. Hacker took the slug dead center in his chest, and was dead before he hit the boardwalk…

Jack again noted that the three men outside his office all resembled Uben Hacker. He knew from the look in their eyes that they wanted vengeance for the death of their brother. He wished Deputies Cade Ryer and Jarrod Benson were there, but he knew he had to go out and face these men alone.

A brisk wind now whistled down the street.

The marshal breathed a prayer for God's protection and loosened his gun in its holster. He walked to the door, pulled it open, and stepped onto the boardwalk, facing them. He thought how odd it was that the smell of blood went with the wind and how the impulse of violence flowed along the street.

FIVE

People on the street had heard the loud shout demanding that Marshal Jack Powell come outside, and they stopped to watch, wide-eyed and tense, as Marshal Powell silently ran his cold gaze over the faces of the three rough-looking men.

As the marshal stepped off the boardwalk, a sudden quiet came over the crowd. For a moment there was a deathly silence. The only sound anyone in the crowd could hear besides the whine of the wind was their own thunderous heartbeat.

The Hacker brothers stood restive, their gun hands dangling over the handles of their holstered revolvers, their eyes fixed on the stolid face of Marshal Jack Powell.

Intent on the three gunmen and the marshal who faced them, no one in the crowd noticed the two riders with badges on their vests riding into town. Deputies Cade Ryer and Jarrod Benson quietly pulled rein and dismounted some fifty feet from the edge of the crowd, their eyes fixed on the scene in front of the marshal's office.

The oldest of the three brothers, who stood between the other two, said, "You know who we are, marshal?"

Jack Powell fixed the man with unflinching eyes and said, "All three of you resemble a man who drew on me and forced me to kill him a couple of weeks ago. You must be Uben Hacker's brothers."

"Yeah, you've got it right. I'm Urich Hacker. The brother here on my right is Ulak, and the one on my left is Unid. Just thought I ought to introduce us before we gun you down for killin' Uben."

In spite of the brilliant noonday sun, death hung over Sacramento's Main Street like a black pall.

Suddenly the sharp voice of Deputy Ryer sliced through the whine of the wind: "Hold it right there!"

Every eye flicked toward the deputy. The crowd scattered like frightened sheep, diving behind wagons and buggies parked along the street and plunging through the doors of nearby shops.

The surprised trio looked toward the sound of the voice and saw the grim-faced Deputy Ryer, sided by an equally grim-faced Deputy Benson. Both lawmen had their guns drawn, cocked, and aimed at the Hacker brothers.

"Listen to me!" Ryer said with even more bite in his tone. "All three of you reach down real slow-like, unbuckle your gunbelts, let them fall to the ground, and raise your hands over your heads!"

A scowl formed on Urich Hacker's face. Below his bushy, grizzled mustache, his lips made a firm, long line. Barely moving them, he whispered to his brothers, "Those tin stars won't open fire with all those people at the windows and behind the wagons and buggies. Let's take 'em out. Ulak, you get the marshal. Unid and I will get those smart-aleck deputies."

Instantly, the Hacker brothers whipped out their weapons.

The deputies' six-guns thundered a fractional fatal fragment of a second ahead of the gunmen's weapons, followed by the repeated roar of Marshal Powell's Colt .45.

Urich's gun exploded wildly, sending the slug into the dust of the street as a bullet ripped into his heart. He went down like a pole-axed steer.

Ulak took two slugs in the forehead. The jerk of his head loosened his hat, and as he was going down, it fell off to let a mane of dirty, matted hair shake loose around his temples.

Unid took three bullets in his chest and one in his left shoulder. The impact lifted him off his feet and hurled him backward as if he had been swatted by some enormous invisible giant. He hit the ground with a loud *whump* and lay still in the grasp of death.

The marshal holstered his smoking Colt .45 and met his two deputies where the bodies of the gunmen lay. He gave them a grim smile and said, "I'm sure glad you two showed up when you did."

The people who had dashed for cover stepped out from behind the wagons and buggies, while the others came out of the shops, their faces pale.

Cade Ryer holstered his smoking gun, looked down at the corpses, then at the marshal. "I'm sure glad we got back here when we did, too, boss."

At the Powell home, because of the number of people Jack and Carrie had invited for dinner that evening, Carrie had asked their fifteen-year-old son, Randy, and eleven-year-old son, Darin, to bring an extra table into the dining room from the back porch before they began the yard work their father had assigned them.

Nineteen-year-old Rena was at her mother's side to help prepare the dinner as soon as the breakfast dishes were done.

Carrie's passion was cooking, and the prospect of having her dining room filled that evening with hungry people brought much joy to her heart.

By early afternoon, mother and daughter enjoyed the myriad aromas filling the house from the kitchen. A large elk roast with many succulent spices was baking in the oven. Baked sweet potatoes and mashed potatoes were ready and being kept hot at the back of the stove.

Carrie stirred the dark gravy while Rena set the tables in the dining room. Carrie glanced over the other pans on the stove. The green beans with stewed tomatoes and onions bubbled, sending off steam, and a pan of black-eyed peas simmered as well.

Carrie made her way into the dining room, where Rena was just finishing up. The two tables were spread with snow-white cloths, embroidered with plum-colored berries and green leaves. The main table had a centerpiece made of pine cones of various sizes placed between trimmed green pine boughs in a brown basket. There were candles in holders at each end of the basket, and the table—as well as the spare table—was set with Carrie's best dinnerware.

Carrie put an arm around Rena and smiled. "You've done a beautiful job, sweetheart. I wish all the dinnerware matched, but hopefully all of our guests will be more interested in what they are putting into their mouths than what they're using to do it."

"I'm sure they will, Mama."

Carrie gave Rena a squeeze. "Well, I need to get back to the kitchen. You go ahead and finish up here."

At that instant, mother and daughter looked at each other wide-eyed as several gun shots filled the air, one after another, echoing through the town.

Carrie licked her lips. "Those shots came from the business district. I hope…I hope your papa and his deputies are all right."

Rena took a deep breath. "I hope so, too, Mama. You've got to tend to the food on the stove. I'll go see what happened. Be back as soon as I can."

"All right," Carrie said, worry pinching her face.

Carrie returned to the kitchen, her heart heavy with fear. She had often wished that Jack would find another line of work, but she could never bring herself to say anything about it. He loved his job, and it was obvious to anyone who knew him that he was cut out to be a lawman.

That evening at the Powell home, Carrie smiled at her hungry guests as they arrived, telling Jack to lead them into the dining room.

Soon the Powells and their guests were seated at the tables in the dining room. Present as guests were Tim and Sally Benson, with their daughter, nineteen-year-old Lucinda, and their son, Deputy Marshal Jarrod Benson. Also present were Pastor Richard Skiver and his wife, Rosie. At the smaller table, Randy and Darin sat with their sister and Lucinda.

When everyone was settled, Jack asked the pastor to lead them in prayer. Everyone bowed their heads, and Pastor Skiver began by emotionally thanking the Lord for sparing Jack's life. He also gave thanks to the Lord for bringing Jarrod and Cade back to town in time to go to Jack's aid, and for seeing to it that the deputies also made it safely through the shootout. Tears were shed around both tables while the pastor prayed. He then thanked God for the food, and amens were spoken by all.

During the meal, they talked about how the West was growing more dangerous as the population expanded.

Jack took a sip of hot coffee, sighed, and said, "It's only going to get worse as more and more people come west. I'm sure glad the town could afford for me to hire Jarrod, and with the growth Sacramento is experiencing, I'm going to need a third deputy in another year."

At the smaller table, Rena's fork dropped from her hand and clattered on her plate. Every eye flashed to her. They all noticed that tears were glistening in her eyes.

A bit embarrassed, Rena sniffed, wiped tears, and looked at her father. "Papa, this shootout today would have had us burying you if Cade and Jarrod hadn't shown up when they did. I—I—" She choked and swallowed hard.

Jack shoved his chair back and stepped to the smaller table, taking hold of Rena's hand. "What, honey?"

She looked up into his eyes, wiped more tears with her free hand, and said, "Papa, I just wish you would resign and make a living some other way. I'm afraid for your life." She cast a tearful glance at Jarrod. "I'm afraid for Jarrod's life, too."

Randy leaned across the table and laid a gentle hand on his sister's arm. "I feel the same way, Sis."

Jack patted Rena's hand, ran his gaze between brother and sister, and said, "Kids, you have to understand something. Ever since I was knee high to a grasshopper, I've wanted to be a lawman. It's the way the Lord made me. I know He cut me out to wear a badge. Somebody has to do it, or the outlaws and killers would be on the rampage worse than they are, and nobody among the decent people would be safe. Besides, I wouldn't be happy doing something else. I'm the man for Sacramento."

Tears misted Carrie's eyes as she said, "Rena…Randy…I'll be honest with you, there have been times when I wanted to say something to your father about getting a safer job. But when I see him pin that badge on his chest every morning and strap on that gun, I also see the look in his eyes. I could never ask him to take off the badge and do something else for a living. I want him to be happy in his work, and I have to agree with him. He's a born lawman. It was his Creator who made him this way. And as far as I'm concerned, he's the best town marshal in the West."

"Amen to that," piped up Pastor Skiver. "I have to agree. Jack was cut out by the Lord to be a lawman, and boy, does the West need more like him!"

"I agree, Pastor," said Tim Benson.

Sally glanced at her husband, then ran her gaze around the room. "I don't mind telling all of you that I was absolutely terrified when Jarrod announced that he wanted to be a lawman. But I couldn't ask him to do something else. He is superbly happy in his work, and can't say enough about how great it is to be one of Marshal Powell's deputies."

Tim looked at Jarrod and said, "Son, if somehow you don't think you're cut out to be a lawman, I'm sure I could get you a job at the sawmill."

Jarrod grinned at his father. "Pop, you're happy sawing wood, and I'm glad for you...but I'm more than happy wearing a badge under my boss, here."

Jack smiled at him. "Tell you what, Jarrod. I was mighty glad to have both you and Cade as my deputies today!"

Everyone in the group cheered and applauded.

Pastor Skiver said, "Jack...Jarrod...do you realize that the Bible calls lawmen God's *ministers*?"

Jack's eyebrows arched. "It does?"

"Yes. Of course, not in the sense that preachers are called ministers, but God ordained civil law, and law officers are ministers of God to keep peace, even those who do not know the Lord."

"I'd like to hear more about this, Pastor," Jarrod said.

The others spoke up, saying they wanted to hear more, too.

The pastor smiled. "All right. When dinner's finished and the dishes have been done, I'll show it to you." He looked at Jack. "May I borrow your Bible?"

"Of course."

When the ladies had done the dishes and cleaned up the kitchen, everyone sat down in the parlor. Pastor Skiver sat in a padded wooden chair facing the rest of them and opened Jack's Bible. Finding the passage he wanted, he ran his gaze over their faces and said, "I'm going to read you Romans 13:1–7. Listen closely. I'll read it to you, then go back and make a few comments.

"'Let every soul be subject unto the higher powers. For there is no power but of God: the powers that be are ordained of God. Whosoever therefore resisteth the power, resisteth the ordinance of God: and they that resist shall receive to themselves damnation. For rulers are not a terror to good works, but to the evil. Wilt thou then not be afraid of the power? do that which is good, and thou shalt have praise of the same: For he is the minister of God to thee for good. But if thou do that which is evil, be afraid; for he beareth not the sword in vain: for he is the minister of God, a revenger to execute wrath upon him that doeth evil. Wherefore ye must needs be subject, not only for wrath, but also for conscience sake. For for this cause pay ye tribute also: for they are God's ministers, attending continually upon this very thing. Render therefore to all their dues: tribute to whom tribute is due; custom to whom custom; fear to whom fear; honor to whom honor.'"

Pastor Skiver ran his gaze over their faces again. "I think you can all get what God is talking about, here. He is speaking of those who are employed to make sure the civil law that man has set up is obeyed. The 'tribute' spoken of are the taxes we pay from which lawmen's salaries are drawn. Civil law, we can see right here, is ordained of God. Those men who wear the badge, if you please, are twice called God's ministers. In Sacramento, the ministers of God are Jack, Cade, and Jarrod."

Jarrod smiled and looked at his parents. "What about that? Your son wears a badge as a minister of God to keep the peace."

"He's right," said the pastor. "It's not only the badge he wears as God's minister, but that gun he wears on his hip. Listen again to verse four: 'He beareth not the sword in vain: for he is the minister of God, a revenger to execute wrath upon him that doeth evil.' Today, Jarrod, when you and Cade unleashed your guns on the Hacker brothers, you were the ministers of God bearing the 'sword.' The 'sword' is the instrument to execute justice in order to keep the peace."

Flipping toward the front of the Bible, the preacher said, "Let me read to you what God says about the use of the 'sword' in Genesis 9:6. He is speaking here to Noah and his sons after the flood, when the human race was to be started again, and He once again establishes civil law. 'Whoso sheddeth man's blood, by man shall his blood be shed: for in the image of God made he man.' This ties with Romans 13:4, where God says the lawman bears not the sword in vain."

Flipping back to the New Testament, Pastor Skiver said, "Elsewhere in Scripture, lawmen are called *magistrates*. Titus 3:1 says, 'Put them in mind to be subject to principalities and powers, to obey magistrates, to be ready to every good work.' Any good Bible dictionary will define a magistrate as a civil official entrusted with administration of laws and justice. That would certainly be the men who 'wear the badge,' if you please."

Jack and Jarrod smiled at each other.

The pastor went on. "The Bible makes it clear that magistrates exist to preserve peace and to execute justice. Now, of course, when men set up laws that are contrary to the laws of God, we are to obey God rather than men, as it says in Acts 5:29. The reason the apostle Paul, for example, spent so much time behind bars was because men had made laws against preaching Jesus Christ and His gospel. So Paul obeyed God rather than men, and had to do jail time for it.

"The greatest commands of men are no weight against the paramount authority of the King of kings and Lord of lords. When, however, the laws of men are not at variance with the law of God, the Scriptures expressly tell us to obey them."

Jarrod waggled his head with a look of superiority on his face and said, "Well, I guess all of you are aware that Marshal Powell and I are ministers of God, and you are all to obey us!"

Everyone laughed, then in a serious tone, Pastor Skiver said, "We should all keep Jack, Jarrod, and Cade before the Lord daily, asking Him to protect them. They do have a dangerous job."

Carrie Powell nodded. "And we all need to pray hard for Cade, that he will open his heart to Jesus. Both Jack and Jarrod have been witnessing to him, and they've told me that he's showing some interest."

"We've laid the plan of salvation before him several times," Jarrod said, "and made the gospel clear to him. He's even asking questions, now, so that's a good sign."

"I'm really glad to hear it," the pastor said. He stood and handed the Bible to Jack. "Well, Rosie and I need to head for home. We sure thank you for the great meal and for the good time we've had this evening."

"Pastor, would you lead us in prayer before you go?" Jack said.

"Certainly. Let's pray."

❧

At the San Francisco city jail, Usel Hacker sat in his cell talking to his three cell mates when a guard stepped up to the cell door and said, "Hacker, you have a visitor."

Usel rose to his feet and stepped up to the barred door. "Who is it?"

"His name's Spencer Halton. He says he's an old friend of yours."

A smile broke over Usel's bearded face. "Well, good ol' Spence! He's been so good to visit me often."

The guard unlocked the cell door, the prisoner stepped out, and the guard closed and locked the door. When Usel was ushered into the visitors' room, he saw his old friend sitting at a barred window. He noted that Spencer Halton had a serious look on his face.

Usel sat down, and the guard told Usel he had ten minutes, then left the room, locking the door behind him. "Nice to see you, Spence," said Usel, looking at him through the bars. "You look awfully solemn. Something wrong?"

"Yeah, pal. Something's wrong. I've got bad news for you."

Usel frowned. "What is it?"

Halton held up the front page of the *San Francisco Chronicle*, pointed to the largest article, and said, "Read it for yourself."

When Usel read of the shootout in Sacramento on Saturday, and of Marshal Jack Powell and his deputies killing his three brothers, his rough features turned crimson. Red rage poured through his heavy eyes as he said, "It was bad enough that Powell gunned down Uben, but now he's killed my other three brothers! My sentence will be up in a few months, Spence. When I get out of this jail, Marshal Jack Powell is a dead man!"

SIX

In Manhattan, New York, on Sunday, November 28, Craig Turley was in the library on the ground flood of the mansion, reading Charles Dickens's latest novel, *Dombey and Son,* which had just appeared in the bookstores.

Craig was engrossed in the book, sitting in an overstuffed chair close to the fireplace where the fire was crackling and putting off welcome heat. But as he was about to start chapter three, he glanced up at the clock on the mantel. "Almost one o'clock," he muttered to himself. "What's keeping them?"

At the same moment, Adelle Brown walked past the open library door in the hallway.

Hearing her footsteps, Craig glanced in that direction and caught sight of the housekeeper just as she was passing from view. "Adelle!" he called.

Adelle turned around and stepped up to the library door. She noticed the agitated look on Craig's face. "Yes, Mr. Turley?"

"Have my father, Maddie, and Kathy returned from church yet?"

"No, sir. Not yet."

Craig shook his head and said, "I wish they had stayed home. Sunday is the day for the family to be together. This church stuff is a waste of time."

Adelle took two steps into the library. "But you know that for some time your father has been wanting to meet Pastor Charles Finney and hear him preach. And so have Maddie and Kathy."

Craig released a petulant sigh. "Does Elizabeth have dinner ready?"

"She does, sir. Since the family isn't back yet, she has put everything on the back burners, expecting they will arrive home any minute."

Craig closed his book and rose from the overstuffed chair. "I'm going to go ahead and eat. I can't wait any longer."

As Craig and Adelle started walking down the hall toward the kitchen, the front door came open and Wallace, Maddie, and Kathy stepped inside. Adelle said in a low tone, "I'll go on to the kitchen, Mr. Turley."

Maddie spotted Craig first, and a bright smile curved her lips. She removed the scarf from her head and hurried toward him. "Guess what, Craig! I walked down the aisle at church this morning and received Jesus into my heart!"

Wallace and Kathy drew up and saw the startled look on Craig's face. When Craig turned his eyes on them, Wallace said, "Son, Kathy and I also went forward during the invitation and received Christ into our hearts as our personal Saviour."

Craig ran his dull gaze over the faces of Maddie and Kathy, then stared silently at his father.

Wallace laid a hand on his son's shoulder. "Craig, I have peace in my heart and mind like I've never known possible. Because of what the Bible says, I know I'm going to heaven when my life is over on this earth."

"Me, too," said Maddie, hopping from one foot to the other.

Wallace let go of Craig's shoulder. "Pastor Finney is a powerful preacher. He preached on the existence of a burning, eternal hell this morning, quoting Jesus Christ Himself straight out of the Bible."

Maddie tugged on big brother's sleeve. "Oh, Craig, I want you to be saved, too, so you can go to heaven with us! Will you ask Jesus to forgive you of your sins and come into your heart like we did? Papa can show you about it in the Bible. Please, oh please, Craig!"

Craig sighed and loosened his little sister's hand from his sleeve. "Maddie, I don't believe in all this salvation, heaven, and hell stuff. I got this clear in my mind when I was in college, and I can't start believing it now, even for *you*, little sister. When a person dies, they go out of existence. There's no such thing as an afterlife."

Kathy took a step closer to Craig. "I used to feel the same way, but I've been wondering of late if I might be wrong. Craig, when Pastor Finney preached this morning, I knew I was hearing the truth. He showed us in God's Word that Jesus came to earth from heaven for the very purpose of shedding His blood and dying on the cross for sinners like you and me. But He didn't stay in the tomb. He arose from the dead and went back to heaven. He is alive today, wanting to save every sinner. He saved me this morning. And now, with my sins forgiven and washed away in Jesus' blood, I have real peace and joy about where I'll go when I die, whenever that happens."

Craig shook his head slowly. "Kathy, how do you know it's the truth just because it came from the Bible? It was written by mortal men."

Wallace said, "Son, the Bible was written by mortal men, yes, but I have long believed what my dear paternal grandmother taught me when I was a boy—that just as the Bible says, God gave those mortal men the words to write and made sure they wrote every word correctly. He has also preserved His Word so we still have it today. The reason that Kathy knew what she was hearing from God's Word is true is that the Holy Spirit of God was speaking to her heart, telling her so. He was doing the same thing to me and to your little sister. I've been such a fool not to take God at His Word a long time ago. Craig, I want you to come to church with us next Sunday and hear Pastor Finney preach. I just know if you'll—"

"What about Harold?" Craig said. "Certainly he didn't stay out in the carriage as cold as it is outside. Did he sit in the service?"

"Yes, he did."

"Did he walk down the aisle and do what you three did?"

"No. He was sitting in the balcony with a man he recognized when we entered the building. I plan to talk to Harold about it, as well as Elizabeth and Adelle. I'd love to see them be saved, too. Now, back to what I was saying. Will you come to church with us next Sunday?"

Craig took a deep breath and wiped a palm over his face. "Dad, if this is what you, Maddie, and Kathy want, that's fine with me. But I'm not interested. Religion just isn't my cup of tea. My philosophy professor at NYU convinced me and many of my classmates that religion is a waste of time. We live, we die, and that's the end of us. Why bother with religion, waste time sitting in church and having religious leaders tell us how we ought to live? I have no desire to be religious."

Wallace shook his head. "Son, what Maddie, Kathy and I did this morning was not become religious. We became children of God by receiving God's only begotten Son into our hearts as Saviour. We've now been born again, as Jesus said we must in order to go to heaven. All of our sins have been forgiven. This isn't religion. This is salvation."

Craig cleared his throat gently. "Dad, like I said, if this is what the three of you want, that's fine. But I'm not interested."

Maddie looked up at the big brother she adored. "Please, Craig. Don't be that way. I want you to be in heaven with me. I love you. And Jesus loves y—"

"Maddie, that's enough. I don't want to hear any more about it."

At that moment, Elizabeth called out, "Dinner's ready, everybody!"

The three new Christians removed their wraps and headed for the dining room with Craig following. Maddie's heart was hurting for the way her big brother had cut her off.

At the dinner table, Wallace, Maddie, and Kathy ate the delicious meal Elizabeth had prepared and chattered happily about their newfound faith. Craig tried to close his ears to their cheerful conversation, but bits and pieces still penetrated his mind. His stomach was churning, and he merely toyed with the food on his plate. Finally, he pushed back from the table and stood up.

All talk ceased as the others looked up at him.

"Please excuse me," Craig said, then turned and hurried out of the dining room.

The trio watched him go, then Wallace said, "We must pray for Craig. He's miserable, and he doesn't even know why."

Maddie left her chair and put an arm around her father's neck. "Papa, the three of us will pray hard for Craig every day, won't we?"

"We sure will, sweetie," said Wallace, patting her cheek.

Maddie worked up a smile. "Then I know that someday he will get saved!"

Wallace put his arm around her and kissed her cheek. "You're right, sweetheart. With you, Kathy, and me praying for him, he will indeed turn to the Lord. Just as the Lord brought us to Himself, He'll do the same for Craig. It may take a while, but we'll keep praying until God brings about the proper circumstances that will cause him to turn to Jesus."

Maddie batted her eyelids. "Could we pray for Craig right now, Papa?"

"Of course. Kathy, come over here, and let's hold each other's hands as we pray."

Kathy moved to the chair close to Wallace, and the three joined hands.

"Kathy, would you like to start?" Wallace said.

Kathy nodded, and as they bowed their heads and closed their eyes, she offered a heartfelt prayer for Craig, asking the Lord to work in his heart and bring him to Himself.

When Kathy had said her amen, Wallace looked down at his little ten-year-old daughter. "Do you want to pray out loud before I do, honey?"

"Yes, Papa," she replied. Maddie squeezed both hands she was holding tightly as she said, "Dear God, thank You for sending Your Son to die on the cross for our sins. Thank You for letting us go to church today and hear Pastor Finney preach. Thank You for saving Papa and Kathy and me. And dear God, I want my brother to get saved. I want Craig in heaven with us. Please—" She choked up, and felt Kathy's other hand touch the side of her face. She opened her eyes and looked at Kathy, who was looking at her through a film of tears.

Kathy kissed her cheek. "Go ahead, honey."

A lump arose in Wallace's throat when he saw the tears streaming down Maddie's cheeks. He caressed the top of her head. "Go ahead, sweetheart."

Maddie sniffed and said, "Dear God, please work in Craig's heart and make him believe Your Bible. Please, please, dear God. I want Craig to be saved and be in heaven with us." She sniffed again and took a deep breath. "I ask it in Jesus' name, dear God. Amen."

It took Wallace a few seconds to gain his composure. Then he prayed, giving thanks for their salvation and asking the Lord to work in Craig's heart as only *He* could, and that they might see Craig open his heart to Jesus.

After Wallace said his amen, he folded Maddie and Kathy in his arms and told them how much he loved them.

They returned to their food, and when dinner was over, Wallace told Maddie and Kathy he was going to retire for the night early. Kathy said she and Maddie would do the same.

Wallace entered his room, closed the door, and dropped to his knees by his bed. He prayed again for Craig's salvation, and he also prayed that he would be able to bring his servants to Christ.

In the girls' room, when the lanterns were out and both were in their beds, Kathy soon heard Maddie's steady breathing. She closed her eyes and prayed in a low whisper, "Dear Lord, I'm asking again that You work in Craig's heart and bring him to the place where he will repent of his sin and open his heart to Jesus. And—and Lord, I pray that after Craig is saved, You will cause him to fall in love with me as I am in love with him so we can marry and have a Christian home together. I ask it in the precious name of Jesus. Amen."

New Year's Day 1848 came, and on Monday afternoon, January 3, in Iowa City, Iowa, it was snowing hard with an icy wind blowing. At Main Street Bank—the town's only bank—the new president's secretary tapped on the door and entered at his invitation.

"Mr. Edwards," said Martha Webber, "one of our farm customers would like to see you. His name is Luke Daniels. His parents banked here for several years before they passed on and left the farm to their son. Luke and Sandra Daniels are fine people and very good customers of the bank."

Vance Edwards pushed aside the papers on his desk and said, "Bring Mr. Daniels in, Martha."

Martha stepped back into her office and said, "Mr. Daniels, Mr. Edwards will see you now."

When Martha ushered the farmer into his office, Edwards rounded the desk, smiling, and extended his hand. "Mr. Daniels, I'm very glad to meet you. Martha gave me a few words about your background just before she brought you in."

"I hope she didn't tell you about all those checks I've bounced over the years."

Edwards laughed. "I guess somehow she forgot to tell me about that! Go ahead and have a seat, Mr. Daniels. What can I do for you today?"

Luke settled on the chair. "Well, sir, I need to explain some things to you."

"I'm listening."

"My wife, Sandra, and I have a sixty-acre farm seven miles north of town. I inherited the farm when my parents died."

Edwards nodded. "Yes, Martha told me."

"On fifty-nine of those acres, we've been raising corn, even as my parents did when I grew up on the farm as a boy."

"Martha told me that your parents had banked here for several years."

"Yes, sir. Sandra and I have a barn, three milk cows, and a team of draft horses. Our two-story farmhouse is well built, and I keep the house and outbuildings in good repair."

The bank president smiled and folded his hands on top of the desk. "I think I know what you're leading up to. You want to borrow money on your farm."

Luke shook his head. "No, sir."

Edwards eyebrows raised. "No?"

"Mr. Edwards, when I inherited the farm from my parents almost twelve years ago, they already had a mortgage on it at the bank here. In order to make it financially when Sandra and I got married, we came in and had a new loan set up in order to lower the payments. We took out a twenty-year loan, and have never so much as been late on a payment in these twelve years."

Edwards nodded. "That's commendable, Mr. Daniels."

"Thank you. Ah…apparently Martha didn't tell you about our big fire last summer."

"No. Tell me about it."

"Well, sir, last August, just before time to harvest the corn, we had a severe lightning storm. I had left a wagon standing in the cornfield about a hundred feet from the fence, and a bolt of lightning struck the wagon, setting it on fire. Sandra and I were in town at the time, and when we arrived home, a stiff wind was blowing, and the cornfield was ablaze."

Edwards shook his head. "Oh, my."

"Fortunately the wind blew the flames away from the house and outbuildings. Neighboring farmers were splashing water on their own crops along the fences to keep them from catching fire. They were able to stop the flames from getting into their fields, but our crop was almost totally burned up."

Edwards leaned toward him, his hands still folded on the desktop. "I'm truly sorry for your loss, Mr. Daniels. So tell me, what it is you need?"

Luke scrubbed a palm over his mouth. "Well, sir, the usual income from the corn crop was a grand total of nothing. We had some savings here in the bank, but most of it's gone now. What I need to ask is, will the bank allow us to wait until our crop is harvested next August to make any more payments on the mortgage?"

The banker ran splayed fingers through his thinning gray hair. He shook his head. "I'm sorry, Mr. Daniels, but that just isn't possible. Since you and your wife have signed the note on the mortgage, the payments must be made as you agreed. I wish I could do it for you, but it would go against bank policy, and I do have to answer to the bank's board of directors. I know what they would say if I let you do as you have requested. I'm sorry, but I just can't do it."

"I understand, sir."

Edwards bit his lower lip. "Mr. Daniels, I almost hate my job when I have to turn down a hard-working man who's the victim of circumstances beyond his control. I just wish it was in my power to grant your request."

"I understand, Mr. Edwards. It's certainly not your fault. My wife and I will just have to trust the Lord to supply our need. We love our farm and this little community. Sandra and I were both born and raised right here. God will make a way according to His will. I just have to believe that."

Luke stood up and Edwards followed suit.

Luke took a deep breath and said, "Thank you for your time, Mr. Edwards. I'll just have to try to find a job so I can have enough income until next summer to make the payments...plus provide for my wife and children."

Edwards walked him to the office door, saying, "I hope you're able to find a job."

Luke managed a thin smile. "Thank you. I have to, sir. I just have to."

A moment later, Luke walked out the front door of the bank, his head bent against the driving wind and blowing snow. While climbing into his wagon, he said, "Lord, help me to explain this to Sandra so she'll understand. And—and please help me to find a good job."

As Luke drove away, he was unaware that the bank president was standing at one of his office widows and looking out at the street. When he saw Luke put the team in motion, his own prayer for provision for this little family wended its way heavenward.

SEVEN

Luke Daniels wiped snow from his face as he guided the wagon team northward along Iowa City's Main Street, still praying that the Lord would help him to find a job. The wind was blowing the falling snow hard against the buildings and buffeting people, vehicles, and horses.

"Lord, guide me as to where I should look for a job," Luke prayed. "I don't know whether to try one of these stores here in town, or to possibly look into working at one of the dairy farms in the area. I really need You to give me wisdom, and to guide—"

Suddenly, his gaze fell on the sign that hung over the double doors of the company that always bought his corn crop each year. It was covered with a thin layer of snow, but the large black letters still stood out:

GANTON'S FEED AND SUPPLY
ROBERT GANTON, PROP.

"Are You telling me something, Lord?" Luke said. "Guess there's one way to find out."

He swung the wagon up to the hitch rail in front of Ganton's, climbed down from the seat, and tied the reins to the nearest post. He spoke to two farmers who were making their way along the snow-covered boardwalk, opened the door, and stepped inside.

Bob Ganton's only employee, Bill Duxbury, was behind the counter. He smiled as Luke was shaking snow off his hat, and said, "Well, howdy, Luke! Think it'll snow?"

"Well, if it doesn't, it's going to miss a good opportunity."

"You're right about that. What can I do for you?"

"I need to see Bob, if he's around."

"Sure. He's in his office. Go on back. Door's open."

"Thanks." Luke made his way toward the rear of the building, passing piles of gunnysacks stuffed full of different grains and shelves loaded with all types of supplies for farm use.

Bob Ganton was just coming out the office door when he saw Luke approaching. "Howdy, Luke. Looks like we're gonna get some snow."

"I'd say so. Got a minute? I need to talk to you."

"Hey, for you, I've even got *two* minutes!"

At the Daniels farm, Sandra Daniels mopped the kitchen floor while her sons—ten-year-old Paul and nine-year-old Silas—were in the parlor.

Tears glistened in Sandra's eyes as she said, "Dear Lord, Luke's no doubt seen the new vice president at the bank by now. He's just got to come home and tell me that Mr. Edwards agreed to let us defer the mortgage payments until harvest time this fall. He's just *got* to."

In the parlor, the fire in the fireplace crackled and popped as it sent out its heat into the room. Paul washed and polished the glass chimneys on the kerosene lanterns one by one while his younger brother used a feather duster on the furniture.

Just as Silas was dusting a small table near the large parlor window, movement outside caught his eye. Through the falling snow, he saw a buggy pull into the yard. "Paul, we've got company."

Paul placed the glass chimney he was holding on one of the mantel lanterns and looked at his brother. "Who'd be coming to visit us on a day like this?"

Silas pressed his face closer to the window as the buggy drew near the front porch. "Well, Pastor and Mrs. Flint would, that's who!"

Paul's eyes widened. "Pastor and Mrs. Flint? Are you sure it's them?"

"Positive," said Silas, heading for the parlor door. "I'll go get Mama."

Silas dashed down the hall into the kitchen just as his mother was wringing out the mop over a bucket. "Mama! Pastor and Mrs. Flint are here."

Sandra's brow furrowed. "Really?"

"Really. They're just pulling up in front of the house. I saw 'em!"

Sandra leaned the mop against the kitchen wall, and while wiping her hands on her apron, hurried toward the front of the house with her youngest son. When they neared the foyer, they saw Paul just opening the door to Pastor Flint and his wife, Caroline.

Sandra rushed up and said, "Well, hello, Pastor…Caroline! Come in! Come in! Boys, take Pastor and Mrs. Flint's coats and hang them on the clothes tree. Here, Pastor, let me take your hat. Caroline, give me your scarf. I'll brush the snow off them and hang them up for you."

After the coats and headgear had been taken care of, Sandra led the couple into the parlor with her sons following.

The instant Caroline stepped into the room, she dashed up to the fireplace, turned her palms toward the crackling flames, and exclaimed, "Oh, this fire feels so good!" She glanced at Sandra over her shoulder. "Looks to me like we're going to have a long, cold, snowy winter." A smile graced her lips. "But that's normal for Iowa, isn't it?"

Sandra smiled and nodded. "Sure is."

Caroline shrugged her shoulders, keeping her palms toward the flames. "Oh, well. It makes us look forward to spring with great anticipation, doesn't it?"

"Sure does," said Paul.

Rubbing her hands together briskly, Caroline left the fireplace and stepped up beside her husband. They smiled at each other, then at Sandra and the boys.

Their beaming countenances began to melt the cold dread in Sandra's heart. "What in the world brings the two of you out on such a cold, blustery day?" She shook her head before either of the Flints could respond. "No, wait a minute! Let me go to the kitchen and get some hot coffee so you can both get some heat inside you. It's already on the stove, so it'll only take a few minutes. Then you can tell me why you're here. Boys, you keep Pastor and Mrs. Flint occupied while I'm gone." With that, she hurried out the parlor door and down the hall toward the kitchen.

Some five minutes later, Sandra entered the parlor to find young Silas sitting between the Flints on the sofa, showing them his art-work from school. Paul looked on from behind the sofa, and all four looked up to see Sandra moving toward them carrying a tray upon which three cups of steaming coffee fragrantly filled the air. There was also a plate of oatmeal cookies on the tray.

"It sure looks and smells good, Sandra!" Pastor Flint said.

She set the tray on a nearby small table, then placed cups in the Flints' hands. Both of them curled their fingers around the warm cups.

Sandra put her attention on her sons. "Boys, I poured each of you a glass of milk in the kitchen, and two cookies each await you. When you've finished, you can come back to the parlor."

After Paul and Silas had left the room, Sandra sat down with a cup in one hand and a cookie in the other. "Now, you've driven all the way out here in that fierce storm. Is there something I can do for you?"

The Flints looked at Sandra with warm eyes as the pastor said, "Before I tell you why we're here, Sandra, I need to ask if the bank cooperated with Luke in deferring the mortgage payments. We've been praying about it since Luke asked us to do so in the service yesterday morning."

"Luke hasn't come back from town, yet, Pastor. I had expected him by now."

"Oh. I figured he was probably out working in the barn. He told me yesterday morning that he's been busy replacing all the floorboards in the hayloft. That's a big job."

"Well, he's been doing that, all right, but the visit with the new bank president had priority this morning." Sandra took a deep breath. "I don't mind telling you, Pastor and Caroline...I'm a bit nervous about how it will turn out with the bank."

The pastor took an envelope from a pocket inside his suit coat and handed it to Sandra. She noted the excitement simmering in his eyes as he said, "Well, even if the bank will let you defer the payments, I'm sure you and Luke can use this, anyhow."

Sandra blinked in puzzlement as the pastor added, "We took up an offering in the service last night after you folks had left for home."

With a shaky hand, Sandra opened the envelope and looked inside. There were several bills of currency. Tears rushed to her eyes. "Oh, Pastor, you didn't have to do this."

He smiled. "Oh, yes I did. The Lord put it on my heart yesterday morning, so before the service last night, I had some of the men tell all the other members to stay around after the service. With you, Luke, and the boys absent, I went over your situation before the people, which they had heard Luke describe in the morning service when he asked for prayer. They all showed concern and gave generously when I had the offering plates passed. There's just over three hundred dollars in the envelope."

Sandra took a deep breath, not noticing her sons coming back into the room. "Oh, praise the Lord! Thank you, Pastor, for being so kind toward us."

"Mama, what are you praising the Lord and thanking Pastor Flint about?" asked Paul.

Silas focused on the envelope in his mother's hand. "What's that, Mama?"

Sandra showed the boys the money, told them how much there was, and explained what the pastor had done. Both boys got excited, and also expressed their gratitude to the pastor.

At that moment above the whine of the wind, everyone heard the sound of a wagon drawing near the house.

Paul dashed to the parlor window and said excitedly, "It's Papa! He stopped at Pastor's buggy, and he's getting out of the wagon. Boy, is he gonna be happy over this gift from the church!"

Sandra ran her gaze between the boys. "You two stay with Pastor and Mrs. Flint. I'll go meet your father at the door."

She hurried into the foyer just as Luke was coming through the door. Not noticing the envelope in her hand, he managed a smile and took her into his arms. After kissing her forehead, he said in a low tone, "I see Pastor is here."

"Yes, and he has Caroline with him. So how did it go?"

Luke cleared his throat, praying in his heart for his precious wife. "Well, honey, not as we had hoped."

"Mr. Edwards turned you down?"

"Yes. He explained that he would have to go against bank policy to defer our mortgage payments. The bank directors would be very upset with him if he had done so. I—I hope you understand."

Sandra smiled. "Well, darling, we certainly couldn't expect Mr. Edwards to go against bank policy and put himself in a bad light with the directors." Her smiled widened.

"What is it, love? You don't seem at all upset about our being turned down at the bank. Do you understand what this means?"

"I know what it means, sweetheart, and I'm so very sorry. But I have some good news." As she spoke, she raised the envelope toward his face. "Take a look inside."

Puzzlement etched itself on his features. He took the envelope in hand and opened it. He looked back at her and grinned.

Sandra quickly told him what their pastor had done and the amount of the offering.

"Well, praise be to God!" Luke said. "He certainly takes care of His children, doesn't He?"

"That He does, darling. Well, we'd better go into the parlor. The Flints and our sons are waiting. You can tell them about Mr. Edwards turning us down."

Luke removed his snow-laden hat and coat and hung them on the clothes tree, then he and Sandra entered the parlor. Paul and Silas ran to their father and hugged him, asking how it had gone at the bank. Luke told them he would explain it to them and the Flints, then shook hands with the pastor and Caroline and expressed his appreciation for the generous offering the pastor had taken for them.

"Luke, I know you must be cold," Sandra said. "While you're explaining what happened at the bank, I'll go get you a hot cup of coffee."

"Sounds mighty good, sweetheart. And when you come back, in spite of what happened at the bank, I've got some good news for you."

"Well, I'm eager to hear it. Be back in a few minutes."

Sandra soon returned, carrying a steaming cup of coffee.

The pastor was saying, "Well, Luke, the same God who put it on my heart to take that offering for you and your family is able to supply the money you need to make those mortgage payments until your harvest comes in early next fall."

Luke grinned as Sandra placed the cup in his hand. "Yes He is, Pastor."

Sandra took hold of her husband's free hand, guided him to the chair next to the one she had been sitting in, and said, "All right, tell me *your* good news."

They sat down side by side, and their sons moved up close to them.

"When Vance Edwards explained that he wouldn't be able to let us defer the mortgage payments, I told him I'd have to find a job. As I was driving toward the north side of town to come home, I prayed that the Lord would guide me as to where to find a job. Even as I was praying, I was about to drive past Ganton's Feed and Supply, and suddenly I knew the Lord was telling me to stop and talk to Bob about hiring me."

Sandra's eyes brightened.

Luke said to the Flints, "I believe you know that Bob Ganton always buys our corn crop every year."

Both nodded.

Luke turned to Sandra. "I told Bob about being turned down at the bank concerning the deferred payments, then I asked him if he could hire me to work for him till spring comes and I have to start plowing, harrowing, and planting corn. And he did."

"Oh, praise the Lord!" Sandra said.

"That's wonderful!" said the pastor.

"Of course, Bob can't afford to pay me real well, but what he does pay me will help us get through the winter, and we should be able to make the mortgage payments. And this money from the church is a big help. Pastor, I'll write a thank-you letter for you to read to the church next Sunday morning."

Pastor Flint frowned. "Luke, I'm glad this money from the church will ease the financial strain, but will you be able to buy groceries and other necessities and still make the mortgage payments?"

Luke met the pastor's gaze for a brief moment, then started to speak. But the pastor cut him off. "I got my answer, Luke. I'll explain to the congregation what you're facing, and we'll take a special offering each week to help you until your next corn harvest."

"Pastor, we can't let you do this. That's asking too much."

"May I remind you that there are many other farmers in the church, and they all know it could have been their crop that burned up. I'm telling you, Luke, they and the other members will want to help."

Luke shook his head. "Pastor, I just can't let you do this. It's asking too much of the church members."

"A couple of weeks ago I preached on Sunday night about Christians helping each other when a brother or sister in Christ is struggling financially. Remember?"

"Yes, sir."

"Do you recall the main text of my sermon?"

"Ah…it was 1 John 3:16 and 17."

"Correct. Let me quote it for you. 'Hereby perceive we the love of God, because he laid down his life for us: and we ought to lay down our lives for the brethren. But whoso hath this world's good, and seeth his brother have need, and shutteth up his bowels of compassion from him, how dwelleth the love of God in him?' Did I quote it correctly, Luke?"

Luke chuckled. "You know you did."

"If one of your farmer brothers in Christ had his crop burn up, would you want to help him?"

"Of course I would."

Flint nodded, flashed a glance to Sandra, then looked back at Luke. "Because you love your brethren in deed and in truth, don't you?"

"I do, Pastor."

"Let me remind you that verse 18, which I also elaborated on in the sermon, says, 'My little children, let us not love in word, neither in tongue; but in deed and in truth.'"

Luke pulled at an ear. "But Pastor, I—"

"Don't rob our church members of a blessing, Luke. The Lord will bless them for this. And I implore you, don't refuse to accept the love of your brothers and sisters in Christ. Let us help you, Sandra, and the boys until you bring in your harvest next fall."

Luke made a choking sound, wiped tears, and looked at Sandra, who was also weeping. "Honey, what can we do when this pastor of ours uses the Word of God on us?"

Sandra brushed tears from her cheeks. "Well, Luke, it looks like we're going to have to let him do what he wants to about leading the church to help us through this difficult time."

EIGHT

On Tuesday afternoon, January 4, 1848, in southeast Australia, middle-aged sheep rancher Charles Wesson and his wife, Marian, were sitting on the front porch of their white frame house enjoying the warm summer air. With them were Lamar and Pauline Prescott, who had recently moved to Sydney from Cairns on Australia's northeast coast. The Prescotts had begun attending the church in Sydney where the Wessons belonged, and the two couples had become friends.

The 800-acre Wesson ranch was located some twenty miles north of Sydney. Charles and Marian had purchased this ranch just over a year ago and were superbly happy raising ten times as many sheep as they had on the much smaller ranch they owned before in western Australia.

Lamar ran his gaze over the vast rolling grassland beneath the shining sun and a sky dotted with puffy white clouds, drained his teacup, and said, "Charles...Marian...this is a beautiful spot. I envy you living out here in the country, away from the noise and crowds of Sydney."

"We sure love it," Charles said. "The Lord has been so good to us. We learned about this place being for sale when we took a boat trip and met the people who owned it. We got to talking, and when they learned that we were sheep ranchers and wanted to get a larger ranch, they told us theirs was for sale. We came here a few weeks later and fell in love with the place. The Lord let us work out financial arrangements with the owners, so we signed the papers to purchase it. When we put our place up for sale, the Lord sent buyers almost immediately. So, here we are."

"Lamar, would you like some more tea?" Marian said.

"No, thank you. Pauline and I had better head for home."

Pauline nodded. "Guess we'd better, dear." Then to Marian: "Honey, the lunch was delicious."

"Next time, it's our turn," Lamar said. "That is, if you don't mind eating in a small house on a main boulevard with city traffic passing by."

"That would not be a problem," Charles said. "We'd love to come to town and have lunch with you."

"All right," said Pauline. "How about a week from today? Lunch at noon?"

Marian smiled. "It's a date!"

The Prescotts rose from their wicker chairs, and the Wessons did the same.

At that moment, Charles noticed a rider on a bay horse coming from the road toward the house. "Marian, Elizabeth's here."

Marian set her eyes on the approaching rider. "Sure enough."

"Who's this?" Pauline asked.

"Her name's Elizabeth Ashlock. She and her husband, Colin, are our nearest neighbors. Their ranch is just south of ours. They're young—in their twenties—but they have the largest ranch anywhere near Sydney. Colin's parents came here from England when he was a teenager, and he became sole owner of their

15,000-acre cattle and sheep ranch when his parents died in a boating accident five years ago. Elizabeth's originally from England too. Colin met her in London a couple of years ago. They got married and Colin proudly brought his bride home to Australia with him."

"Colin's quite busy with the ranch, and even travels a lot," said Marian, "but Elizabeth rides over here at least once a week to spend some time with us. We've witnessed to both of them, but so far we haven't been able to win them to Jesus. But we'll keep praying and trying. Elizabeth and I have become very close. She says I remind her of her mother, which makes her miss her mother more, but in other ways, she says it's a comfort to be close to me."

"On several occasions Elizabeth has told both of us how lonely she is here," Charles said, "being so far from home and in such a different culture. She loves Colin dearly, and she's trying very hard to adjust to Australia and life on the ranch. But it's difficult for her with Colin so busy with his work and traveling as he does."

The young woman on the bay mare drew up to the front of the house. Lamar and Pauline moved toward the porch steps, and Charles and Marian followed.

Elizabeth Ashlock dismounted and brushed wrinkles from her riding skirt as the two couples descended the steps.

Marian hugged Elizabeth and introduced her to the Prescotts. After greetings were exchanged, the Prescotts boarded their buggy, and as they were pulling away, Pauline said, "Don't forget—lunch at our house a week from today. See you in church!"

Marian took hold of Elizabeth's arm, and when she looked into the young woman's eyes, she could tell that she had been crying. "Come up and sit on the porch, honey."

"Is something wrong, Elizabeth?" Charles asked. "You seem upset."

They reached the porch, and Elizabeth gave Charles a weak smile that failed to make its way to her eyes. "Could—could we sit down and talk?"

"Of course," said Marian as she guided her to one of the white wicker chairs. "Just sit there and cool off a bit, dear. You stay with her, Charles. I'll go get us some nice cool lemonade, then we can talk."

Charles sat next to Elizabeth, who removed her broad-brimmed hat, wearily leaned her head back against the chair, and fanned her face with it.

"Rather warm today, isn't it?" Charles said.

"I've still not gotten used to these Australian summers. We had a much milder climate in England."

Charles nodded. "I'm sure that's true." He paused, then said, "Colin's working hard today as usual, I suppose."

Elizabeth kept fanning her face with the hat. "Yes. As usual."

After a few more minutes, Marian pushed open the screen door and moved toward Elizabeth and Charles, carrying a tray with glasses of cool lemonade and a plate of gingersnap cookies.

Elizabeth laid aside her hat.

Marian placed the tray on the small table and handed Elizabeth a glass and two cookies. "Here you go, dear. Just sip and munch. I'm of the mind that food and drink will always bring comfort to someone who's troubled."

"Thank you, Marian."

Marian sat in the wicker chair on the other side of Elizabeth as Charles lifted a glass of lemonade from the tray and picked up two cookies.

"Now, tell us what the problem is and how Charles and I can help," Marian said. "We're always here for you, dear."

Elizabeth's face turned the color of milk and she cleared her throat gently. "Charlie…Marian…since I've become acquainted with you this past year, I've found you to be such kind and considerate people. I definitely need help, and the reason I rode over here today is to share my problem with you about Colin." Elizabeth felt her bottom lip quiver and she touched it with a trembling hand. "Colin…Colin is making my life miserable because of—" She choked and swallowed hard. "Because of his insatiable avarice. He is by far the wealthiest rancher in this part of Australia. No other ranch within five hundred miles has this much land, stock, nor hired men."

Elizabeth took a deep breath to steady herself, then sipped some lemonade. Her color seemed to improve, and she went on. "Colin is already a multimillionaire, but the only thing he thinks about is getting a whole lot richer. You know that terribly expensive seventy-foot steam and sail ship he calls the *Bristol*? Well, he leaves me for weeks at a time to sail to other countries so he can make investments that he hopes will increase his wealth. Even…even when he's home, he pays little mind to me. He's too busy with his cattle and sheep, doing whatever he can to see that they multiply and make him more money.

"I need to know what to do. I feel left out and unimportant, and it's tearing me to pieces. If…if I died, Colin probably wouldn't even spend the money to buy a coffin or purchase a burial plot. He'd just lay my body on top of one of those big rocks on his ranch and let the birds eat it."

Tears were glistening in Elizabeth's eyes.

Marian left her chair, put an arm around Elizabeth's neck, and kissed the brokenhearted woman's cheek. "I'm so sorry your life has turned out this way, Elizabeth."

Charles reached over to pat Elizabeth's arm. "May I remind you, Elizabeth, that Marian and I told you and Colin the very first time we met that we are born-again Christians and that we base our lives on the Scriptures. Without Jesus Christ in our lives, none of us can know true satisfaction in our hearts and souls."

Elizabeth looked off in the distance for a few seconds, then said, "I've thought a lot about what you and Marian have told Colin and me about Jesus and our need to know Him as our Saviour. And I will think more about it, too. I just have never heard it put like you put it. I mean, I believe in God. And I believe in Jesus."

"That's fine, honey," Marian said, "but there's more to it than just believing that the Father exists and that His Son exists. You must do as the Bible says. You must repent of your sin and receive the Lord Jesus into your heart as your own *personal* Saviour."

Elizabeth nodded. "Marian...Charlie...I appreciate both of you so much. I promise. I will continue to think about this. The reason I came over here to talk to you is because you seem to know a whole lot about life and its problems."

Charles smiled. "We know what we know because we've learned it from God's Word after becoming His born-again children."

Elizabeth thought on those words for a few seconds, then said, "Charlie, does the Bible say anything about greed and its results?"

"It sure does."

"Tell me what it says."

"I'll do better than that. I'll go get my Bible and let you read what it says."

At the Ashlock ranch, tall, slender Colin Ashlock had gathered all twenty-six of his hired men under a stand of trees near the barn. Among the group gathered in the welcome shade of the trees were his ship captain, Henry Briggs, and four crewmen who always went along whenever Colin got an urge to sail. Otherwise, Briggs and the crewmen labored on the ranch along with the other hired men.

Running his gaze over their faces, Colin said, "Men, I want to let you know that Henry and the crew and I are going to sail the *Bristol* up to the Solomon Islands where I'm going to meet with some businessmen I've been dealing with through the mail. These men want me to invest in a new manufacturing company in Honiara, the capital city. If the company is all they say it is, I could make millions on the investment. I want to check it out and look their plant over."

Colin's sheep foreman, Walter Robbins, said, "I hope it works out for you, Mr. Ashlock. What does this company manufacture?"

"Construction machinery and farm implements. There's a real need for it in that part of the Pacific."

"Sir, when do you want to leave?" Henry Briggs asked.

"Day after tomorrow at dawn, Henry. You and your crew can have the ship ready to go by then, can't you?"

"Oh, yes, sir. We'll need to get a load of coal on board, plus some food and supplies. But we can easily be ready."

"Good. That's when we'll sail, then."

At the Wesson ranch, Elizabeth Ashlock was impressed with the Bible's warnings about the pitfalls that lay in the path of the person who lived only for the riches they had obtained or wished to obtain.

"Thank you, Charles, for showing me these Scriptures," Elizabeth said, smiling at him. "I wish you could show them to Colin."

"I'd be glad to if he'd let me."

Elizabeth glanced at Marian, then back at Charles. "Could the two of you come to the ranch to talk to Colin?"

"We'd be glad to," Marian said. "We don't want to see your marriage destroyed by greed."

Tears misted Elizabeth's eyes. "Oh, thank you. Colin already knows I'm unhappy, and he knows why. I'll tell him you're coming to see us because I came to you for advice. Could you possibly come for dinner this evening?"

Marian looked at her husband and he nodded.

Elizabeth thumbed the tears from her eyes and said, "Wonderful! I'll have our cook prepare a special meal for you." She sighed. "Well, I'd better head for home. Can you be there by six-thirty?"

"Sure can," Charles said.

The Wessons walked Elizabeth to her horse. She hugged both of them, thanked them for their kindness, mounted up, and rode away.

The Wessons stood on the porch and watched her until she passed from view.

Charles then turned to Marian. "Well, honey, let's go spend some time praying about this."

As Elizabeth trotted her horse along the road toward the gate of the Ashlock ranch, she felt a slow ruffle of apprehension go through her. How would Colin react to what the Wessons were going to say to him, and to the Scriptures Charles would show him?

She shook her head and said to herself, "Something's got to happen, or this marriage is over. I love Colin with all my heart, but

I can't go on living like this. Please, Colin, what the Wessons are going to tell you makes sense. Just listen to them, will you?"

Moments later, Elizabeth rode onto the Ashlock ranch and trotted her horse down the wagon trail toward the house. She let her eyes roam to the vast herd of sheep on one side of the place, and the herd of cattle on the other.

When she neared the ranch house, she saw her husband standing near the front porch, talking to one of his hired men.

She guided the horse toward the barn, but when Colin saw her, he signaled for her to come to him. Her heart skipped a beat as she turned the horse toward him. Colin's features were like stone.

The hired man walked away as Elizabeth pulled her horse to a halt.

Colin stepped up as she dismounted, the stony look still on his face. "Where have you been?"

Keeping her voice steady, she replied, "I went over to the Wesson ranch to talk to Charlie and Marian."

"Why didn't you tell me you were going?"

Elizabeth forced a smile. "Well, darling, Frank and the maids knew I was going. You were busy at the barn, so I told them where I was going so if you asked, they could tell you."

Colin's cold stare was still on her. "Well, I need to talk to you," he said curtly.

NINE

Colin's impudent attitude and the harshness in his voice scraped like flint on Elizabeth's senses, and struck fire within. "I wasn't aware that I had to check with you before I took a ride. I don't like being treated like a child. As I said, Frank and the maids could have told you where I was if you had asked them."

Colin frowned. "You should have told me you were going."

She gave him a petulant look and said, "Before we talk, I'll take my horse to the barn. I'll be right back."

"I'll take the mare to the barn later!" Colin snapped. "I want to talk to you right now."

Elizabeth shrugged. "Whatever you say."

"Let's sit here on the steps," Colin said, gesturing toward the wide stairs that led up to the mansion's porch.

When they were seated, Elizabeth looked at him and waited for him to speak.

"You need to know that my ship crew and I are leaving on Thursday morning at dawn to go to Honiara so I can look into that investment that I told you about a few days ago. Remember?"

"Yes."

"If it's as good as it looks, I can make millions."

"So how long will you be gone?"

"It'll probably take at least two weeks. Maybe three."

"Haven't you got enough money without this venture?" she said.

"Why does my desire to increase my net worth always have to be a problem to you?"

She looked him square in the eye. "Because for one thing, you don't *need* any more money. You've already got more than you could ever spend if you lived to be a hundred and fifty years old! And for another thing, your endless search for greater riches leaves me here alone."

He stared at her silently.

She took a sharp breath. "Colin, do you have any idea how lonely I am? I left everything and everyone that I've ever known and loved to marry you and come to this place. The Wessons are the only friends I have. You and I never leave this place together to visit anyone. In fact, we never leave this ranch together to go *anywhere*. You sail the *Bristol* all over this part of the world to lay hold on more riches while I sit here and pine away alone."

"What do you mean, 'alone'? My hired men and their families are here, as well as the servants."

"Well, they're acquaintances, dear husband, but they're not friends. I can't confide in them and find solace in them when I'm so lonely for you. The only human beings I can confide in and get solace from are the Wessons." Tears filled Elizabeth's eyes. "Even when you're not out sailing the oceans, you're away from the house most every day, working to increase your wealth on the ranch. Most days, I hardly see you."

Colin shook his head. "So I've never done a thing for you, huh?"

She wiped tears and sniffed. "I don't mean that. Of course you have. Colin, you've been very generous with me when it comes to material things. I have more than a woman could ever dream of, but I love you, and as I've told you before, I need to be with you. I need to have your attention on me a lot more than it is. After all, I *am* your wife."

Colin squared his angular jaw. "You ought to be happy that you're married to a wealthy man. I indeed have showered you with anything and everything you could ever want or need. As my wife, you're a very rich woman, Elizabeth."

She bit her lower lip and burst into sobs.

Colin touched her shoulder. "Why can't you be satisfied with everything I've given you?"

Tears streamed down Elizabeth's cheeks. She took a trembling breath and said, "Colin, all of the wealth in the world cannot buy love or happiness. Why is money so much more important to you than anything else? My companionship, for instance."

Colin sighed and shook his head. "You just don't understand, Elizabeth."

"I sure don't! That's why I'm asking you. Why is money more important to you than anything else? I need the love and affection of my husband, as well as time with him. Why don't you need that from me?"

"I do, but I want to build up a fortune while I'm young and able to do it. Why don't you try to understand that?"

Elizabeth wiped her tears and set her reddened eyes on him. "I have tried to understand it, Colin, but my loneliness overrides it. I need you close to me. I don't want anything to happen to our marriage." When those words came from her mouth, she blinked, sniffed, and said, "Oh. I need to tell you that I invited the Wessons over for dinner this evening. I believe they can help us."

"Help us? They're nothing but ignorant religious fanatics, Elizabeth."

"No! They are good people, very wise people. And they care about others. That's why they talked to you and me about Jesus Christ and salvation. They don't want us to go into eternity without being ready to face God."

Colin rubbed the back of his neck and let out a sigh.

Elizabeth touched his arm. "Colin, I went over to talk to the Wessons because I wanted their help. I wanted them to help us save our marriage."

"So our marriage is in danger of falling apart, is it?"

"I wish it weren't, but it takes *two* to make a marriage a success, and I'm having to handle it alone. I want our marriage to work, Colin, but it can't when you ignore me most of the time while being obsessed with becoming richer."

"You want too much from me! I'm busy. I can't hang around the house with you all the time!"

More tears glistened in Elizabeth's eyes. "I can't stand this much longer, Colin. You know we don't spend a total of two waking hours alone together in a week. I want the Wessons to counsel us because I don't want our marriage to break up. Will you at least talk to them with me when they're here tonight?"

"I'll treat them courteously. That's all I can promise."

He rose to his feet and moved toward Elizabeth's bay mare. Without another word, he took the reins in hand and led the mare toward the barn.

Elizabeth stood up and watched him walk away. Wiping more tears, she said in a low voice, "Colin Ashlock, if this doesn't change, I'm leaving you."

cℵɔ

That evening, just before six-thirty, Elizabeth was at the parlor window, watching for Charles and Marian Wesson's buggy to appear.

Colin sat nearby in an overstuffed chair, looking over a sales report on some sheep his foreman, Walter Robbins, had sold at a good price a few days previously.

One of the maids, Sally Thurston, stood at the parlor door, waiting for her mistress to tell her the guests were arriving. Sally knew that Mr. Ashlock would not allow his wife to greet the guests at the door. It must be done by one of the servants.

At that moment, Elizabeth turned from the window and said with a lilt in her voice, "They're coming, Sally!"

"Yes, mum," Sally said and hurried toward the door.

Colin laid the papers aside, left the overstuffed chair, and walked to the window where Elizabeth was peering through the sheer curtains at the Wessons as they were mounting the steps to the front porch.

Colin looked out at them and said, "Oh, no, Charles has his Bible with him. He's probably gonna preach that 'get saved' stuff to us again."

"It's just because he cares about us," Elizabeth said. "Please don't be rude to him."

"I already told you I'll be courteous."

The Wessons passed from view, and Colin and Elizabeth heard Sally greeting them at the door.

Elizabeth took her husband by the hand and led him to the center of the room, where they stopped, facing the open door.

Footsteps were heard, then Sally appeared, smiling, with the Wessons behind her and said, "Mr. and Mrs. Ashlock, your friends are here."

Colin stepped forward and shook hands with Charles, then took Marian's hand, did a slight bow, and also welcomed her.

They went to the dining room, and as they began to eat, Colin's nerves were on edge. Charles had laid his Bible on a small table near where he was sitting, and Colin was sure he and Elizabeth were going to get another sermon about opening their hearts to Jesus.

During the meal, Charles and Marian talked to the Ashlocks about sheep and cattle ranching, and other related subjects. The cook and one of the maids were in and out of the dining room, and the Wessons wanted privacy when they talked about spiritual matters.

When the meal was over, the Ashlocks led the Wessons to the parlor, and they sat down together. Elizabeth noticed Colin warily eyeing the Bible in Charles's hand and elbowed him to make him stop. Colin gave her a sheepish grin.

There was silence at first, then Elizabeth said, "Charles…Marian…I had a talk with Colin when I got home this afternoon. I told him exactly the same things I told you about my loneliness and unhappiness, and that I feared our marriage was in trouble. I made sure he understands that, as I see it, I am number two in his heart, and his wealth and the desire to obtain more of it is number one."

"Really, Elizabeth, you didn't have to bother these people about how you feel," Colin said. "You and I can work it out."

"Well, I hope you do work it out, Colin," said Charles. "But Marian and I want to help if we can." He looked at Elizabeth. "Did you tell Colin that you asked me if the Bible says anything about greed and its results?"

"No. There hasn't been time for me to tell him about that."

Colin eyed his wife and frowned. "You asked him *what?*"

"I asked him if the Bible has anything to say about greed in a person's heart, and the results of that greed. He showed me some Scriptures on it, and I want him to show them to you."

Colin felt a surge of anger boil up within him. "Oh, so you want him to preach to me because you think my desire to become more wealthy is just plain greed."

"What else could it be?"

"I told you what it is, and you still don't understand. I simply want to build up a fortune while I'm still young and able to do it."

Elizabeth's eyes flashed fire. "Nonsense! You already have more money than you could spend in two lifetimes, Colin! You don't need any more money. What drives you to keep piling up more wealth is plain old-fashioned greed. And your excessive desire for money is about to drive me out of my mind!"

Charles took hold of his Bible. "Colin, Elizabeth is right. You're already a multimillionaire, aren't you?"

"Yes."

"Then it is indeed greed that drives you to gain more wealth at the risk of losing your marriage. Elizabeth has a right, as your wife, to expect that you will put more attention on her and give her more of your time." He opened his Bible. "Let me show you what God says about greed in a person's heart."

Colin licked his lips. He wanted to tell the Wessons to leave, but refrained.

"Listen to this, Colin. Proverbs 15:27 says, 'He that is greedy of gain troubleth his own house.' Can you see the truth in those words? Your greed—your insatiable desire to continually become richer—is troubling your own house. Your marriage is on shaky ground because of it. It certainly has caused trouble between you and your wife, according to what she has told Marian and me."

Charles flipped back to the New Testament. "Colin, let me

read you the parable that Jesus told of the greedy rich man in the twelfth chapter of Luke. I already read it to Elizabeth earlier today. It's in verses 16 through 21.

"'And he spake a parable unto them, saying, The ground of a certain rich man brought forth plentifully: And he thought within himself, saying, What shall I do, because I have no room where to bestow my fruits? And he said, This will I do: I will pull down my barns, and build greater; and there will I bestow all my fruits and my goods. And I will say to my soul, Soul, thou hast much goods laid up for many years; take thine ease, eat, drink, and be merry. But God said unto him, Thou fool, this night thy soul shall be required of thee: then whose shall those things be, which thou hast provided? So is he that layeth up treasure for himself, and is not rich toward God.'

"Colin, did you notice how quickly the greedy man lost his riches when God took him into eternity, saying, 'Thou fool, this night thy soul shall be required of thee'? He couldn't take his riches with him when he died, and neither can you."

Colin could only stare silently at Charles.

Marian spoke up. "Jesus made it clear there, Colin, that it's better to be rich toward God than to ignore Him and cling to your earthly treasures. According to Scripture, the only way you can be rich toward God is to make His Son your Saviour."

Again, Colin remained silent.

Charles said, "Let me read you something else in Proverbs that I read to Elizabeth earlier. This speaks of those who have flocks and herds—livestock. Like *you* have, Colin. Proverbs 27:23 and the first part of verse 24: 'Be thou diligent to know the state of thy flocks, and look well to thy herds. For riches are not for ever.'

"Listen to that last statement again, Colin. 'Riches are not for ever.' Let's face it. Whatever earthly things we possess, we lose them when we die…and so often, they are lost while we live. You shouldn't set your heart on your earthly possessions, nor wrap your life up in gaining more possessions. The right thing is to open your heart to Jesus and be saved. As Marian pointed out, that will make you rich toward God."

Colin's face went dark red.

Elizabeth saw it, and a shudder ran through her and her heart began to pound.

"I have my own ideas about riches and piling up all I can, Charles," Colin said. "I will go on as I have been doing. And I also have my own ideas about death and eternity. I don't believe that Bible, and I don't want to hear any more!"

Charles held his voice calm as he asked, "But what about this problem between you and Elizabeth, Colin?"

Colin rose to his feet. His features were redder than ever. "I don't want to be rude to you people, but this conversation is over." With that, he stormed out of the room.

Tears filled Elizabeth's eyes and she pressed a palm over her mouth.

Marian said, "I'm sorry for the heartache you're facing, dear, but believe me, if you would open your heart to Jesus and receive Him as your Saviour, He would be there to help you."

Elizabeth wiped tears and drew a trembling breath. "Marian, I'm just not in a frame of mind to make that move right now."

Charles was on his feet. He laid a hand on Elizabeth's shoulder. "We can't force you to get saved, little lady. We'll go now, but could we pray before we go?"

Elizabeth nodded. "You may."

Charles prayed, asking the Lord to work in Colin's and Elizabeth's hearts to bring them both to Himself. When he had finished praying, Elizabeth walked the Wessons to the front door, thanked them for coming, and bid them good night.

❧

At the breakfast table in the Ashlock mansion the next morning, all Colin could talk about was the proposed financial venture in Honiara, Guadalcanal. Elizabeth barely picked at her food and listened silently.

Colin noted it and scowled. "Elizabeth, why can't you at least try to understand what I'm doing? The more money I make, the richer you are, too!"

Elizabeth looked across the table at him. She swallowed with difficulty, but could not find her voice. She stood up, met his questioning gaze for a few seconds, then turned and left the dining room.

When she stepped into the hall, two of the maids were there. One of them asked if she was finished with her breakfast. Elizabeth nodded and headed down the hall toward the spiral staircase. One of them called, "Is Mr. Ashlock finished, too?"

Elizabeth looked back, hunched her shoulders, then hurried toward the staircase. With tears washing her cheeks, she ran up the stairs and bolted toward the master bedroom.

In the dining room, Colin took his last bite of scrambled eggs, finished his coffee, and stepped out into the hall. The two maids were there, wondering what to do. Colin said, "We're finished, girls. You can clean up the table now."

Colin left the house, went to the barn, saddled up, and rode with his cattle foreman, Clyde Devore, to look over the herd.

When Colin and Clyde returned some four hours later, Colin entered the mansion at the back door and stepped into the kitchen. Frank Coleman was busy at the stove, preparing lunch. He turned, set his eyes on his employer, and said, "Mr. Ashlock, were you aware that Mrs. Ashlock was going to hitch up a pair of horses to one of the wagons and drive it, herself?"

Colin frowned. "Well…no. She did this?"

"Yes, sir. I didn't even know she knew how to hitch a team to a wagon, but she did it. It puzzled me, too, because she had two bags with her. You know, the kind that you put clothes in when you travel."

"She did?"

"Yes, sir. I have no idea where she was going. But I didn't think it was any of my business to stop her and ask."

Colin shrugged. "Well, Frank, I'm not going to try to find her. She'll be back."

That evening, when Colin came into the mansion from the barn for supper, he found the cook in the kitchen as usual, and said, "Frank, do you know if Elizabeth came back?"

"She didn't, sir. A couple of maids were just in here and said they were looking for Mrs. Ashlock and couldn't find her anywhere."

Colin nodded. "I'm going upstairs to wash up. Guess you can tell the maids to set only one place at the table for dinner. Looks like I'll be eating alone."

He made his way up the spiral staircase, washed up in the bathroom attached to the master bedroom, then entered the bedroom. His eye caught the sheet of paper that lay on the dresser.

He picked up the paper and read the message Elizabeth had left for him:

Colin—

I am going back home to England. By the time you read this, I will already be at sea. Our marriage is over. You will find the wagon and team at the docks. Good-bye.
Elizabeth

❧

Early the next morning after Colin had eaten his breakfast, he called for all members of the house staff to meet him in the parlor.

When everyone was there, gathered in a half-circle facing him, Colin said in a dull tone, "Mrs. Ashlock has left me and gone back to England. She left a note saying our marriage is over. I'm sure all of you knew that Mrs. Ashlock was very unhappy. I should never have married her in the first place. She is too self-centered. My ship crew and I are leaving immediately for Sydney to board the *Bristol* and sail to the Solomon Islands. Take care of the house, and I'll see you when we get back."

Colin wheeled and left the room. The house staff looked at each other in sadness.

Frank Coleman shook his head. "Poor little dear. Miss Elizabeth is such a lovely young lady. She brought a graciousness to this house that was certainly lacking before."

"For sure," Sally Thurston said. "Too bad Mr. Ashlock is so blinded by his riches that he couldn't see what a prize he had in Miss Elizabeth."

The head housekeeper nodded. "Well, back to our work, my friends. There's nothing we can do about it. We don't want him getting upset at us. We all need our jobs."

TEN

In early afternoon on Sunday, January 23, 1848, at Sutter's Fort, James Marshall stood at the docks on the American River with his employer, John Sutter. The brilliant California sunshine flickered on the surface of the river, highlighting the white foam that collected along the bank.

While they waited for Sutter's steamboat operator, Zack Clements, to bring the boat to the docks from the company's boathouse, the slender, forty-five-year-old Sutter thanked his mill foreman for spending the past four days with him at the fort.

James smiled. "Well, Mr. Sutter, since I now have Tim Benson to handle things at the mill when I'm gone, I can come and stay a few days every once in a while. I've really enjoyed it, and I think you and I have done some excellent planning for making the mill pay off even better in the future."

"I agree, James. And I sure am glad you hired Tim. He's been a genuine asset to Sutter's Mill."

"That's for sure. Wire me whenever you need to get together with me again, and we'll set a time. I'm so glad we have the telegraph between the fort and the mill now. It really helps us to stay in communication."

"Yes, it does. Thanks to Mr. Samuel B. Morse, I don't have to wait until I get a letter from you to send Zack upriver to pick you up in the boat."

At that moment, the sound of the small steamboat's engine met their ears. Sutter turned and looked at the boat as it pulled out of the boathouse and started down the river toward the docks.

James looked at his boss, whom he admired very much. Having been an officer in the Swiss army, John Sutter carried himself erect, in the military manner. His blond hair curled above his ears and across the top of his broad forehead, giving him the appearance of a Teutonic Napoleon. He kept his side-whiskers and mustache neatly trimmed, imperial fashion.

Zack Clements guided the boat up to the nearest dock, looked up at the mill foreman, and smiled. "All right, James. I'll take you home now."

The next morning, Monday, January 24, just before 7:00, James Marshall arrived at Sutter's Mill in the light of the rising sun. Wearing his mackinaw, he walked alongside the gurgling race toward its confluence with the American River.

The night had been quite cold, and James saw a rime of ice covering the rocks where the water had splashed. When he reached the headgate, he closed it, wanting to let the water's depth go down in the waterway so he could make sure nothing had entered that would clog it up.

"Well," he said to himself as he walked toward the lower end, "it looks good so far."

He walked on, eyeing the waterway closely. When the water

was at a depth of six inches, he said, "Still looks all right. Everything is just as it should—"

He stopped abruptly where the rime and water still in the bed of the channel gave a gleam to the pebbles and sand at the bottom in the morning sunlight. He blinked as a few particular sparkles caught his eye. He squinted at the sparkling segments that reflected the sunlight.

"I'd say that those are glittering pieces of quartz, but they're too shiny for quartz."

James dipped his hand into the water and pulled out two pieces of the shiny metal, each about the size of a silver dollar. He examined them closely and shook his head. "It can't be. Naw, it can't be."

James picked up a fist-sized rock from alongside the waterway and laid one of the shiny pieces on top of a large rock imbedded in the ground. He pounded on the gleaming metal piece and found that it could be beaten into different shapes, but did not break or split no matter how hard he pounded.

He shook his head. "Naw, it can't be."

He laid the other shiny piece on the large rock, pounded it hard, but again found that he could beat it into various shapes without it breaking or splitting.

He reached into the water and took out several more pieces of the gleaming metal. He pounded them with the rock as he had done the others, and the result was exactly the same.

James held all of them in his hands, moving them so as to cause the sunlight to flash off them. "This is no average metal. It sure looks like—no. Impossible." He shook his head. "It can't be *gold*. Can it?"

James placed the battered pieces in his mackinaw pockets and took more from the bottom of the channel, also placing them in his pockets.

He hurried to the headgate and opened it, letting the water gush into the channel, then made his way toward the mill buildings where employees were gathering for the day's work. When the men saw him, they welcomed him back.

He greeted them warmly, then headed for his office. He was almost to the building that housed the office when he saw Tim Benson coming his way. When Tim caught up to him, they entered the building together as Tim asked, "Everything all right at the race?"

James nodded. "All's clear, and the water's running swift and beautiful. You can get the men started with the saws."

"Will do," said Tim, as he veered off and went into his own office.

James entered his office, closed the door behind him, then took off his mackinaw. He removed the shiny metal pieces from the pockets, placed them in a small cardboard box, and closed the lid.

The mill's telegraph key was in James's office. He sat down at the table that held it, and quickly sent a wire to Sutter's Fort by Morse code, telling John Sutter it was necessary that he return to the fort as soon as possible. He needed to see him about something very important. It just might be very good news.

Some twenty-five minutes later, a reply came back from Sutter, saying he already had Zack Clements in his boat, heading upriver to get him.

It was going on one o'clock in the afternoon when James Marshall entered John Sutter's office, carrying the small cardboard box.

Sutter looked up from some papers he was studying and said, "Ah, James! Come and sit down."

James eased onto the straight-backed wooden chair that stood in front of the desk and laid the box on his right leg.

"All right," said Sutter, "what's this emergency that might be good news?"

James lifted the box toward his employer. "Look in here."

Sutter set the box on the desktop and opened the lid. The instant his eyes caught the glitter of the metal, he looked at James. "What's this?"

"Well, sir, I think it just might be gold."

Sutter's eyebrows arched and his eyes widened. "Gold?"

"Yes, sir."

"Where'd you find it?"

"I was checking out the race early this morning as usual, when I spotted these glittery little fellows staring up at me. I know a little about minerals, and I know that gold can be beaten into different shapes, so I tried it with those crinkled-up pieces, beating them with a rock. As you can see, they're not broken or split in any way. Do you know somebody we can take it to who knows how to determine if it is gold?"

"Don't need to take it to somebody. My *Encyclopedia Americana* has a section describing the properties of gold, and how to learn if metal that looks to be gold actually is."

Sutter left his desk and walked to a large bookshelf across the room. "I've spent a lot of time reading it, just to learn how it's done. Never thought I'd actually do an experiment myself."

He took the proper volume from the shelf and headed back toward his desk. "We'll have to get some nitric acid. We can get some at the apothecary shop here at the fort."

Sutter sat down and opened the book to the proper section. He read the description of the properties of gold to James, then together they compared the battered pieces and those untouched by the rock.

After careful examination, and checking the encyclopedia repeatedly, Sutter set bright eyes on James and said, "Sure appears that we've got gold on our hands. Let's run over to the apothecary and get that nitric acid. Then we'll know for sure."

When they returned to the office, John Sutter and James Marshall laid the shiny pieces of metal on a table. Sutter set the bottle of nitric acid on the table and said, "All right, James. We'll follow exactly what the encyclopedia says we're to do. Remember?"

"Yes. We're to place the metal in a glass bowl and cover it with the nitric acid."

"Right. I'll get a bowl from my apartment. Be right back."

Sutter hurried away and was back in less then four minutes.

"All right, James," he said, placing the bowl on the table and picking up the bottle of acid. "The encyclopedia says if the pieces of metal remain in the acid for a half hour without being discolored by it, what we have in our hands is real gold."

"Yes, sir."

Sutter opened the bottle and poured acid into the bowl until all pieces of the metal were submerged. He stared down at the bowl and said, "We'll wait a full hour, just to be sure."

The two men sat down and talked about what it would mean if the metal pieces were real gold. Sutter said excitedly that if they were, the mountains, hills, and streams in that part of California would no doubt hold plenty of gold. Certainly Sutter's Mill and the surrounding river and land could be chock-full of it.

James felt his own excitement, knowing that if what Mr. Sutter had just said about Sutter's Mill was true, he would probably get a share of the gold.

When the hour had passed, they stepped out behind the

office, and Sutter carefully poured the acid from the bowl. A gleam filled his eyes when he held the bowl before his mill foreman. "Look, James, no discoloration! It's gold! Real gold! We're rich, James! We're rich! What you have found—according to the *Encyclopedia Americana*—is gold of the finest quality! We're rich! We're rich!"

James smiled to himself. He liked the way his boss was saying, "*We're* rich!"

John Sutter accompanied James Marshall back to the mill the next morning in the boat piloted by Zack Clements. The foreman ordered all the employees of the mill to assemble in the building that housed the offices, and after greeting the men warmly, John Sutter asked James to tell the men about his discovery the previous morning.

The men listened intently as James described finding the metal in the water channel and testing it by pounding it with the rock. He felt sure he had found gold and had returned to Sutter's Fort to tell Mr. Sutter about it. Sutter then told them of the nitric acid test, and that James most definitely had discovered gold.

The men cheered and shouted for joy.

By that evening, the news of James Marshall's discovery had spread all over Sacramento. By noon the next day, the news had reached San Francisco and soon spread all over the city.

When news of the gold discovery at Sutter's Mill floated down the Sacramento River to the more populated regions of California, men openly began to make plans to go to the American River and seek gold.

California's governor immediately called for a meeting of his legislature. They established rules for staking claims along the American River, and even on land, since there was little doubt that gold was also in the Sierra Nevada Mountains and streams, and in the hills and streams in the Sacramento area. The governor assigned men of the California militia to oversee the establishing of claims, and to see that legitimate claims were not infringed upon by illegal "claim jumpers."

During February and March, men came from all over California to dig and pan for gold. The golden news began to spread to other American territories and states. Soon it was in newspapers from coast to coast.

Newspaper reporters began interviewing national leaders and the general public on James Marshall's discovery at Sutter's Mill and publishing their statements. The newspapers found that most people were skeptical that real gold had been found.

Some national leaders declared that what James Marshall found in the waterway at Sutter's Mill was only pyrite—"fool's gold"—a common sulfide mineral. Others declared it was only yellow mica, a hydrous silicate mineral of little value. Other national leaders said that the whole thing was just a real estate promotion to bring people to the San Francisco–Sacramento area.

However, by the end of March, a great number of Californians had staked claims along the American River and in the mountain streams that fed the river, and were finding gold. Small numbers of gold seekers were making their way to the area from many parts of the country in spite of the national attitude toward James Marshall's story.

At the San Francisco City Jail on Monday, April 3, two guards stood before the desk of the jail superintendent as he closed a folder and said, "All right, gentlemen. You can let him out of his cell and usher him out of the building. He has served his time."

The guards walked together into the cellblock, and one said to the other, "I'll be plenty glad to be rid of him. He's too smart to do anything that would lengthen his time in here, but I get so tired of his cynical attitude and his vile mouth."

"Yeah, me too," said the other guard as they turned a corner and headed down a long row of cells.

When they drew up to Usel Hacker's cell, he was standing at the cell door, looking at them through the bars with a smirk on his face. His long, matted hair covered his ears and lay on his shoulders.

The guard with the key unlocked the door and said, "Okay, Hacker, you're now a free man."

"Yeah, and I'm plenty glad to get outta here!" He fairly spit the words.

As the guards escorted Usel through the jail toward the front door, there was only one thing on his mind: *Kill Sacramento's town marshal.*

When they reached the front door of the building, one of the guards opened it and said, "Better think about the time you spent in here, Usel. You go back to committing robberies, you'll get caught just like you did before, only next time, we'll lock you up and throw away the key."

Usel gave him his evil smile. "You'll never lay eyes on me again, pal." He stepped out into the sunshine and, without looking back, walked away from the jail.

Usel slowly moved along the street, running his eyes to the horses at the hitch rails. When he saw a big long-legged black stallion with a white blaze and stockings, he stopped and smiled to himself. In the saddle scabbard was a rifle.

The stallion was tied between two other horses. Usel eased up to him, quickly untied the reins from the hitch rail, and guided him back from between the other two horses. Looking around to make sure no one was watching him, he put his left foot in the stirrup, swung into the saddle, and casually trotted the big black out of San Francisco.

That evening in Sacramento, Marshal Jack Powell, his wife, Carrie, their daughter, Rena, and sons, Randy and Darin, welcomed their guests as they arrived for dinner.

Pastor Rich Skiver and Rosie had drawn up to the Powell home in their buggy at the same time as Carrie's brother, Tim Benson, his wife, Sally, and their daughter, Lucinda, had arrived in theirs.

As the Skivers and the Bensons entered the house, they talked excitedly about the meal they were anticipating, agreeing that Carrie's cooking was marvelous.

Tim smiled at Carrie, who was blushing, and said, "Sis, you really should open a café. With your cooking, you'd be rich in no time."

"That's right, Carrie," Rosie said. "People would desert the other restaurants in town and stand in line to get into the famous Carrie's Café!"

Carrie laughed. "Sure, I'd enjoy running a café, but I've got enough to do without that." She then looked at Tim and said, "Speaking of getting rich, big brother, how about the gold John Sutter has you men at the sawmill taking out of the river? Is he going to share it with you?"

"As a matter of fact, we had a meeting at the mill this morning with Mr. Sutter himself. The first week of February, he had staked out a big claim along the river by the mill and had a few of the employees panning for gold each day for a couple of hours. We turned the gold over to James Marshall, and James put it in a safe place each day. We figured it was all going to Mr. Sutter.

"Well, Mr. Sutter announced this morning that the gold we've panned thus far has been put aside for future improvements on the mill property and the Sutter's Fort property. Then he told us that starting tomorrow, each one of his employees at the mill will be allowed to stake his own smaller claim within the big one. How about that?"

Carrie's eyes sparkled. "Wonderful, Tim!"

During the meal, the discussion turned to the attitude of people all across the country toward the gold strike. They marveled that so few people believed that real gold had been discovered in the American River.

"That really amazes me," Tim said. "But at the mill, we're learning every day that more and more Californians from farther north and all the way south to San Diego are showing up to stake claims, both on the American River and its tributaries in the Sierra Mountains."

"I'm hearing this same kind of report here in town, too, Tim," Jack said. "I'm sure that little by little, it will get out that genuine gold is being found in California. When people across the country realize it, many of them will be coming to get rich."

"Yes, sir," said Tim. "It's going to happen. I've got a feeling that someday this gold strike of James Marshall's will be so big, it'll go down in the history books!"

ELEVEN

While they all enjoyed the delicious meal at the Powell home in the residential section of Sacramento, Usel Hacker rode into town beneath a starlit sky, guiding the black stallion slowly along Main Street, which was lighted by street lamps. As he ran his eyes from one side of the street to the other, he noted that very few people were moving about.

When he drew up to what seemed to be the main intersection in Sacramento, Usel noticed three men standing on the corner under a street lamp, talking. Two of them were middle-aged, but Usel noted that the third man was younger, and wore a badge on his chest.

He rode on by, turned onto the intersecting street, and as soon as he was past the pharmacy building on the corner, he pulled rein and slid from the saddle. He tied the big black to a hitching post, then stealthily made his way in the shadows to the edge of the building, where he could hear the lawman and the two older men talking.

Usel soon picked up that the young lawman's name was Jarrod.

"One of Powell's deputies," he told himself as he turned and walked back to the black stallion. He mounted up and guided the horse back onto Main Street. When he reached the middle of the next block, he pulled rein when by the light of the street lamps, he saw a sign hanging over a door:

MARSHAL'S OFFICE
Jack Powell, Town Marshal

Usel muttered curse words under his breath. "Tomorrow," he hissed. "You die tomorrow, Powell. Vengeance will be mine."

Just before eight o'clock the next morning, Sacramento's marshal and his two deputies rode up in front of the marshal's office and dismounted. On the roof of the mercantile store directly across the street, Usel Hacker was bent low, cocked rifle in hand, watching them.

He recognized the deputy named Jarrod and heard the other young man wearing a badge call the older man Marshal.

Burning hatred swirled up inside Usel, causing him to grip the rifle so hard that his knuckles turned white. He had planned to simply identify his target, then follow him when he left the office later and gun the marshal down when he was alone, making his escape free of any complications.

But the hatred that flared up inside him was so consuming, so terrible, so reckless…that he decided to kill him now.

The three lawmen had tied their horses to the hitch rail and were heading toward the office door.

Usel Hacker's lips curved in a wicked grin as he drew a bead on Jack Powell's back and aimed for the spot that would send the slug right through his heart.

He squeezed the trigger.

The rifle thundered, shattering the morning's silence as Marshal Jack Powell went down. The loud, sharp sound rocked the street and echoes clattered along the boardwalks.

The deputies whipped out their guns while they pivoted around.

The rifle thundered again, and a second bullet buzzed past Cade Ryer's ear just as Jarrod Benson's Colt .45 roared, sending hot lead toward the crouching figure on the mercantile's roof.

The slug shattered wood, sending sharp fragments into Hacker's eyes. He let out a howl, ducked down as Deputy Benson fired a second shot his way, and crawled to the rear of the roof.

Jarrod saw the gunman duck and disappear. He said, "Cade, see to the marshal. I'm going after him!"

Jarrod darted across the street as townspeople looked on from the boardwalks, their eyes bulging and their hearts pounding. He ran between the mercantile building and the clothing store next to it. When he reached the alley, the gunman was still blinking at the wood fragments as he mounted the black stallion, clinging to the rifle.

Hacker wheeled the horse, intending to gallop from the alley, when suddenly he saw the young deputy standing spread-legged in his path, Colt .45 in hand. It was lined directly on Usel's chest. The muzzle seemed to be gaping at him hungrily with a widening mouth.

"Drop that rifle, mister! *Now!*" Deputy Benson barked.

Hacker reluctantly let the Browning slip from his fingers.

When it clattered to the dirt, Jarrod said, "Now, get off the horse and put your hands in the air."

Still blinking at the fragments that burned his eyes, Usel Hacker eased out of the saddle and planted his feet on the ground, fixing the young deputy with a hard glare. His hands hung at his sides.

"I said put your hands in the air!"

Usel lifted his hands above his shaggy head.

Jarrod took a few steps closer, studying the gunman's features closely. "You have to be related to the Hacker brothers who got themselves killed here in November."

The grim-faced gunman sneered. "Yeah. They were my brothers."

Jarrod held the Colt .45 on him steadily. "So what's *your* name?"

"Usel."

Jarrod removed the handcuffs that hung on his belt. "Turn around and lower your hands behind your back."

When Usel didn't respond, Jarrod said, "Don't tempt me to crack your skull, Hacker! You shot my boss. It wouldn't take much to get me riled beyond control."

The stubborn look faded from Usel's face.

"If Marshal Powell dies, you'll hang, mister. And I'll volunteer to be there and drop the noose over your head. Now, do as I tell you! Turn around and lower your hands behind your back!"

Usel Hacker reluctantly obeyed, and Jarrod snapped the cuffs on Usel's wrists.

In front of the marshal's office, the crowd looked on breathlessly as Dr. John Alford—one of Sacramento's three physicians—knelt over the fallen marshal, using his stethoscope to listen for a heartbeat. Deputy Cade Ryer knelt beside the doctor, his own heart racing as he noted that the rise and fall of the marshal's chest had ceased. He could still feel the breath of the bullet that had missed his left ear by a fraction of an inch. The hum of it also remained in his memory.

A woman in the crowd gasped when Dr. Alford eased back and shook his head. He solemnly hung the stethoscope on his neck, removed his spectacles, and pinched the bridge of his nose between his forefinger and thumb. "He's dead, Cade."

The words hit the crowd like a sledgehammer. Women began to cry, and men stood frozen in shock.

Cade fought back waves of nausea and bit his lips. "I'll go see if Jarrod needs my help, Doctor."

As Cade rose to his feet, a man moved up from the crowd and said, "Dr. Alford, I'll go bring the undertaker."

The doctor nodded. "Thanks, Walt."

Cade turned to head across the street, but halted when he saw Jarrod crossing the street beside a long-haired, bearded man, his gun aimed at the man's side. It was obvious that the man's hands were cuffed behind his back.

As Jarrod drew up with his prisoner, he glanced down at the unmoving form of Marshal Jack Powell, ran his gaze to the doctor, then to Cade, who said with tight throat, "Marshal Powell is dead, Jarrod. Walt Kramer has gone to get the undertaker."

Jarrod swallowed hard and looked down at the dead marshal. His breathing became uneven as he turned to his prisoner and said, "Let's go inside, Usel. There's a cell waiting for you."

Cade frowned as he studied the killer's rough features and said, "Jarrod, he's got to be a Hacker."

"He is. Name's Usel. He came here to have his vengeance on Marshal Powell and you and me for taking out his brothers back in November. C'mon, Usel. Let's go."

"I'll go in with you," Cade said. "Nothing more I can do out here."

They ushered their prisoner through the marshal's office to the cell block at the rear, removed the cuffs, and locked him in a cell.

Cade studied Usel's watery, bloodshot eyes. "Got something in your eyes, Hacker?"

"Wood splinters from the bullet I shot at him when he was on the roof of the mercantile," Jarrod said.

Cade gave the prisoner a cold look. "Well, splinters in your eyes won't seem so bad when you face what's coming to you. I'll tell you right now, mister, you will face Judge William Stedman for killing Marshal Powell. Believe me, Judge Stedman is the no-nonsense type. After the jury declares you guilty, he'll sentence you to the gallows. Count on it."

As Cade and Jarrod moved into the office, Cade touched his left ear and said, "Jarrod, that bullet barely missed my ear. I came mighty close to getting killed, myself."

Jarrod laid a hand on his shoulder and looked deep into his eyes. "Cade, I'm mighty glad it missed you. Marshal Powell was ready to die, but you're not."

Cade swallowed hard. "I...uh...I need to give it more thought."

"No, you need to open your heart to Jesus and let Him save you. Heaven is forever, Cade, and so is hell. I'm so glad I know that Marshal Powell is in heaven."

Cade met Jarrod's gaze, then looked down at the floor.

Jarrod squeezed the shoulder he was touching, let go, and said, "Well, I've got to go to the Powell home and break the news to the family."

"I've been the marshal's deputy longer than you have. Can I go with you?"

"Sure. And once that's done, I'll go break the news to my own family and to Pastor and Mrs. Skiver. You can come back here to the office."

"That'll be fine. Let's go."

Two days later, the church building was packed as Pastor Rich Skiver preached the funeral service for Marshal Jack Powell.

The Bensons sat with Carrie, Rena, Randy, and Darin on the second row of pews in the center section.

The pastor began his message by reading passages of Scripture about life, death, and eternity, and of the necessity of being born again to go to heaven. He then read to them how Jesus had shed His blood and died on the cross to provide salvation for the human race. He explained that to be saved we must repent of our sin and receive the crucified, risen Christ into our heart as Saviour. Then he spoke about what an excellent lawman Jack Powell had been, and spent time elaborating on his commendable role as a husband and father.

Carrie and her children dabbed at their tear-filled eyes as the pastor spoke so tenderly about Jack.

Pastor Skiver then said, "Let me say, however, that even more important than these laudable things I have just dwelt on in Jack's life, is the fact that he was a born-again child of God. As a teenager, he came under the preaching of the gospel in a Christ-honoring church in his home town of Kansas City, Missouri, and opened his heart to Jesus. And I'm so glad he did, because I can say that Jack is now in heaven with the Lord, the angels, and the born-again children of God who have gone on before us."

All over the audience, heads were nodding while people wiped tears from their faces.

Pastor Skiver dabbed at his own tears, looked at the Powell family, and said, "Carrie...Rena...Randy...Darin...because you also are born-again children of God, you will one day have a great reunion with your beloved husband and father in heaven."

In the audience, Cade Ryer kept thinking of how close that bullet came to his head, and where he would be at that very moment if he had been killed. Cade knew he would be in hell, and it felt like an iceberg had settled in his stomach.

The pastor closed his sermon and said they were going to have one verse of an invitation song. Those who wanted to receive Christ as their Saviour were invited to walk the aisle and church counselors would meet them at the front to pray with them.

The audience was asked to stand, and when the pump organ began to play, Cade Ryer hurried down the aisle. Several others followed.

Since Jarrod Benson was one of the church's counselors, and a close friend of Cade, the pastor directed Jarrod to talk with Cade.

When each person had been led to Christ at the altar, the counselors filled out cards so the pastor could read off the names of those who had come forward. Immediately after the pastor had announced the names and the audience rejoiced with them in their salvation, he dismissed the service and told everyone to follow the funeral procession to the cemetery, where there would be a brief burial service.

When the burial service was over, the people in the crowd passed by the Powells and the Bensons to express their condolences.

Carrie Powell valiantly greeted each friend that came to her, but when the last person had passed by, the grief in her aching heart overwhelmed her, and she struggled to keep from bursting into uncontrollable sobs. Leaving the Bensons and her children together in their sorrow, she took a few steps toward the rectangular hole in the ground, where her husband's coffin would soon be lowered. *Oh, Jack, how will I ever be able to go on without you? You were my everything. My whole world revolved around you. What am I to do, now?*

Cade Ryer saw Carrie standing alone, staring down at the yawning grave, with tears flowing down her cheeks and dripping off her chin. He walked up beside her and placed a strong arm around her shaking shoulders. "Mrs. Powell, I'm so terribly sorry about your loss. This town will never be the same with Marshal Powell gone, but I need to tell you something."

Carrie looked at Cade through her tears as he pulled a clean white handkerchief from his hip pocket and extended it to her. She accepted it with a trembling hand, and mopped the tears from her face. Sighing deeply, she looked Cade in the eye and gave him the ghost of a smile. "What is it, Cade, that you need to tell me?"

"Ever since I have known Marshal Powell, he has been witnessing to me about Jesus, and about being saved. But I was too proud and stubborn to listen. It took his death to make me stop and think about it. Mrs. Powell, if it weren't for your husband and his faithfulness to the Lord, I would not have walked the aisle today and received Jesus as my Saviour. I would still be headed for hell.

"Your husband was a wonderful man, Mrs. Powell. He was strong in his faith, and many times I heard him share it with others. I just wanted you to know that if it hadn't been for him, I would still be lost and headed for hell. Jarrod has talked to me, too, since becoming a deputy, but it was Marshal Powell who talked to me for so long. And he was such an example to me of what a Christian should be."

Looking into the young man's tear-misted eyes, Carrie felt

God's peace flood her soul. "Cade, thank you so much for telling me this."

This time, a full, genuine smile formed on her lips as she reached up and hugged him.

That evening at the Powell home, Tim Benson told his sister that he knew with Jack's income gone, she and her three offspring were going to have a hard time. He assured her that the Bensons would help them all they could.

Pastor Skiver and Rosie were there, and the pastor told Carrie that the church would do what they could to help them.

Carrie thanked Tim and the pastor, and said, "Since Jack's death, Tim, I've been thinking about your casual comment the other night about opening up my own café. If I had the money, that's exactly what I would do."

Tim smiled at her. "Tell you what, sis—if my claim on the American River does well, Sally and I will give you the money to open the café."

"You *are* kidding, aren't you, big brother?"

"No, he's not," Sally said. "Tim's serious about helping you, and so am I. I was thinking the same thing while you were telling us your thoughts about opening your own café."

Tears welled up in Carrie's eyes. "I've already been praying that the Lord would make your claim pay off in a great way. Now, I'll pray even harder!"

Everyone laughed, and it felt good after the day of sadness.

At the courthouse the next morning, Usel Hacker stood trial before Judge William Stedman and a jury of twelve men. Both

Cade Ryer, who had been sworn in as marshal the day before, and Jarrod Benson testified against Usel Hacker as the man who had killed Marshal Jack Powell.

It took the jury less than ten minutes to return to the courtroom and to declare Hacker "guilty as charged." Judge Stedman sentenced him to hang at sunrise the next day.

That afternoon, Marshal Ryer entered the cell block with Pastor Richard Skiver at his side. There were two men in cells who were there for public drunkenness and disturbing the peace on Main Street the night before. They were both sleeping on their cots as Marshal Ryer led the preacher up to Usel Hacker's cell.

Usel was sitting on his cot, staring into space. Hearing the footsteps, he looked up at the marshal and the man with him.

"Usel," said Cade, "this is Pastor Skiver. He'd like to talk to you."

Hacker rose from the cot and stepped up to the barred door. He noted the Bible in Skiver's hand. His eyes narrowed and became cold and menacing as he snorted and said, "Preacher, eh? Well, holy reverend, I don't wanna talk to you."

The pastor looked at him compassionately. "I care about where you're going when they hang you tomorrow, Mr. Hacker. I'd like to read some Scripture to you. I want to show you that God loves you, and that He sent His only begotten Son into the world to die on the cross and—"

"I don't wanna hear it! Get outta here!"

"But, Mr. Hacker, if you die without Jesus Christ as your Saviour, you'll go to hell tomorrow morning. Just let me—"

"I said get outta here! I don't wanna hear none of that Bible stuff! When a person dies, they go out of existence. There ain't no heaven, and there ain't no hell."

"You're wrong about that, Mr. Hacker," said the pastor, lifting his Bible to open it. "Let me show you what God says."

. Usel Hacker's face turned crimson. He swore vehemently at the preacher, screaming at him to get out of his sight. "You deaf, mister? I said get outta here!" Then to Cade, he screamed, "Get him outta here, Tin Star! I don't have to listen to him!"

"Looks like he's not going to listen to you, Pastor," Cade said.

Tears showed in Richard Skiver's eyes. "I'm afraid you're right. Thanks for letting me try, anyway."

Usel Hacker watched as the marshal and the preacher passed through the door that led to the office. When the door clicked shut, he swore in that direction, then whirled and sat once again on the cot.

The next morning at sunrise, Usel Hacker was hanged for his crime, and his body was buried in a section of the cemetery set aside for executed criminals.

TWELVE

News continued to spread across the United States and its territories about California's gold strike, but most of the country was still skeptical that real gold had been found. Newspaper columnists continued to insist that it was just a scheme to draw people to California in order to boost the territory's economy.

At the capitol building in Washington DC on Thursday morning, July 6, 1848, the men of the United States Congress gathered in the assembly hall for a special session called by President James K. Polk. As they sat down in their usual seats, they noticed that on the platform, the Speaker of the House was talking with an army officer they did not recognize.

A moment later, the Speaker motioned for the man in uniform to take a seat just to the rear of the podium, then the Speaker gestured toward a door to the rear of the platform and said, "Gentleman, I present to you, the president of the United States!"

The congressmen and army officer rose to their feet and applauded as President Polk appeared with Vice President George M. Dallas at his side, along with another congressman. Dallas and the congressman stepped to the army officer and greeted him, shaking his hand, while the president stepped up on the podium.

The speaker smiled at Polk, stepped off the podium, and took a seat with the other three men.

President Polk, at fifty-two years of age, was completely gray-headed, and this, with the strain he was carrying over the present Mexican-American War, made him look much older.

The congressmen were still standing and applauding him. He smiled and motioned for them to sit down. When they had done so, and the assembly hall was silent, Polk said, "Gentlemen, I have called this special session of Congress in order to give you information about the alleged gold strike in Sacramento, California, at Sutter's Mill. As you know, there has been conflict over this since it began over six months ago. You are about to learn that the gold strike is no longer alleged. It is fact."

There was a soft buzzing among the congressmen.

Polk turned and motioned for the army officer to come to him.

When the middle-aged man in uniform stepped up beside the president, Polk ran his gaze over the faces of the attentive congressmen and said, "Gentlemen, I want to introduce to you Colonel Richard Mason, military governor of the territory of California. Three weeks ago, I received a telegraphed report from Colonel Mason after he had made a tour of California's gold fields along the American River in the Sacramento area. The report convinced me that the gold strike is indeed genuine. I wired him back and asked him to come to Washington and present his report to you. He has also brought some actual gold samples taken from various spots along the banks of the American River."

The president remained at Mason's side as he began his report by holding up a map showing Sutter's Mill and the exact spot where James Marshall first found gold. Next, he showed them the gold samples, explaining that he had presented these to mineral experts in California, who examined them carefully. The experts performed every test possible on the samples and pronounced them genuine gold, saying each sample was remarkable for its density, malleability, ductility, and freedom from rust.

President Polk then urged Congress to join him in confirming the discovery of gold in California. There followed a unanimous vote of Congress to join the president in making the official declaration that the California gold strike was indeed genuine.

At the Daniels farm just outside of Iowa City on Monday afternoon, July 17, Sandra Daniels was preparing the evening meal for her family and their dinner guests, Pastor Bryan and Caroline Flint, when a sharp pain pierced her left side. She gasped, placed her hand over the spot, and lowered herself onto the nearest kitchen chair. Beads of perspiration popped out on her brow. She wiped them away with the corner of her apron and sighed.

What can be causing this pain? I've had several of these spells in the last few weeks.

Within a few seconds, the pain eased. She decided to rest there on the chair a little longer before returning to her work.

Maybe I should see the doctor, but we really can't afford it. It's probably nothing serious, anyway. Maybe I just strained a muscle from pulling weeds or working in the garden. With summer on us, I've hardly had a moment to rest. I won't mention it to Luke. He's already got enough of a burden to carry with his job and all the heavy work on this farm. I'm sure it will go away in time.

Sandra took a deep breath and returned to preparing supper.

⌭

That evening at the dinner table, Pastor Flint offered a prayer of thanks for the food, then everyone dug in.

When she had barely tasted the food, Caroline Flint said, "Oh, Sandra, this is delicious!"

Sandra smiled at her. "Nothing fancy, Caroline. Just fried chicken and fresh vegetables from the garden."

"Well, you sure have a way of making fried chicken and fresh vegetables exceptionally delicious, my dear."

"That big garden must be a lot of work, Sandra," Bryan said.

"Well, it is, Pastor, but my boys help me a great deal with it. They lug all the water for me, and they also help me at planting and harvest time." She smiled lovingly at her sons. "And something else…Paul and Silas are real good at weeding, too."

The pastor looked at the brothers and nodded. "Good boys, that's what you are."

"They sure are, Pastor," Luke Daniels said. "The Lord has been so good to Sandra and me, giving us hard-working boys like these."

Paul and Silas looked at each other and grinned.

As the meal progressed, the pastor brought up how proud he was that Luke had led Bob Ganton to the Lord back in May, along with his wife.

"Pleasure was mine, Pastor. It's a joy to see them growing so well in their spiritual life."

"Well, I'm not telling you anything you haven't seen for yourself, but the Gantons have sure become faithful members of the church. But here's something you don't know. Bob has offered to pay for the new wing we need to build onto the church building."

Luke's eyebrows arched. "Well, praise the Lord!"

"The way the church is growing, we need that new wing desperately," Sandra said.

"I'm going to announce it to the church Sunday morning," Bryan said. "I think we can have the wing done and ready to occupy by late September." The pastor set questioning eyes on Luke. "New subject. What do you think about your corn crop?"

"Well, it's not looking as good as I had hoped. I'm thinking that it might take the ground another year to recuperate from last year's fire."

When the meal was over, the men and the boys went out on the front porch to enjoy the evening breeze while Sandra and Caroline cleared off the table and washed and dried the dishes.

Some forty minutes later, as the last dish was dried, Caroline laid a hand on Sandra's arm, her brow furrowed. "Honey, I couldn't help but notice this evening that you look awfully tired."

Sandra smiled at her. "Oh, I'm a little tired, but with Luke working so many hours in town, the boys and I try to do as much of the farmwork as we can. We all work *overtime,* I guess you would say. But it's just necessary right now."

Caroline patted the arm she was touching. "Well, summer won't last forever. I know you have to do as the old saying goes, 'Make hay while the sun shines.'"

Sandra laughed. "How right you are! Well, let's go out and see what our menfolk are talking about on the front porch."

As Sandra and Caroline made their way toward the front of the house, they saw Paul and Silas just starting to climb the stairs.

"Where are you boys going?" Sandra asked.

"We knew you and Mrs. Flint would be coming out about now," Paul said. "Silas and I figured you adults would want to spend some time together without kids around, so we're going up to our room to play some games."

"Maybe it's the other way around. Maybe you kids would rather spend some time together without adults around."

"Why, Mama, how could you think such a thing?" Silas said.

The four of them laughed, then the boys bounded up the stairs.

The Flints stayed another hour or so, then thanked the Daniels for the enjoyable evening, climbed into their buggy, and drove away.

Luke and Sandra stood on the front porch watching the Flint buggy until it passed from view, then Luke said, "Sweetheart, there's something I'd like to discuss with you. Let's go into the parlor."

As they moved through the front door and headed for the parlor, he took hold of her hand. "You remember back in February when we first learned about the gold strike in California? We talked about maybe going out there if it proved to be a good strike."

"I remember," she said. "But we also learned that a number of people were warning that it wasn't a genuine gold strike."

Luke let go of her hand and motioned for her to sit down on the sofa. He picked up a newspaper from a small table and headed toward her. "Well, this afternoon I heard talk that the *Iowa City Press* had a story about President Polk and Congress saying that they now know it is a genuine gold strike. I bought a copy before heading home after work."

He sat down beside her and held the newspaper so she could see the headlines on the front page. He then read the accompanying article to her, which told of the president and Congress declaring the gold strike to be valid.

He read on as the article quoted California government reports that some of the gold seekers were beginning to strike it very good.

Sandra looked at her husband. "So what are you thinking now, honey?"

"Well, I'm thinking if we learn in the next few months that the strike is getting better, I'd like to sell the farm, go to California, and get in on it."

She nodded silently.

"For sure," said Luke, "our corn crop this year isn't going to be very good. I don't like to take the money the church keeps giving us, but with our present income, we have no choice." A light glinted in his eyes. "However, if we went to California and did well, we could live a whole lot better than we are right now."

Sandra could sense the excitement in Luke's voice, and a tiny quiver of fear slithered down her back.

In Manhattan, New York, on Tuesday morning, July 18, Craig Turley was busy at his desk when he looked up to see Charlotte McClain enter his office, carrying the morning editions of both the *New York Tribune* and the *New York Herald*. As she laid them on the corner of the desk, she said, "Well, it looks like all that talk about California's gold strike is a fact."

Craig looked at her skeptically. "Sure, Charlotte. Sure. I've been telling you all along that it's just a scheme to draw people out there to beef up the economy. When I hear that President Polk and Congress have declared it to be true, I'll believe it."

Charlotte giggled, and a mischievous look came into her eyes. "Then, boss, you'd better believe it. Just take a gander at the front pages of both these papers!"

With that, Charlotte left his office, laughing.

Craig picked up the *Tribune* first because of his trust in Horace Greeley. He was stunned to read the headlines proclaiming the California gold rush to be the real thing, and he quickly read the article about the president and Congress declaring that the claim of pure gold being discovered in the American River and in its tributaries in the Sierra Nevada Mountains was true.

He read the front-page article three times, then checked the *Herald* and found it almost identical.

In both articles, Craig learned that any citizen of the United States or its territories could stake a claim along the river or the creeks in the Sierras. Those who staked claims legally would be protected by the newly organized Miners' Security Association, which was backed by California Territorial law.

Craig's heart leaped in his chest at the prospect.

That evening at supper in the Turley mansion, Wallace brought up the article he had read that morning in the *New York Tribune* about the validity of California's gold strike. He asked Craig if he had seen it.

"Sure did, Dad. Charlotte brought me both the *Tribune* and the *Herald* morning editions as usual, but she made a point to impishly poke fun at my previous statements that it was all a hoax."

Kathy and Maddie looked on, smiling, as Wallace chuckled and said, "Craig, when this news spreads across the country, there'll be so many people going to California that they'll trample each other!"

"You're probably right, Dad." Inside, Craig was feeling that he just might like to try it.

"You wouldn't want to go out there to California and try to gather up lots of gold, would you, Craig?" Maddie said.

Big brother reached across the corner of the table and pinched Maddie's ear playfully. "If I did, would you want to go with me?"

"And get trampled to death?"

Craig laughed. "Our esteemed father was speaking figuratively, honey. Nobody's really going to get trampled to death."

Maddie glanced at her father and saw that he was smiling. Then she looked at Craig. "Really? Nobody's gonna get trampled to death?"

Craig shook his head. "No."

Maddie's eyes lit up. "Well, then, sure I'd like to go with you. Of course Kathy would have to come, too. She's my very special governess."

"Well, that would be all right, Maddie. So since I'd certainly let Kathy go with us…will you promise to go if I decide to make the trip?"

"Only if you'll promise to go somewhere with me, first."

"And where would that be?"

"To church."

Craig's eyebrows arched. "To church?"

"Uh-huh. You haven't ever met Pastor Finney. I want you to meet him. Please say you'll come to church with us, Craig."

Craig laughed. "Maddie, I've got too much to do. I don't have time to go to church with you."

"Craig, only those people who have their names in the Lamb's Book of Life will go to heaven when they die. Don't you want your name in that book?"

Kathy and Wallace exchanged glances as Craig looked at his little sister, perplexed.

Maddie went on. "Craig, just think of what's happened to

Harold, Elizabeth, and Adelle in these past few weeks. Their names are in the Lamb's Book of Life because they opened their hearts to Jesus. Right in that book, it has those names along with Wallace Turley, Kathy Ross, Maddie Turley, and all the other saved people: Harold Wilkins, Elizabeth Loysen, and Adelle Brown. It sure would make all of us happy if you'd get saved and the name Craig Turley was written in there, too."

Craig was still speechless.

Like Maddie, Kathy also desperately wanted him to become a Christian, and almost as desperately wanted to hear him say that he was in love with her. He was always very attentive to her, and in many ways showed her that he was fond of her, but Kathy wanted him to be saved, and to fall in love with her. She had daydreamed often of the two of them having a Christian home and raising their children in the nurture and admonition of the Lord.

Later that evening, Kathy and Craig happened to meet in the hall that led from the foyer to the rear of the mansion.

Kathy smiled and said, "Since we're alone at the moment could I ask you something, Craig?"

"Of course."

"I saw the look in your eyes when you and your father were talking about the California gold strike. Would you really like to go out there and try to find gold?"

"Kathy, I'm too busy being first vice president of the Turley Corporation."

Kathy sighed with relief. "Good. I want you to keep on being too busy as first vice president of the Turley Corporation. I think an awful lot of you, Craig. I don't want you to go away and live somewhere else."

He patted Kathy's upper arm and said, "I think an awful lot of you, too."

Later that night in her room, Kathy relished Craig's tender touch in the hall and the words he spoke when he did it.

In his own room, Craig lay in the darkness and pondered the newspaper articles about the California gold strike. He would stay abreast of how the strike was going over the next few months. If there were reports of big strikes, this just might be his way of making his own fortune and not having to live under the shadow of his wealthy father. Craig also thought about Kathy. He had long sensed how she felt about him and reminded himself that he could fall in love with her if he wasn't careful. *But what would Dad think of my falling in love with Maddie's governess?*

THIRTEEN

At dawn on Wednesday morning, October 4, in Sacramento, California, Carrie Powell awakened and noted the brightening sky through her bedroom window. Her mind was instantly on Jack and how very much she missed him. Seconds later, her thoughts went to the struggle she and her children were having to pay their bills and keep food on the table.

The past six months had been difficult. Jack's salary as marshal had barely been enough to meet the family's needs before he was killed. Carrie and her children had very little to fall back on when Jack was suddenly taken from them. Carrie scrimped in every way she could, and scratched out a meager living by cleaning houses and doing laundry for five of Sacramento's wealthy families. Rena and the boys pitched in, doing odd jobs around town to pick up what money they could.

Carrie was so exhausted at the end of each work day that when she went to bed at night, she immediately fell asleep. Night after night, she dreamed of Jack and woke herself up, crying. Morning always came too soon, and after a time of prayer, she wearily crawled out of bed to begin another lonely, work-filled day. Tim and Sally did all they could to help Carrie and her children, but they had little money left over after paying their own bills.

As sunrise came that Wednesday morning, Carrie talked to the Lord, asking for strength and wisdom. When she finished praying, she crawled out of bed to begin another day.

That evening, Carrie, Rena, Randy, and Darin were just finishing supper when they heard a knock at the front door of the house. Darin jumped up and hurried out of the kitchen. When he opened the door, he smiled broadly. "Hi, Uncle Tim!" He then called loudly over his shoulder, "Mama, it's Uncle Tim!"

"Bring him on back, honey," Carrie said.

When Darin and his uncle entered the kitchen, Tim saw his sister's weary, pinched face, and his heart ached for her. "Sis, could you and I go out on the front porch? I want to talk to you."

"Go ahead, Mama," Rena said. "The boys and I will do the dishes and clean up the kitchen."

Carrie thanked her, then poured Tim a cup of coffee and handed it to him. She filled her own cup, and they walked to the front of the house together and sat down side by side in rocking chairs on the front porch. Both took sips from their cups, then Carrie said, "What's on your mind, big brother?"

Tim's face brightened and his eyes sparkled. "Little sis, I've got great news, and I couldn't wait to come over here and tell you about it! I can tell the kids later, but I just have to share it with you first."

"Well, tell me!"

He leaned toward her, meeting her questioning gaze. "I struck it rich on my claim this morning! I mean *rich*! When I found this huge deposit of gold about ten o'clock, I showed it to James

Marshall. He sent for Hal Mason, one of the government officials who works at the claim office. Mason's an expert in gold mining. He came and looked at it, and told me the claim is going to produce gold hand over fist!"

"Oh, Tim, I'm so very happy for you! Sally must be thrilled!"

"That she is. She would've come with me, but she's looking after that sick neighbor, Mrs. Walden at the moment."

"Bless her."

"Carrie, you remember Sally and I told you that if we hit it big, we'd set you up in the café business."

Carrie shook her head. "Now, Tim, you don't have to do that. I know Sally has family back East who need help and—"

"Sis, Sally and I have talked about this ever since I started panning and digging on the claim. We want to do this for you. You *do* still want your own café, don't you?"

"Of course I do, with all my heart. But—"

"No buts, little sister. You and the kids have been working your fingers to the bone to scratch out a living ever since Jack went to heaven. Sally and I know you'll make a very good living running a café. We want that for you."

Tears welled up in Carrie's eyes. "Oh, Tim, how will I ever be able to thank you?"

"It'll be thanks enough just to be certain you have plenty of money to live on, and to see you as happy as I know you'll be doing the thing you do best...cooking. Jack will be pleased, I know, when he looks down from heaven and sees you running your very own café."

She placed her coffee cup on a small table beside her rocking chair and stood up. Tim also rose to his feet, set his cup next to hers, and opened his arms to receive the hug he knew was coming.

When Carrie had hugged him tight for a long moment, she

eased back and looked into his eyes, blinking at her tears. "I'm sure the children and I will do well with the café, but I want it understood that when we can do it, we're going to pay you back."

Tim shook his head. "No you won't. This isn't a loan. It's a gift, free and clear. No strings attached. Now, for some time I've been looking for just the right lot on Main Street for Carrie's Café, and I think I've found it. You know that lot at Third and Main, right across the street from Sacramento Bank and Trust? The one that's had the for sale sign up for three or four months?"

"Yes, but that location has to be very expensive, Tim. I'll have to find something else to—"

"No, you won't. Sally and I bought it for you this afternoon. The deed is already in your name. Now, tomorrow, I'm going to talk to Bill Madison at Madison Construction Company and hire him to build your café for you. We'll go together, and you can tell him what kind of building and floor plan you want."

Carrie's tears spilled down her face. She reached up, cupped his face in her hands, and kissed his cheek, moistening it with her tears. "Tim, you're the best brother in all the world. And Sally's the best sister-in-law. I thank you with all my heart. And until I can tell her in person, you pass on what I'm saying, all right?"

Tim grinned. "All right."

Carrie reached up and brushed her tears from his cheek. "Oh, Tim, I promise I will make you proud. This café will be a family affair. Rena will be totally involved, and the boys will work in the café as much as possible when they're not in school. And it goes without saying that you and your family will always be welcome to a free meal, and will have a table waiting!"

"We'll pay our way at Carrie's Café, sis. I know you'll give it all you've got, but as soon as you can afford it, I want you to hire some more help. I want you to enjoy running your café, but I also want you to have some time for yourself. I want you to live life to the fullest once more, and maybe someday even fall in love again."

Carrie bit her lips and blinked at new tears. "That...ah...doesn't seem possible right now, Tim. But maybe someday, if the Lord has that in His plan for my life."

On Saturday morning, November 25, 1848, in Sacramento, a festive celebration was taking place on the southwest corner of Third and Main Street, directly across the street from the Sacramento Bank and Trust Company. It was the grand opening of Carrie's Café.

A great number of new people were now in Sacramento, having come from other parts of California to get in on the gold strike. A large crowd stood on the boardwalk and in the dust of the street in front of the café as Carrie Powell publicly thanked Tim and Sally Benson for their kindness to her.

Standing with Carrie were Rena, Randy, and Darin, smiling broadly.

At the forefront of the crowd stood Marshal Cade Ryer, Deputy Jarrod Benson, and Ryer's new deputy, Bruce Follmer, who had military experience in the recent Mexican-American War.

Also standing near Carrie were Pastor and Mrs. Skiver and the chairman of the town council. When Carrie finished her brief speech, she nodded at the chairman, and he stepped up and told the crowd how pleased he and the other council members were to see such a fine eating establishment opening for business that day.

The crowd cheered.

The chairman then called on Pastor Richard Skiver to come and lead in prayer, asking God to bless Carrie and her family in their new endeavor.

Pastor Skiver moved to the center next to Randy Powell, ran his gaze over the crowd, and said, "Folks, before I pray, I want to make it clear that Carrie's Café will not sell alcoholic beverages."

"Hallelujah!" shouted a middle-aged man in the crowd.

Another man cried out, "God bless you for that, Carrie!"

Other voices called out their agreement.

Pastor Skiver then asked everyone to bow their heads. He prayed loud enough for all to hear, thanking the Lord that He had made it possible for the young widow and her children to go into business, and asked Him to bless them abundantly.

When the pastor said his amen, Carrie smiled at the crowd and said, "It's too late for breakfast, but we'll be open by eleven o'clock. Come on back for lunch!"

On Friday, December 1, in southeast Australia, Colin Ashlock returned to his ranch after riding his choice stallion into Sydney on business. He also had picked up the mail. He guided the stallion off the road onto the lane that led to the large ranch house and outbuildings which stood in a huge patch of trees.

It was a beautiful summer day with a soft warm wind blowing across the rolling grassy hills. The land was golden beneath the burning sun. Cattle and sheep dotted the vast pastures and broad-winged birds of various descriptions ruled the sky. Puffy white clouds drifted on the lofty winds, patching the earth with drifting shadows.

Tall trees grew along the lane, and Colin smiled as he let his gaze drift over the creek that ran alongside the lane, then glimpsed the house and buildings through wind-stirred branches, heavy with green leaves. He loved this marvelous country, which he gladly called home.

When he rode up to the corral where several of his hired men were stacking hay, he asked them to find the others and bring them all to the back of the ranch house. He had good news for them, and would be on the back porch, waiting.

Colin drew his horse to a halt at the back porch, left the saddle, and mounted the steps. He took the mail into the kitchen and laid it on a counter, then returned to the porch, keeping one piece of mail in hand: a brown envelope.

In less than twenty minutes, all of the hired men were gathered in a half circle at the back porch. Colin stood on the porch, smiled at them, and lifted up the brown envelope. "I picked up the mail when I was in town, men. In this envelope is my first dividend check from the new company in Honiara. It's a substantial amount, and I'm going to share a portion of it with each of you as a bonus for your hard work and your faithfulness to me."

The men spoke up one by one, thanking their boss for his generosity.

Colin's cattle foreman, Clyde Devore, said, "Mr. Ashlock, we're all so proud to be employed for such an energetic and aggressive man. Do you have any new money-making projects in mind?"

"Yes I do, Clyde. I'm presently doing some studies on business opportunities in the Hawaiian Islands, as well as New Guinea and Borneo. I'll let all of you know if I decide to make a journey to those places. Our lady *Bristol* is always ready to sail the high seas!"

"And so are her captain and crew!" Henry Briggs said.

"I'm sure glad of that, Henry. Where would the *Bristol* and I be without our captain and crew?"

Colin was almost to the barn, leading his horse, when he looked up and saw a buggy coming down the lane from the road. He recognized the horse and the buggy as belonging to Charles Wesson, and though he could not make out who the driver was as yet, he was sure it was Charles. *Oh, no. Not more of that Bible stuff.*

Colin halted the stallion at the barn door, then turned to see the Wesson buggy drawing close. Charles lifted a hand and waved at him.

Colin did not wave back.

As Charles drew up and pulled rein, he smiled and said, "Hello, Colin."

Colin nodded but did not smile.

Charles stepped out of the buggy and offered his hand. "Good to see you, Colin. It's…ah…it's been a long time."

Colin shook his hand briefly and nodded. "Mm-hmm."

"Marian and I were saddened when we learned that Elizabeth had—had—"

"Left me?"

"Yes. I…just wanted to come by and see how you were doing, and ask if…if there has been any communication between you and her."

"None, Charles."

"Too bad. I was hoping maybe she would come back."

"No chance of that."

"I see. I'm so sorry."

"That's life."

Charles met his gaze head-on. "Colin, have you given any consideration to the things Marian and I talked to you and Elizabeth about?"

"You mean that salvation stuff?"

"Yes."

Colin shook his head. "No. I've told you before that I don't believe that stuff. The Bible isn't true."

"How about that verse I showed you from Proverbs 15? 'He that is greedy of gain troubleth his own house'? Your greed cost you your marriage, Colin. Isn't that true?"

Colin looked at him coldly.

"I'm trying to get you to see that when God's Word speaks, it is always true. Well, wasn't it your greed for more riches that kept you so busy that you had no time for Elizabeth? Isn't that why she left you and went back to England?"

Suddenly Colin's eyes flashed with fire. "It's none of your business, Charles. Now, I'll thank you to get back in your buggy and get off my property."

Tears misted the older man's eyes. "I'm trying to help you, Colin. You need to face the fact that God's Word *is* true. The most important thing is that you realize it's true when it says plainly that if you die without the Lord Jesus Christ as your Saviour, you will spend eternity in a burning lake of fire. I just don't want you to die lost, Colin. Please let me go over some salvation Scriptures with you again. I can't let you—"

"Get off my property! I don't want you here, and I don't want any of that Bible nonsense!" Colin wheeled, took his horse's reins, and led him inside the barn. Colin stepped back to close the door and saw Charles standing there, wiping tears. "I said get off my property! *Now!*"

On Saturday December 9, at the Turley Department store in Manhattan, New York, Charlotte McClain entered the first vice president's office and laid the morning editions of the *New York Tribune* and the *New York Herald* on the corner of the desk. "Mr. Turley, you really should read the article by Horace Greeley on the front page of the *Tribune*."

Craig looked up and smiled. "What's it about?"

"Well, you've shown so much interest in the California gold strike ever since it happened almost a year ago, I thought you'd be interested in Mr. Greeley's latest comments. It looks like that gold strike is going to be more than anybody ever thought it could be. Read it. You'll see."

Charlotte wheeled and left his office as Craig picked up the *Tribune* and noted the bold headlines on the front page: "**The Age of Gold!**"

In the center of the page, one of the newspaper's artists had sketched a large picture of two miners leaning over a sluice box on a river bank. Both men were smiling joyfully at what they saw in their shiny metal pans.

Craig glanced at the front page of the *Herald*. There was nothing about the gold strike at all.

Tossing the *Herald* aside, he read the caption under the sketch, written on the front page of the *Tribune* by Horace Greeley:

This editor and publisher is deeply stirred by the new excitement in California. In this country we are on the brink of the Age of Gold! Many gold seekers in Sacramento and in the nearby Sierra Mountains are making amazing gold strikes. I am told that California is expecting gold to be found in the next four years equal to at least ONE THOUSAND MILLION DOLLARS being added to the general aggregate of gold in circulation.

Craig's heart was pounding. He closed his eyes and whispered, "Craig, ol' boy, I think you've found your answer. If you go out there and stake your claim, a great portion of that thousand million dollars can be yours! You won't be the kid with the silver spoon in your mouth any longer. You'll make your own fortune and be rich all on your own!"

He opened his eyes, looked at the front page of the *Tribune* again, and banged his fist on the desktop.

"Yes! This is it!"

Craig eased back in his chair, folded his hands behind his neck, and stared at the ceiling. "Just think of it," he whispered to himself. "Your very own fortune, dug out of the ground and maybe dipped out of some stream with your own hands!"

That evening at bedtime, Maddie held Craig's hand as the Turley family and Kathy Ross climbed the winding staircase. She looked up at him and said, "Craig, do you love me?"

He looked down and grinned. "Do I *love* you? You know the answer to that, don't you?"

"I want to hear it."

Craig squeezed the hand he was holding as they climbed higher. "Of course I love you, baby sister."

"Do you love me enough to do me a real big favor?"

"Of course. What is it?"

"Will you go to church with us tomorrow?"

Craig noticed Kathy's eyes on him as Maddie waited for a reply.

He bent over and kissed Maddie's forehead. "I have too many things to do tomorrow, little sister. I simply won't have time to go to church. But just because I can't go to church with you doesn't mean I don't love you. Okay?"

Wallace and Kathy had stopped on the stairs also. They looked on as disappointment showed in the child's eyes.

"Okay."

Wallace prayed in his heart, *Lord, please bring Craig to the place where he won't make excuses. I want so badly for him to hear Pastor Finney preach.*

FOURTEEN

On Monday morning, December 11, a large group of men gathered in front of the Miners' Association office in Sacramento, California. They had arrived over the weekend, having come from many parts of California to make their fortunes in gold. Some had their families with them. Others had come alone.

The Association president, Clark Fletcher, had already explained the legal process of staking claims and was schooling the new hopefuls in digging and panning for gold. When he was finished, he said, "The amount of gold that is being found in the American River and the mountain streams that feed it is astounding. Any man by common industry can make fifty dollars a day or more, depending on the situation on his claim."

The hopeful men looked at each other, smiling.

At the south edge of Sacramento, two brothers from Moreno Valley in southern California were busy on the bank of the American River, panning gold. Ed and Lou Conley, both in their thirties, had come to Sacramento only a week previously and were quite satisfied with their claim, which had been assigned them by the Miners' Association. So far, they had accumulated over $400 in gold, according to the government-appointed assayer in Sacramento.

The Conley brothers worked side by side as they knelt on the river bank, scooping up gravel and sand with a mixture of glittering pieces of gold.

Lou dipped a fresh pan full, and his eyes widened. "Hey, Ed! Look! There's almost as much gold as sand this time!"

Ed looked at the contents of the pan and a smile spread over his face. "Wow! That's amazing, Lou. I—"

"Hey! What're you doin' on our claim?" came a loud voice from behind them.

They looked around to see two men staring at them with fire in their eyes. One was easily thirty years older than the other one. The older one spoke again. "You two claim jumpers are askin' for trouble!"

Both Conley brothers stood up, and Ed said, "Excuse me, mister. What're you talking about? My brother and I were assigned this claim a week ago by Clark Fletcher, president of the Miners' Association. He told us that a man and his son had been working the claim, but had suddenly decided to leave."

"Well, I'm Jason Muller and this is my son, Harold. We laid claim to this section in October. We left a couple weeks ago to go into the mountains and see if we could find a spot that would give us more gold faster." His eyes narrowed and his jaw tightened. "You two can leave, now, and we want that gold in those pans."

"Now, hold on!" Ed said. "This is our claim, legally. See that sign over there that's got our names on it?"—

Father and son glanced at the sign on a post that had been driven in the ground. Harold Muller said stiffly, "Well, Ed and

Lou Conley, we don't care about that sign. This is *our* claim. Get off it!"

Lou jutted his jaw. "We aren't getting off it! Like my brother just told you, this is our claim, and we came by it legally!"

A sneer curled Jason Muller's lips and his eyes went flat and cold. He stomped up until he was within arm's reach of Lou and unleashed a right cross that sent Lou staggering backward.

Ed lunged for Jason and drove a smashing right to his ribs, then cracked him with a left hook that put him down. Harold headed for him, roaring like a wild beast, but was stopped short with a powerful blow by Lou, who was full of fury.

As the Mullers scrambled to their feet spitting out violent words, the sound of horses' hooves on the soft bank of the river filled the air, followed by a loud voice, "Hey! Hold it! What's going on here?"

All four men looked to see two men with badges on their vests and guns on their hips, who were sliding from their saddles. They recognized the special law officers who had been hired, along with many others, by the Miners' Association to keep the law in the gold fields.

Jason Muller held his aching jaw and spat, "These two claim jumpers need to be arrested, Lance!"

Lance Williams looked at his partner, Rex Patton, who was shaking his head, then said sternly, "Jason, Ed and Lou are not claim jumpers. You two vacated this claim at least two weeks ago without notice to the office. Mr. Fletcher granted this claim to the Conley brothers legal and proper."

Jason's face went beet red as he still held his jaw. "What're you talkin' about, Lance? All we were doin' was takin' a few days to scout out a possible better claim in the mountains."

"You didn't talk to Mr. Fletcher about this, did you?"

"Well, no, but—"

"Then by leaving this claim without his permission, you forfeited it."

"Says who?" snapped Harold.

"Says the *law!*" Rex Patton said. "That was explained to you the day you were assigned this claim."

Fire smoldered in Jason's eyes. "Well, I don't remember it."

"Neither do I," Harold said.

"Well, if you weren't listening, that's your problem," Williams said, "but the law says a claim is valid only as long as it is being exercised. That means *physically worked*. Neither an individual nor a company can set aside property to be worked later or randomly. The law says if the claim isn't being worked regularly, it can be assigned to someone else."

"Well, we left the sign with our name on it right over there where theirs is now," Jason said. "They should be arrested for throwin' it away."

"Ed and Lou didn't throw it away, Jason," Patton said. "Mr. Fletcher came out here to this spot to make sure you weren't occupying it and working the claim. He pulled up the stake and took it back to the office. If you want it, go talk to him about it. And let me warn you...if you give the Conley brothers any more trouble, you'll find out what the inside of Marshal Cade Ryer's jail looks like."

Father and son exchanged glances, then Jason said, "We won't give 'em any more trouble." He ran his heavy gaze to the Conley brothers. "I'm sorry. You won't see us around here again."

Ed and Lou Conley thanked the officers for their help and watched as they mounted their horses and rode toward town with Jason and Harold Muller riding their own horses beside them.

❧

On Tuesday morning, December 12, in Manhattan, Craig Turley was busy at his desk, preparing some papers for his father when Charlotte McClain came into his office with the morning editions of the *New York Tribune* and the *New York Herald.* She paused before returning to her office. "Mr. Turley, do you know what El Dorado is?"

"In what context?" he asked.

"When the subject is gold."

Craig's brow furrowed. "What do you mean?"

Charlotte opened the *Tribune.* "Here on the front page, Horace Greeley writes about the California gold strike and says thousands of people are being drawn to the new El Dorado." She handed him the open paper. "See for yourself."

Craig scanned the headline, ran his gaze down the article, then looked up at Charlotte. "Well, I remember El Dorado from studying history in college. It's the legendary land of the Golden Man, a place of gold in massive amounts sought by Spanish Conquistadors in the New World beginning in the mid-sixteenth century. Its imaginary location shifted as new regions were explored when there was supposed to be a great deal of gold in the area."

Charlotte nodded. "I'd heard that El Dorado was something legendary, but didn't know what it was. Well, I'll leave you to your work."

Craig watched her disappear into the hallway, then moved the papers he had been working on, spread the *Tribune* in front of him, and began to read:

We Americans are fairly afloat. We don't see any links of probability missing in the golden chain by which Hope is drawing her thousands of disciples to the new El Dorado, where fortune lies abroad upon the surface of the earth as plentiful as the mud in our streets, and where the old saying "a pocket full of rocks" meets a golden realization.

The perilous stuff lies loose upon the surface of the ground, or only slightly adheres to rocks and sand. The only machinery necessary in the new gold mines of California is a stout pair of arms, a shovel, and a tin pan. I encounter many young men these days desiring to make their fortune. To them I say, Go West, young man, go West!

Craig stared at those final words of advice from Horace Greeley and said aloud, "I will, sir! I will!"

He folded up the newspaper, placed it on a small table behind the desk, then quickly finished the work his father had assigned to him.

For the next several days, Craig Turley pondered Horace Greeley's words, "Go West, young man, go West!" He worked at devising just how to tell his father that he was going to follow Mr. Greeley's wise counsel.

On December 14, there was another article by Horace Greeley in the *Tribune* on the gold strike in California, and another on December 18.

Three days later, Craig stepped into the hall with a folder in his hand and walked the short distance to Charlotte McClain's office. He paused at Charlotte's desk, noting that the door to his father's office was closed. "Is someone in there with Dad?"

"Yes, sir," Charlotte said, "but I don't think your father and Mr. Horace Greeley will mind if you interrupt them."

Craig grinned, walked to the office door, and tapped on it lightly.

"Come in, Charlotte," Wallace Turley said.

Craig opened the door and stuck his head into the room. "I'm not Charlotte, but I have these Jersey City papers ready for you."

"Come in, son."

Horace Greeley rose from the chair in front of the desk and extended his right hand. "Nice to see you, Craig."

"Nice to see you too, sir."

Craig laid the folder on his father's desk, then turned again to the owner of the *New York Tribune*. "Mr. Greeley, I've been keeping up with your articles on the California gold strike. The one that really spoke to me was December twelfth's morning edition, when you said, 'Go West, young man, go West!'"

"I didn't mean *you*, Craig!" Greeley said. "I was speaking to those young men here in the East who want to make their fortune. You already have yours."

Craig looked at his father. "Dad, can the three of us talk about this right now?"

Wallace looked at Greeley. "Do you have the time?"

Greeley nodded. "Of course."

Craig sat down in the chair next to Greeley's and said, "Mr. Greeley, I was born into a wealthy family, as you know. I've had a good and wonderful home, so please don't misunderstand me. You see, all my life I've been the kid with the silver spoon in his mouth. You know what I'm saying?"

"Of course."

"Mr. Greeley, I love my dad, and I deeply appreciate him providing my education at NYU and giving me the position of first vice president in the corporation." He smiled at his father, then looked back at Greeley. "But you see, sir, for a long time there's been a burning desire inside me to make my own fortune. It has grown stronger ever since I first heard of the gold strike in California. I haven't talked to Dad about California yet, so this is all news to him, too. I feel I must leave the Turley Corporation and become wealthy by what I accomplish with my own brain and hands."

Greeley noted the strained look that captured Wallace's features.

Craig looked into his father's eyes. "Dad, I'm going to go to California, stake my claim, and dig myself a fortune in gold."

"Craig," Horace Greeley said, "I think you should have talked to your father about this before you set your mind to do it."

Wallace looked at Craig. "I really wish you had, son."

Craig sighed. "Dad, I'm sorry to break it to you this way, but with Mr. Greeley here, and his call to young men to go west, it seemed the best time to do it."

"Tell you what, gentlemen," said Greeley, rising from his chair. "I really think the two of you should talk about this without my presence. I really do need to get back to the office."

Father and son stood up and shook his hand.

"Mr. Greeley, thank you for those enlightening articles you've been writing about California's gold strike," Craig said.

Greeley chuckled. "Well, Craig, with all the information I'm receiving from the California newspapers, I'm not calling it the gold strike anymore. It's the gold *rush*! People are heading that way from all over the country by the thousands. I don't doubt at all that as the news spreads around the world, there will be foreigners who will come and go after gold in California, too."

Wallace frowned. "Do you think they will be allowed to, Horace?"

"Yes, I do. It would hurt our relationship with other nations if our government denied their citizens the opportunity to make their fortunes. Our president and the other national leaders will realize this, and grant permission, I feel sure."

As Wallace was nodding, Greeley said, "My friend, I hope you won't hold it against me that Craig used my presence and newspaper articles to break it to you that he's going west. As I said, when I urged young men to go west, I didn't have Craig in mind."

Wallace smiled and shook his head. "I'm not holding anything against you, Horace. As I think about it, I can see Craig's side of the matter. I just hate the thought of his leaving home."

When Horace Greeley was gone, Wallace looked across his desk and said, "Son, I've learned from the Bible that a man has to be careful that he doesn't set his heart on riches. If they come because he has worked hard and been successful, okay, but it can be dangerous to live just for the sake of wealth."

Craig rubbed the back of his neck. "Dad, I simply want to become rich on my own, just like you did...only in another way."

Wallace took a deep breath. "I'm concerned about what you could be getting yourself into out there in California. I know there's a lot of gold in those rivers and streams, but with so many thousands of people pouring in there, everyone cannot strike it rich. You need to seriously think that over. Getting there will be difficult, by itself, but from what I've heard and read, the living conditions for the most part are pretty deplorable, too. I read in the *Herald* last week that there's already sickness and disease among those gold seekers who have settled in the Sacramento area, not to mention the men who have been killed as a result of the greed that goes along with a race for gold."

Craig noted the ashen look on his father's face, and he leaned forward in his chair. "Dad, you told Mr. Greeley that you can see my side of the matter."

"Yes. But like I also said, I hate the thought of your leaving home."

"I appreciate the thought, but try to see this through my eyes. I'm grateful for the wonderful life you've given me, but there's just something inside me—a voice that I have to listen to. I have to go to California, Dad. I must make my own fortune. Please try to understand."

A slight smile creased Wallace's face. He placed both hands on top of his desk and pushed himself to his feet. Craig also stood up.

Wallace rounded the desk, opening his arms. Craig walked into them, and Wallace pulled him close, patting his back. He squeezed Craig tight, then drew back so he could look into his eyes, while gripping his shoulders. "Son," he said, his voice cracking slightly, "I do understand your wanting to make your own fortune in life. I did that. I'm proud of you. It sure won't be the same around here without you, but always, *always* know you are welcome to come back here at any time. I'll have to put another man in your position, but you'll still have a job if you need it."

Craig embraced his father again, then looked into his eyes and said with a slight break in his voice, "Thank you for understanding."

Wallace swallowed with difficulty. "So when do you plan to leave?"

"I'm not sure yet. I need to look into it and find the best way to go. Mr. Greeley would probably be able to tell me how to find out."

"Well, keep me posted, won't you? And, son, I think it would be best to wait until you have a date of departure settled before we tell Maddie, Kathy, and the rest of the household." He paused. "And for that matter, before we tell anyone here at the store, too."

Craig nodded, then father and son embraced again, finding a new respect for each other.

When Craig left the room, closing the door behind him, Wallace stood staring at the door. He blinked at the moisture that had welled up in his eyes. "Please, heavenly Father, go with him. Out there in the West, bring my boy to Yourself."

Horace Greeley had been back in his office almost two hours when his secretary came in to inform him that Craig Turley was there to see him. He told her to bring the young man in, and welcomed him as he entered. Greeley had Craig sit down in front of his desk, then eased into his chair and asked what he could do for him.

Craig explained that his father had given his blessing on his going to California, then said, "Mr. Greeley, can you tell me what's the best way to travel from here to California?"

Greeley leaned on the desktop with his elbows. "Well, Craig, some easterners are taking ships down the east coast and around the southern tip of South America, then north all the way to San Francisco Bay. None of them have reached San Francisco, yet. The average time of travel this way is ten to eleven months."

Craig smiled. "Well, I'd rather go straight west overland than take such a long route."

Greeley wheeled his chair around, lifted a thin paperback book from the shelf behind the desk, and handed it to Craig. "This is a new publication by a man named Joseph Ware of St. Louis, Missouri.. It gives several routes to travel overland, depending on where you're starting from."

"*The Emigrant's Guide to California*...looks like just what I need. How much is it?"

"No charge. Mr. Ware sent me several copies for free, figuring I might know some people who would need them."

FIFTEEN

That night in his bedroom—after the rest of the family and the servants had gone to bed—Craig Turley left all three lanterns burning so he could see to read the *Emigrant's Guide to California* while sitting up in bed.

He found that the thin volume contained every point of information needed for the emigrant who desired to travel across the country to the San Francisco–Sacramento area from anywhere within the United States and its territories.

The information included routes, distances, water, grass, timber, and crossing of rivers and mountain passes. It gave altitudes with a large map of the routes that was folded up inside the book. The book also gave full instructions for testing and assaying gold.

Craig carefully went over each route laid out by Joseph Ware, wanting to decide before going to sleep which one he would follow. When he had gone over the routes several times, he took pencil and paper and wrote down the route he had chosen. By that time, he was getting sleepy. He told himself that he would go over the route with his father the next evening, so his father would know how long it would take him and approximately where he would be at any given time during the long journey. He decided that he should plan to head west by the first of February.

He had learned in the book that in traveling by covered wagon, he would average twelve miles per day. He would take a Baltimore and Ohio Railroad train from New York City to Wheeling, Virginia, on the Ohio River. He would purchase a wagon and two-horse team in Wheeling and begin his slow journey from the west bank of the Ohio River to Sacramento, California. According to Joseph Ware, at an average of twelve miles per day, Craig would arrive in Sacramento in late August or early September.

Craig folded the slip of paper containing his chosen route and slipped it inside the book. He snuffed out the three lanterns and lay on his back in the dark, satisfied that he had planned his journey correctly. He snuggled down into the covers, feeling drowsiness coming on.

However, for a few minutes sleep eluded him as he thought about how he would miss his father and Maddie. He bit down on his lower lip then swallowed hard. His thoughts went to Kathy. There was a strong stirring in his heart as he contemplated being away from her.

Craig shook his head and said in a whisper, "I can't let sentimentality keep me from reaching my goal. I've got to go to California and make my fortune. Within two or three years, I'll be one rich man, and—and I will not have inherited my riches. I will have gained them by my own initiative and hard work. The 'silver spoon' will remain in New York."

During breakfast the next morning, Craig was quieter than usual. Wallace knew why, but did not let on. Maddie and Kathy both noticed it, but did not ask Craig why he was not as talkative as was typical for him.

Later, when Wallace and Craig entered the Turley Department Store and headed up the stairs toward the offices, Craig said, "Dad, I've done my homework for the journey to California."

Wallace gave him a sidelong glance. "Oh? How?"

"Well, yesterday after you and I had our talk, I went over to the *New York Tribune* office. Mr. Greeley gave me a new book written to help the gold seekers who want to get to California from all over the country. I mapped out my route, and I'd like some time alone with you this evening after supper to go over it."

They topped the stairs and Wallace said, "Sure, son. Let's plan to meet in the library right after supper."

That evening, Craig was quiet again during the meal. Finally, Kathy set concerned eyes on him across the table and said, "Craig, are you all right?"

He gave her a surprised look. "Why do you ask, Kathy?"

"Well, you just haven't been yourself for a couple of days now. Maddie and I have both noticed it, and we're worried about you."

Maddie was nodding her head. "That's right, big brother. Kathy and I are both worried about you."

Wallace concentrated on his food, keeping his eyes on his plate.

Craig swallowed the mashed potatoes he was chewing, cleared his throat, and gave Maddie and Kathy a weak smile. "Well, ladies, I appreciate your concern, but there's nothing wrong with me. I've just had a lot on my mind lately."

"Big brother, you're not still dreaming about all that gold in California, are you?" Maddie said teasingly.

Craig's head jerked up at the question. He stared at her blankly, but did not reply.

In the moment of dead silence, Maddie decided to change the subject. "Craig, this is Friday."

He let a grin curve his lips. "I'm fully aware of that, baby sister."

"Then you know that tomorrow is Saturday."

Craig's grin widened. "Well, it is unless somebody has changed the days of the week."

Maddie giggled. "That hasn't happened, big brother. Tomorrow is Saturday, all right. So what's the next day?"

"Sunday."

"Right! Will you go to church with us on Sunday, Craig?"

"Can't, sweetie. I have more important things to do."

Maddie's lower lip stiffened and stuck out. "That's what you always say. What could be more important than going to church and learning about Jesus?"

Craig picked up his coffee cup and sipped slowly.

Maddie and Kathy exchanged glances, then everybody went back to their food, and soon the meal was over.

Wallace stood up, ran his gaze from Kathy to Maddie, and said, "Craig and I have some business to talk over this evening. We'll be in the library if you need us."

After they left, Maddie and Kathy looked at each other, perplexed.

Maddie frowned. "Something's wrong, I don't care what Craig says, Kathy."

"Well, sweetie, I guess it's none of our business, or he would have told us what's bothering him. How about you and me play a game or two of dominoes before bedtime?"

Maddie flashed her a warm smile. "Sounds good to me. Of course, I should warn you…I'm going to beat you tonight!"

Kathy laughed, took her hand, and they left the dining room.

⚭

When father and son entered the library, Craig noted that the fire was dwindling. He headed for the fireplace, saying, "Go ahead and sit down, Dad. It looks like Harold forgot to stoke up the fire before he went to eat supper with Elizabeth and Adelle. I'll throw on a couple of logs."

Craig tossed the logs in the fireplace, then went to where his father had seated himself on the sofa and eased down beside him.

"All right, son," Wallace said. "You understand that talking about your leaving home and going to California isn't easy, but tell me your plan."

Craig opened the travel guide he was carrying and took out the paper he had drawn up. He then removed the map and spread it between them so they could both see it. "I've found, Dad, that the best route for me is to take a Baltimore and Ohio Railroad train from Manhattan to Wheeling, Virginia. Wheeling, as you can see here on the map, is on the Ohio River. This is the farthest point west that the railroad goes. The book tells me that because emigrants are passing through Wheeling, wagon makers and horse dealers are there to sell them wagons and horses for the journey to California."

"I don't doubt that."

Craig went on. "I've written out the route I've chosen on this piece of paper, and after I tell you the amount of time it takes to make this trip, you'll be able to have a good idea where I'll be each day. I'll buy my wagon and team there at Wheeling and follow the trail overland to Sacramento as Mr. Ware recommends. He urges all of those making the journey to travel with other California-bound emigrants in wagon trains for safety's sake."

"Makes good sense."

"And that's what I'll do." Craig put a finger on the map. "So, in the wagon train, I'll travel across northern Ohio and Indiana, and pass just south of Chicago. Like I said, I have all of this written on this piece of paper."

Wallace nodded. "All right."

"From Illinois, the route will take the wagon train across Iowa, just past Iowa City, then across Nebraska Territory. Using this route, we'll avoid high passes in the Rocky Mountains by traveling across southern Wyoming Territory to Salt Lake City, Utah. Mr. Ware tells in the book that Salt Lake City was founded just last year."

Wallace nodded. "I did read that in one of the newspapers."

"From there," said Craig, running his finger along the trail on the map, "we'll cross the Great Salt Lake Desert, then angle across Nevada Territory southwestward to the Sierra Nevada Mountains, and over them straight to Sacramento."

Wallace made a smile. "Well, one thing for sure, you'll be one tired young man when you get there."

"No doubt. But it'll be worth it when I make my fortune in gold. Mr. Ware says in here that when traveling overland by wagon, the average distance covered in a day's travel of twelve hours is twelve miles."

Wallace's eyebrows arched. "Only twelve miles in twelve hours? That's only one mile an hour."

"I thought the same thing when I first read it, but Mr. Ware explains that there are various stops during that twelve hours to cook meals, water, feed, and rest the horses, and tend to other necessary things that naturally come up on the journey. One of the most frequent stops is to repair or replace wagon wheels. Rough country takes its toll on wheels and axles. Mr. Ware points out in here, also, that there are lots of rivers and creeks to cross, and with wagons, it takes a lot of time to do that."

Wallace nodded. "I never thought about most of these things, son. I guess twelve miles a day is about all a wagon train can expect to cover."

"By my calculations, the journey will take me some two hundred and eight days. I want to give you a month to find a replacement for me here at the store, so I'm planning to head west by the first of February. Mr. Ware says there are wagon trains leaving Wheeling three or four times a week. If I can average twelve miles a day with the wagon train I join, that would land me in Sacramento in late August or early September."

Wallace frowned, looked at the map, and said, "Let's go over this one more time. I want to make sure your calculations are correct."

Craig grinned. "Sure."

Maddie and Kathy were playing dominoes upstairs, and Kathy was winning every game. She looked at the child with concerned eyes. "Honey, you're not playing like you usually do. You warned me that you were going to beat me tonight. Is...is it Craig?"

Maddie bit her lips and tears misted her eyes. She nodded. "Yes. I'm so afraid that he's going to go to California, Kathy."

"Do you want to talk to him some more?"

"Uh-huh."

"Well, since I'm not actually family, it might be best that you go down alone and talk to him and your father."

Maddie sniffed and ran a hand over her nose. "All right."

Father and son were just finishing rechecking Craig's calculations when there was a knock on the library door.

Wallace looked in that direction. "Come in!"

Maddie came through the door and moved toward the sofa. Tears were evident in her eyes.

"What is it, sweetie?" Wallace asked.

"I...I want to talk to Craig, Papa."

Craig remained on the sofa, but opened his arms to his little sister. She moved into his arms, and he sat her on his lap. "What is it, honey?"

Maddie sniffed and looked up into his eyes. "You're going to go to California, aren't you?"

Craig glanced at his father, who mouthed, *Don't tell her, yet. I want to tell her, myself. In the morning. It's best it comes from me.*

Craig nodded, pulled Maddie close to him, and said, "Baby sister, I just can't discuss it with you right now. Okay?"

A pout formed on her mouth. "When can we discuss it?"

"We'll all talk about it in the morning, honey," spoke up Wallace. "You go on back upstairs, now. Don't worry. Everything will be all right."

"All right, Papa." Maddie reached up and hugged Craig's neck with all her might. "I love you, big brother."

Craig kissed her cheek. "I love you, too, little sister."

Maddie left Craig's lap, hurried across the room to the door, and passed from view.

Wallace smiled at his son. "I'm very glad you and Maddie are so close."

"She's one special little girl, Dad. I hope you can help her understand why I'm going to California."

"I'll do my best. Craig..."

"Yes, Dad?"

"I'm very concerned about what might happen to you if you make this fortune you're going after."

Craig's brow creased. "What do you mean?"

"Since I've come to know the Lord and have been studying the Bible, I've seen in there what riches can do to a person if they get the wrong kind of hold on him."

Craig licked his lips nervously as his father rose from the sofa, picked up a Bible that lay on a nearby table, and sat down again. "There's something I want you to see in here, son."

Wallace scooted up close to Craig so he would be able to see the passage he wanted to show him. He turned to James chapter five.

"Look here at verses one through three. God is speaking in this passage to rich men who have ignored Him and His Word, and have built their lives on their riches instead of on the Lord Jesus Christ. Read them to me, son."

Reluctantly, Craig read them aloud to his father: "Go to now, ye rich men, weep and howl for your miseries that shall come upon you. Your riches are corrupted, and your garments are moth-eaten. Your gold and silver is cankered; and the rust of them shall be a witness against you, and shall eat your flesh as it were fire. Ye have heaped treasure together for the last days."

Wallace said, "Craig, there are multitudes of detrimental things that riches can do to a person whose goal is to become wealthy. A person like that definitely lives his life apart from Jesus Christ. This wastes that person's life, no matter how much money they accumulate. As we have just seen here in the Bible, that person's riches are corrupted in the eyes of God."

Craig shook his head. "I don't see it that way, Dad. I simply want to be wealthy so I can enjoy the good life, and have the satisfaction of knowing I became wealthy by my own initiative and hard work."

Wallace started to say something else, but Craig cut him off.

"Dad, I'll stay until Friday, February 2, in order to give you time to replace me. I'll leave on the third, and take a train to Wheeling as I explained to you."

Wallace sighed. "Son, I told you I can understand your wanting to make your own fortune, but since you will not open your heart to Jesus, I'm afraid of what will happen to it and to you." He paused, then said, "It would mean so much to me if I knew you were saved, and I knew that no matter what happened in this life, you and I would be together in heaven."

It was Craig's turn to sigh. "I'm glad for you—and for Maddie and Kathy—that you have this belief that seems to give you so much satisfaction. But it's not for me."

Wallace wiped a tear from the corner of his eye. "I'll tell Maddie, Kathy, and the servants in the morning that you'll be leaving February 3. I want Maddie and Kathy, especially, to have as much time as possible to prepare themselves for your departure."

SIXTEEN

The next morning at the breakfast table in the dining room, Wallace Turley prayed over the food, thanking the Lord for His generous provision for them. As soon as he closed the prayer, Maddie looked at her brother, then set her gaze on her father and said, "Papa, you told me last night in the library that we would talk about Craig and California. Can we talk about it now?"

At that moment, Elizabeth came in from the kitchen and moved toward the table.

Wallace saw her and whispered, "After breakfast, Maddie. Not now."

Elizabeth drew up and said with a smile, "So how is breakfast?"

"It's delicious as always, Elizabeth," said Kathy.

The others agreed.

Elizabeth looked at each one. "Anybody need anything?"

When no one answered, Wallace said, "Looks like we're all set, Elizabeth. Thank you."

When the cook had left the room, Wallace said, "Maddie, I don't want to talk about Craig and California with any of the servants within hearing distance. I want you and Kathy to hear about it first. Now, go ahead and eat your breakfast. We'll talk when we're finished."

Maddie's face pinched. "He—he's going to California, isn't he?"

Wallace gave her a stern look. "I said we will talk about it when we're finished eating breakfast."

Maddie nodded. "Yes, sir."

Kathy felt a knot form in her stomach. Both she and Maddie picked at their food until Wallace and Craig were finished.

Wallace noted that both young ladies were leaving food on their plates, and said, "All right. We can talk about Craig and California now." He took a deep breath. "Yes, Craig is going to California with the intention of getting in on the gold strike and making his own fortune."

Big tears welled up in Maddie's eyes.

"Now, I want to make it clear that even though I would rather my son stay here and go right on working as my first vice president, I do understand his need to make his own way in life. I did that myself. Craig and I had a long talk last night. It's no secret that my greatest desire for him is that he become a child of God, but I cannot force him to receive Jesus into his heart."

Sister and governess both looked at Craig. He glanced at them, then looked away.

The tears were now spilling down Maddie's cheeks.

Kathy felt a lump rise in her throat and tears warm her eyes. She bit the inside of her cheeks to keep from crying.

Maddie was using her napkin to wipe the tears from her cheeks as Kathy asked, "So, when are you leaving for California, Craig?"

"I—I'll be leaving February 3. I want to give Dad time enough to replace me."

Maddie left her chair and threw her arms around Craig. "No! No! I don't want you to go! Please don't go, Craig!"

Craig hugged her and kissed her forehead. "Maddie, you heard Papa say he understands why I need to do this. As a young man, he left his family to make his own fortune, and I need to make my own fortune, too. Please try to understand. It isn't that I want to leave home, but the gold strike—or should I say, the gold *rush*—is in California."

Maddie sniffed, choked slightly, and said, "I—I'll try to understand, Craig. At least you'll be here for Christmas."

He kissed her forehead again. "I sure will. And Maddie, one day I'll come home to see you after I've made my fortune."

Craig noticed that Kathy was thumbing tears from her cheeks.

"And Kathy, I'll be back to see *you*, too."

Kathy looked into his eyes and nodded.

Maddie asked, "How long will it be till you come back, Craig?"

"Well, from what I've learned, it will probably take a couple of years to amass my fortune once I arrive there, which will be in late August or early September. And then once I have enough gold, it will take me about eight months to make the trip home."

Maddie blinked and her eyes widened. "But that means it will be more than three years before I see you again! I'll be a teenager by then!"

"I know, but it's just going to take time to do all the things I need to do."

Maddie looked at her father.

Wallace said, "Honey, Craig's mind is made up. We can't stop him. It's his life."

Maddie looked back at Craig. Her chin quivered and her voice shook as she said, "Will you write to me?"

"Of course I will. I can post letters along the way telling you about my traveling adventures, so in a sense, you can experience them, too. Then when I get to Sacramento, I'll write and tell you my mailing address, and then *you* can write to *me*."

Maddie wiped the last traces of tears from her face and hugged her brother tightly around the neck. "Craig, once we have your California address, I'll write you a letter every day, and send them at the end of each week. How does that sound?"

Craig patted her back. "That sounds just about perfect, squirt."

Maddie let go of his neck and kissed his cheek. "It's a deal, big brother."

Wallace stood up and said, "Well, Craig, you and I had better get ready to go to work."

Kathy also rose to her feet. "Maddie, we need to go upstairs so I can put your hair in braids like you said you wanted."

Kathy took her by the hand, and they left the dining room just ahead of the men. As they climbed the winding staircase, Kathy was doing a valiant job of holding herself together. But what she wanted to do was to find a private place where she could have a good cry.

Some forty minutes later, Kathy stepped out of her room into the hallway at the same time Craig came out of his room, ready to go to work. Her room was closer to the stairs, so when she saw him coming, she stopped and waited.

When Craig drew up, he saw tears misting Kathy's eyes. "What is it, Kathy?"

She sniffed. "Oh, Craig, I'm going to miss you so much."

He smiled thinly. "I'm going to miss you, too."

Craig started to move toward the stairs, but she touched his arm to stop him, and said with a quavering voice, "I have to tell you how I feel."

"Hmm?"

"I've been falling in love with you for some time. I…I just haven't found the right moment to tell you until now."

Craig looked into her glistening eyes.

Kathy went on. "I have been praying for two things. One, that you would open your heart to Jesus. And two, that you would fall in love with me. Excuse me for being so bold to say this, but that's how it is."

Craig was trying to think of what to say to her when he heard his father call out from downstairs, "Craig, you ready? Time to go!"

Craig looked toward the staircase, gave Kathy a delicate embrace, and said, "Kathy, you are very special to me." With that, he wheeled and hurried away.

Kathy hurried back into her room, threw herself across her bed, and sobbed.

When Craig hurried out the back door of the mansion, Harold Wilkins was already in the driver's seat, holding the reins, and Wallace was seated behind him. Craig hopped in next to his father, saying, "Sorry, Dad. I had to spend a couple of minutes with Kathy in the hall upstairs."

Wallace's lips were pressed thinly. He nodded.

Harold put the horse in motion, and as the buggy turned onto the street, he spoke over his shoulder. "Mr. Craig, while we were waiting for you, your father told me about your plans to go to California."

"Oh?"

"Uh-huh. I wish you well, Mr. Craig."

"Thank you, Harold."

"We'll all miss you, sir."

"I'll miss you, too."

Soon they were in heavy traffic, and with the sounds of the street in their ears, Craig leaned close to his father and asked, "Did you tell Elizabeth and Adelle, too?"

"Yes. I figured it was best that they all know about it now, since it's no longer a secret."

At the end of that work day, as Harold was driving Wallace and Craig home, Wallace said, "Son, I talked with Dirk Reyes this afternoon about your plans to go to California. I offered him your job, and he gladly accepted the promotion."

"Well, good. I figured Dirk would be your first choice, since he's second vice president, although there are some other good men in the corporation who could handle the job." He paused, then added, "Dirk deserves the position more than anyone else, though."

"That's how I feel about it."

Christmas came that following Monday, and as the Turley family and Kathy Ross gathered at the huge, brightly decorated tree in the parlor, it was a bittersweet time. Behind the gaiety of opening gifts was the dismay that Craig would soon be gone.

Craig had gone out of his way to buy more gifts than ever before, doing his best to make this an especially happy Christmas for them all to remember. He knew the years he would be away at holiday time would be different for all of them—including himself.

Maddie loved each gift from her brother, but her favorite gift was her very own stationery with her name and address imprinted on each sheet of paper and on the flap of every envelope.

Craig smiled and said, "Now, little sis, you will have no excuses. You have plenty of paper and plenty of envelopes. Once I let you know where to send my mail, I'll expect letters from you every week, as you promised."

Maddie hugged him, then looked into his eyes and said, "You'll get those letters, big brother. And I want answers, too."

"Yes, ma'am. You shall have them."

The New Year arrived, and on Wednesday afternoon, January 17, 1849, Craig was at his desk, showing Dirk Reyes how to handle certain parts of the first vice president's job. Charlotte McClain entered the office. Both men looked up as she said, "Mr. Turley, your father wants to see you in his office right away."

"All right, Charlotte." Then to Dirk: "We'll take up where we left off tomorrow morning."

Dirk nodded. "That's fine."

Craig entered his father's office to find a stranger seated with his father on the sofa by the window.

Both men rose, and Craig suddenly realized he had seen the tall, slender, balding man before—in front of Broadway Tabernacle. *He's the pastor of Broadway Tabernacle…Charles G. Finney.*

"Son, I want you to meet my pastor," Wallace said, smiling broadly.

Craig painted a smile on his face and extended his right hand. "Pastor Finney."

Finney smiled in return as they clasped hands. "Craig, I'm glad to finally get to meet you. Your father, Maddie, and Kathy have spoken of you often."

Though the ice that had formed in his stomach chilled him, Craig kept his smile. "I'm glad to meet you, too, sir."

"Craig, last Sunday I told Pastor Finney about your plans to leave for California soon," Wallace said, "and I asked him to come by the office so he could meet you before you leave."

Craig noticed Finney reach down and pick up his Bible from the sofa seat. He drew a short breath and said, "Well, Pastor Finney, I'm sure you and Dad have plenty to talk about. I'll just excuse myself."

Wallace shook his head. "No, no, son. Please sit down here with us. Pastor Finney would like to talk to you."

Along with the icy feeling in Craig's stomach, there was now a touch of nausea.

The pastor and Wallace sat back down on the sofa, and Craig reluctantly took a seat in an overstuffed chair facing them.

Wallace noted that Craig's face had turned a bit pale.

Finney smiled at Craig. "You are aware, I'm sure, that your father, your sister, and Kathy became born-again children of God several months ago. And that more recently, all three of the servants in your house have been born again."

Craig nodded, avoiding the preacher's steady gaze. "Yes, sir."

"Well, Craig, I'd like to talk to you about your need to be born again."

Wallace jumped up and picked up the Bible that lay on a small table nearby. He handed it to his son, saying, "It will help if you can follow in here what Pastor Finney will be reading to you from his Bible. They were produced by the same publisher, so the page numbers are the same."

Opening his Bible and telling Craig where to turn, Charles Finney very kindly and compassionately showed Craig the passage in John chapter three where Jesus told Nicodemus, "Except a man be born again, he cannot see the kingdom of God." He went on, then, and showed him that as the Lamb of God, Jesus shed His blood on the cross for a lost, sinful world, died, was buried, and arose from the dead. Finney showed Craig what God said about all unbelievers spending eternity in the lake of fire and made it clear that the reason God sent His only begotten Son into the world was to provide the one and only way of salvation for lost, hell-bound sinners. He showed him 1 John 4:14—"And we have seen and do testify that the Father sent the Son to be the Saviour of the world."

He set steady eyes on Craig. "Do you see that? Jesus is *the* Saviour of the world. Not one among many. *The* Saviour. There is only one. Do you see that?"

Craig nodded. "Yes, sir."

Letting it soak in, Finney said, "Craig, just like the rest of the human race, you are a sinner in need of salvation…of being born again. You need to repent of your sin and receive the Lord Jesus Christ into your heart as your Saviour."

Craig cleared his throat gently and said, "I'll give it more thought one of these days, Pastor Finney, but all I can think about right now is getting to California and making my fortune."

Finney shook his head. "Craig, you know who you remind me of?"

"No."

"You remind me of the prodigal son that Jesus told about in Luke chapter fifteen. Have you ever read or heard the story?"

"I've heard *about* the story, sir, but I've never actually heard the story or ever read it."

Finney opened his Bible again, told Craig what page to find, and when he had found it, Finney said, "All right, you follow along as I read it aloud."

When they finished reading the story, Finney said, "The prodigal finally realized that he had been a fool to rebel against his father's way of life and leave home. And as we have read, he hurried home, asked his father's forgiveness, and was welcomed with open arms."

Craig stiffened. "Pastor Finney, I mean no disrespect, but I don't think it's fair of you to compare me to the prodigal son. Just because I'm going to California to make my fortune doesn't mean I'm rebelling against my dad. Since I was very young, I was known as the kid with the silver spoon in my mouth because I was brought up in a well-to-do home. I want to get rich by what I do with my own intellect and my own two hands."

"Son, Pastor Finney is merely trying to keep you from making the same mistake the prodigal son did," Wallace said. "Remember the passage of Scripture I showed you in James about the miseries that can come upon rich people who live for their treasures rather than living for the Lord?"

Craig nodded. "I remember."

"Son, you could go to California, strike it rich, then lose all of it because you've turned your back on the Lord."

"Dad, I'm not turning my back on God. I said a little while ago that I'd think about all this salvation stuff later."

"But you see, Craig," spoke up Finney, "the gospel has been presented to you right here today. If you don't say yes to Jesus and open your heart to Him, in His eyes you are saying no. The Bible is very clear on that."

"Craig, what a tragedy if you strike it rich out there, then lose it all," Wallace said. "I ran onto another passage of Scripture on this subject recently. I want you to see it."

Craig stood up. "Dad, I don't want to hear any more about it."

Wallace's eyes filmed with moisture as he said, "I just don't want you to make a mistake and mess up your life."

Touched by his father's tears, Craig sighed, sat back down, and said, "All right, Dad. I know you have my best interests at heart. Go ahead. Show me this latest Scripture that you found."

SEVENTEEN

Wallace Turley turned to Pastor Charles Finney. "May I borrow your Bible? I want Craig to follow along as he has done with you."

Pastor Finney smiled and handed his Bible to Wallace, who opened it to Proverbs 23. He looked at Craig. "It's Proverbs 23:4 and 5, son. Page 944."

Pastor Finney prayed in his heart and looked on with the hope that young Craig Turley would turn to Jesus.

When Craig had found the page and put his finger in the margin beside the two verses, Wallace read it aloud: "Labour not to be rich: cease from thine own wisdom. Wilt thou set thine eyes upon that which is not? for riches certainly make themselves wings; they fly away as an eagle toward heaven."

Wallace looked at Craig, who was already looking at him. "Do you see it, son? If you work at getting rich for the sake of proving you can do it on your own and center your life on the riches, even as God says here, those riches can sprout wings and fly away just as an eagle flies toward heaven. You can end up poor and hungry like the prodigal son."

Craig frowned. "Why is it wrong to work hard to be wealthy if I come by it honestly?"

"Wallace, may I answer Craig's question?" Charles Finney said.

"Of course, Pastor. Go ahead."

"Craig, this passage does not forbid industry and honest, diligent toil to live comfortably above poverty, but it warns against excessive desire for wealth and the burning lust of greed, which so often results in total loss."

Craig nodded. "Pastor Finney, I can see that greediness could so warp a man that he becomes selfish and insensitive to others around him. I will not be that way when I make my fortune. I just want to lay hold on all the wealth I can by industry and honest toil, and enjoy the fruit of my labor."

Finney glanced at Wallace, then back at Craig. "Think on those words you just said, Craig. '*I just want to lay hold on all the wealth I can…*' When would you have enough? When would you say, 'I don't need any more money'?"

"Well, I really can't say, sir. I guess I'd just have to steadily keep my eyes on my needs and desires as the wealth accumulated."

"That's dangerous, Craig. God says in His Word that the human heart is deceitful. Your heart can tell you things that aren't true. It can cloud your vision and make you believe things that are not so. You just said you would have to keep your *eyes* on your needs and desires. Proverbs 27:20 says, 'Hell and destruction are never full; so the eyes of man are never satisfied.' True satisfaction can come only to those who have Jesus Christ in their hearts. When He comes into our hearts and into our lives, everything changes. Old things are passed away, and all things are become new, and we have a satisfaction that the person outside of Christ can never fathom. Our hearts and our eyes find complete satisfaction in Jesus and the salvation He gives us."

Craig stared at him blankly.

"Craig, remember what God said about your eyes in Proverbs 23:5: 'Wilt thou set thine *eyes* upon that which is not?' How quickly riches can disappear! If we build our lives on what wealth we can attain, rather than on Jesus Christ, those riches have the ability to make themselves wings and fly away. Then what does that once-wealthy person have? Nothing. But when we build our lives on Jesus and the salvation He has given, Jesus does not fly away, and neither does our salvation. We have Him and our salvation forever."

Craig still stared at him, but a thoughtful expression replaced the blank one.

"Let me tell you a story," Finney said. "Actually, it's an old legend that came out of Russia many years ago. A young Russian man fell heir to his father's small farm when his father died. His mother had died giving birth to him. The young man was no sooner in possession of this land when he began to dream eagerly of how he could add to it. He wanted *more* land…all he could possess. He felt if he had all the farmland he could possess, he could become a very rich man.

"One morning, Craig, this young Russian was standing in the local cemetery at his father's grave. He had gone there every day since his father's death to pay honor to him. While standing at the grave, the young man saw a stranger dressed in black, standing a short distance away, looking at him. By his clothing, the young Russian thought the stranger must be very wealthy.

"The stranger then came to him and said, 'Young man, I would like to make you an offer.' 'What is that, sir?' asked the young man. The stranger said, 'I will give you, free of charge, all the land adjacent to one side of the cemetery that you can walk over in one day. But no later than sundown, you must be back at the very place you started from —which is right here at your father's grave. If the sun has dipped completely beneath the western horizon before you return, you will get nothing.'

"The young man wondered how the stranger knew the grave was his father's, but the offer had his full attention. He looked eagerly over the rich fields before him, wondering why this stranger would want to give away his valuable property. Believing, however, that the offer was valid, he told the stranger he would begin right now. He revealed to the stranger that his plan was to cover a parcel of ground fifteen miles square. This would give him sixty miles to traverse before sundown. Instead of walking, he would run as fast as he could.

"The stranger smiled and told him he had better get started; it was already nearing midmorning. The stranger advised the young man that he must mark the ground as he covered it, so he would know that he had actually done so.

"The young man hurried away. His greed pushed him relentlessly for the rest of the day. In the last moments of sundown, terribly fatigued, he came staggering into the cemetery toward his father's grave as the stranger watched him. He was breathing raggedly, ready to faint, but summoned all of his remaining energy and rushed toward the grave.

"As he reached the grave, the top rim of the sun was barely visible. He saw a cruel, cynical smile on the face of the stranger, whom he thought was the possessor of the fifteen square miles of rich, fertile land. Puffing hard, he pointed toward the sliver of sunlight still showing on the western horizon, and said hoarsely, 'I made it! I made it!' The stranger's smile broadened as he said, 'Yes, you made it.'

"Suddenly the young man clutched his chest, gasped, and fell dead on the ground. The stranger in black, who was Death, looked down at the lifeless form and said, 'I offered you all the land you could cover by sundown. With your excessive greed, you found what that is: *six feet long by two feet wide.*'"

There were a few seconds of absolute silence, and both Pastor Finney and Wallace could tell that the story had an impact on Craig. But he quickly shook it off. He looked at Finney and said, "That's only a legend, Mr. Finney."

"Yes, that's so. But what a powerful testimony to the truth of Proverbs 23:4 and 5. Without a thought of seeking the wisdom of almighty God, that young man used his own frail wisdom and labored to be rich. His riches sprouted wings just as he staggered into the cemetery, and flew away as an eagle toward heaven when he fell dead on the ground."

Craig's features were pallid, and he felt nerves twitching throughout his body. He tried to smile, but the smile was brittle. "It's been nice to spend a little time with you, Mr. Finney." Then to both men: "Please excuse me. I need to get back to my office. I have a lot of work to do."

"Sure, son," said Wallace. "Be sure to think Pastor Finney's story over, with its application to Proverbs 23:4 and 5. Think about those wings of riches."

Craig nodded, then turned and left the office.

Wallace turned to Pastor Finney. "Your story affected him, without a doubt."

"Yes, I could see that, Wallace. Let's pray for him right now."

The two men knelt at the sofa, and Pastor Finney led in earnest prayer for Craig, asking the Holy Spirit to drive the truth of the gospel into his heart and draw him to Jesus.

When the amen was said, and the two men stood up, Finney patted Wallace's shoulder and said, "Don't give up on him. The prodigal son finally came to himself and went home to his father."

Wallace grinned. "Yes, he did, didn't he?"

❧

In Sacramento, California, on Friday evening, January 18, two men stood in the shadows across the street from Carrie's Café. Main Street stretched away both directions under great blinking white stars. People were moving along the boardwalks, and a few horse-drawn vehicles rattled along the dusty street.

No one noticed the two men in the shadows keeping their eyes on the café. Through the two windows that faced the street, they could see that the place was packed.

Judd Chaney pulled his pocket watch from a vest pocket, angled it toward the nearest street lamp, and said, "It's two minutes till nine o'clock, Blackie. That there cash register has gotta be jam-packed with money."

Blackie Bollin's eyes were narrow and intent as he observed Carrie's Café. "Now's the time, Judd. We're gonna make us a big haul tonight. Let's go."

Inside the café, Rena Powell was at the cash register, waiting on customers who had just finished their meals. Randy Powell, who had recently turned sixteen, was in the kitchen helping his mother clean up, since it was closing time. Darin Powell was busing tables. Just as he was beginning to wipe one of the tables clean with a wet cloth, he saw two rough-looking men come in, their eyes roaming around the café.

Darin dropped the cloth on the table, stepped up to the men, and said, "Sorry, sirs, but we're closed."

In the kitchen, Carrie Powell was washing dishes while Randy emptied a pan of beans into a large jar on a counter next to the cookstove. Suddenly, they heard a loud male voice bark, "We ain't wantin' to be served, kid! All we want is that money in the cash register!"

Another male voice commanded everyone to lift their hands above their heads and freeze.

Carrie and Randy looked at each other, eyes wide. Randy dashed to the large pass-through and cautiously looked at the scene. One glimpse of the two robbers holding their guns on the patrons and the look of terror on Rena's face at the cash register impelled him to go to the cupboard and take a revolver out of the drawer. When he saw the frightened look on his mother's face, he whispered, "I've got to stop them!"

Bending low, Randy hurried back to the pass-through. He cocked the Colt .45, aimed it at the man who was approaching Rena, and bellowed, "Hold it right there! Both of you drop your guns, or I'll cut you down!"

Blackie Bollin was almost to the cash register. Judd Chaney stood just inside the door.

Blackie squinted at Randy and growled, "Don't be a fool, kid. You can't hope to get both of us before one of us blows your head off."

"I may be a kid, mister," snapped Randy, breathing heavily with a flush of heat on his cheeks, "but my dad was marshal of this town, and he taught me how to use a gun. Drop your guns, both of you, or else!"

Blackie's gun hand came up, but before he could squeeze the trigger, Randy's .45 roared, and the robber fell to the floor. Men gasped and women screamed. Judd whirled, bolted through the door, and ran down the street.

The men in the café who wore guns whipped them out and headed for the door. Randy was picking up Blackie's gun off the floor when one of the men looked at the fallen robber and said,

"He's still breathing, Randy. Watch him."

As the armed men dashed outside, they saw Marshal Cade Ryer running down the street toward them. He had been in conversation with a man and his wife further up the street when the report of Randy's Colt .45 echoed among the clapboard buildings.

When the marshal was almost to them, one of the men said, "Marshal! Two men just tried to rob the café! Randy shot one inside! The other one's trying to get away! He ran that way, toward—"

The man's words were cut off by the sound of a galloping horse coming to a skidding halt just around the corner, and a man shouting, "Hey! Look out!"

"Go back to the café and stay with Randy till I come back," Marshal Ryer said. With that, he dashed to the corner, where some of the other café patrons were standing over a man who lay in the dust of the street, moaning. The rider of the horse, who was one of the gold miners in the area, was bending over him.

As Ryer drew up, one of the men told him that the man on the ground was the other robber. This gold miner came down the cross street on his horse at a gallop, and in the robber's hurry to escape, he stepped right in the path of the galloping horse.

The marshal handed the man a key and said, "Have some of these other men go with you and take this man to my office and keep him there. I'll check on the other one and be there shortly. Have somebody go get my two deputies, and they can put this one in a cell."

"Will do, Marshal," said the man.

Seconds later, Marshal Ryer entered the café to find Carrie Powell standing beside Rena as they looked down at Randy, who was kneeling over the bleeding, unconscious robber. Most of the women patrons were still seated at their tables, waiting for their husbands to return.

"Darin went to get one of the doctors, Cade," Carrie said.

Cade nodded, then knelt down beside Randy and looked into the face of the fallen robber. There was a bullet hole in his right upper chest, and his coat was soaked with blood.

The marshal then turned to Randy. "They told me outside what you did. That took quick thinking and courage."

"I had to stop them, Marshal. I couldn't let them take our money."

Cade laid a hand on the teenager's shoulder. "You did an excellent job. This robber and his partner will both go to prison, thanks to you. If you were five years older, I'd hire you to be one of my deputies."

Carrie looked down at the marshal. "I'm sure when he turns twenty-one, he will want you to make him one of your deputies. He's got the itch to wear a badge, just like his father did."

Cade squeezed Randy's shoulder. "Well, my friend, on your twenty-first birthday, I'll be offering you a deputy's badge."

In Manhattan, New York, the days passed quickly, and before the Turley household was ready, it was the evening before Craig was to board the train for Wheeling, Virginia.

Elizabeth Loysen had prepared a special meal of Craig's favorite foods and his favorite dessert.

When the Turleys and Kathy Ross entered the dining room, they noted that the table was adorned with a new creamy-white tablecloth, with napkins to match. Elizabeth and Adelle Brown had the table set and the food on the table. The aromas that filled the air made everybody smile. Wallace had invited the cook, the housekeeper, and the handyman, Harold Wilkins, to eat with the family and Kathy.

As the group was sitting down, Craig eased onto his usual chair at the table and smiled at Elizabeth. "If it's half as good as it looks and smells, it's going to taste great!"

"I wanted to give you a good sendoff," she said.

Wallace looked around and said, "Let's pray."

Heads were bowed, and there was a tremor in the heartsick father's voice as he asked for God's blessing on the food and for his son's safety as he traveled to California.

It was a somber occasion as they ate the delicious meal, but each person tired to bring some measure of levity to the conversation. Elizabeth, Adelle, and Harold recalled pleasant incidents concerning Craig in his growing-up years.

Kathy was rather quiet and had little appetite as she thought of all the lonely, empty days ahead with Craig gone.

Although Maddie's heart was breaking, she did her very best to be cheerful. She knew she would miss her brother desperately and could not imagine what her life was going to be like with him thousands of miles away. These thoughts brought a lump to her throat. She wanted Craig to have happy memories of this night, so she did not allow herself to break into tears.

At one point, the conversation dwindled. Wallace broke the silence by saying, "I learned from Horace Greeley just yesterday that since the California gold rush is escalating so rapidly, the U. S. Postal Service has declared that all the passenger ships that leave the east coast for San Francisco will carry the mail for the people in that area. No mail sent to those Forty-niners, as they are now called, will be carried cross-country to California. Horace said it will take an average of ten to eleven months to get the mail there, but at least it's going. He told me that he's going to have an article about it in the *Tribune* within a day or two."

Maddie frowned. "Papa, will the ships bring back mail from

the people who are digging for gold in California?"

"Mr. Greeley didn't mention that, but I suppose they'll have to."

Maddie looked at her brother. "Craig, as soon as you get to California and start digging for gold, I want you to write and let us know how it's going, even though it will take a long time for your letters to get here."

Craig smiled. "Of course I'll write, baby sister."

"And you promised that when I write to you, you'll write me back."

"I did, and I *will*."

The next morning, Craig placed his briefcase and one suitcase in the buggy, and said his good-byes to the cook and housekeeper. Then he turned to find Maddie standing right behind him, just ahead of her father and her governess.

When Craig gathered his little sister in his arms, she clung to him and began to wail as if her heart would shatter into pieces. "Oh, Craig, are you really sure you have to go? Can't you stay here and let everything be as it's always been? Please, Craig! Please don't go!"

The tears that Maddie had so bravely held back the night before refused their captivity this time. She put her hand to her face and tried to brush them away, but they just kept coming.

Craig held her tight and said softly, "Maddie, don't carry on so. You'll make yourself sick, and I don't want that. Yes, I'm sure I have to go. I know it seems like I'll be gone a long time, but I promise that if you stay busy with your studies, do your schoolwork, and learn all that Kathy wants to teach you, the time will hurry by. I'll be back before you know it!"

Maddie choked on her tears and valiantly gained control. She mopped the tears on her cheeks with a hankie Kathy put in her hand. There was still a sob in her quavering voice as she looked into her brother's eyes and said, "Since you promise the time will hurry by if I stay busy with my schoolwork, I promise I'll be good and work hard on my lessons. Only—only the next time you see me, I'll already be a young woman."

A wayward tear glided down Maddie's cheek. She dashed it away with the hankie.

After Wallace and Craig had said good-bye to each other, embracing and pounding one another on the back, Kathy stepped up to Craig and placed a folded note in his hand. "Please read this later."

He smiled at her, placed the note in his shirt pocket, and folded her into his arms.

As they were embracing, Kathy whispered in his ear, "I love you, Craig. I'll be praying that you open your heart to Jesus. I'll also be praying that you will make your fortune quickly, and hurry home. I—I will miss you terribly."

Craig squeezed her tight, looked into her tear-filled eyes, and whispered, "Kathy, I will miss you very much."

Craig climbed into the buggy, and Harold put the horse in motion.

The others stood on the porch and waved as the buggy reached the street and wheeled to the left. Craig waved back as the buggy turned at the corner and vanished from sight.

Wallace wiped his own tears as he beheld the tears in the eyes of Maddie and Kathy. "Well, enough of this," he said as he hugged his daughter with one arm and Kathy with the other. "We each have work to be done and lives to be lived. We can't go around with these long faces forever." A smile lighted up his features. "That wouldn't be pleasing to the Lord. All three of us love Craig and will miss him. We've already agreed that our prayers will follow him wherever he goes. Won't it be wonderful when the Lord answers those prayers and puts circumstances in Craig's life that will bring him to Jesus?"

"Papa," said Maddie, "the Lord can really do wonderful things like that, can't He?"

"He sure can, honey. I just thought of a Scripture verse that I read in my devotions a couple days ago. Psalm 72:18. I committed it to memory on the spot. 'Blessed be the LORD God, the God of Israel, who only doeth wondrous things.'

"Did you girls hear that? He only doeth *wondrous* things! That's because He is such a wondrous, magnificent, amazing, marvelous, astounding God! He, indeed, has done wondrous things for the three of us already. And because of our prayers, He's going to do wondrous things in Craig's life."

The hopeful threesome let the peace of God take control of their hearts, and a glad smile lit up each face as they moved inside the mansion.

Less than two hours after he had told his family and Kathy goodbye, Craig Turley was aboard the train, sitting on a seat, alone.

While looking out the window and watching the busy streets of New York City pass by, he suddenly remembered Kathy's note. He reached into his shirt pocket and took out the folded slip of paper.

Tears moistened Craig's eyes as he read Kathy's words of love, saying she would never love anyone but him.

He took a handkerchief from his hip pocket and wiped his tears. He knew in his heart that he would fall in love with Kathy if he was around her much longer.

He took a deep breath and whispered to himself, "Right now, you must concentrate on making your fortune."

EIGHTEEN

It was twilight on Sunday, February 4, as the train pulled into Wheeling, Virginia. When the big engine ground to a halt in the depot, Craig Turley noticed a man standing on the platform in lantern light, holding a large sign that read:

CALIFORNIA GOLD RUSH
TRAVELERS GATHER HERE

Craig took his briefcase from the rack above and joined the line of people in the coach as they filed toward the front. When he stepped down from the coach, he hurried to the baggage coach, picked up his suitcase, and quickly made his way to the man who held the sign.

He was the first one to draw up to the man, who smiled and said, "California gold rush?"

"Yes, sir."

"All right. Just wait right here. When the rest of them gather, I'll give instructions."

Craig nodded and set his suitcase down. He looked around

and saw other people coming that way from the baggage coach. Some were young couples with children tagging along. Eight men walked together just behind the others.

When all had gathered around the man with the sign, he asked how many covered wagons and horse teams were to be purchased for the journey to California. Craig learned that there would be seven wagons in their wagon train. Four of them would be occupied by men with their wives and children. Two wagons would be occupied by four men each, who had left their families at home. Seven of the eight men were venturing to California with the hope that they could return home with plenty of money for their families. The eighth was an older man, who had identified himself as Richard Dawson, a farmer from upstate New York. He explained that he was a widower, and his plan was to remain in California after he struck it rich.

The seventh wagon would be Craig's.

The man with the sign then explained that a small settlement occupied the Ohio side of the Ohio River. The group would be ferried across the river the next morning at seven o'clock, where they could purchase their wagons and horses from the dealers in the settlement. They would also be able to purchase food, cookware, bedding, and other necessary items at the settlement's general store. He explained that Wheeling had three hotels, but recommended that they all stay at the Bellaire Hotel, which was just a block from the depot and closest to the dock where the ferry would pick them up in the morning. He gave them directions to the hotel and the dock, and the travelers walked together toward the Bellaire Hotel in the light of the street lamps.

As the group moved toward the hotel in the crisp night air, Craig stepped up beside Richard Dawson and said, "Mr. Dawson, my name is Craig Turley. I'm from Manhattan."

Dawson nodded. "Glad to meet you, young man."

"You said you're a farmer from upstate New York?"

"That's right. Near Syracuse."

"Well, sir, I know very little about horses and wagons. Could I get you to help me in the morning when I make my purchase?"

"Of course. I'll be glad to help you outfit your wagon, too, if you wish."

"Oh, that would be great! I'd really appreciate it. I've read as much as I could about wagon trains before starting on this trip, but I know I'm going to need help."

Richard Dawson looked at this young man and told himself that he would have pity on the city boy and take him under his wing on the long journey.

At precisely seven o'clock the next morning, the travelers, dressed warmly, were ferried across the Ohio River. A brisk wind was blowing. The air was very cold, and the gray sky above promised snow.

With Richard Dawson's guidance, Craig Turley purchased a sturdy covered wagon and a strong-looking pair of horses. The wagon was equipped with a large water barrel attached to its side, as well as a good supply of firewood.

Richard volunteered to ride with Craig the first day so he could teach him how to handle the horses, and Craig gladly accepted. The farmer told Craig he had explained to his traveling partners that he was going to help the young man from Manhattan along the way, and they were glad to see him do it.

Richard drove the wagon to the general store, where Craig purchased the necessary equipment, groceries, cookware, and bedding as directed by his new friend. Then they carried it to his covered wagon and stowed it inside.

When Richard had placed the last sack of goods inside Craig's wagon, he smiled and said, "Well, there you go, lad. As I told you, I'll ride with you today, so I can help you learn how to handle the horses. And tomorrow morning when we pull out from wherever we camp for the night, I'll have our wagon right behind yours so I can keep an eye on you and help you if you have any problems."

Craig smiled broadly. "Thank you so much, Mr. Dawson. You've already been a great help to me, and I appreciate it."

Richard laid a work-worn hand on Craig's shoulder and gave him a lopsided grin. "Glad to help, my boy. I hope this journey to gold country proves to be real profitable for both of us."

Moments later, the wagons were lined up to pull out.

Wind-whipped snow was beginning to coat the canvas covers of the wagons, but it did not bother the occupants of the wagon train. Heading west into the hills of Ohio, they endured the storm with dreams of gold strong in their minds.

At the Turley mansion on Tuesday evening, February 6, Wallace, Maddie, and Kathy sat down at the dinner table. Wallace prayed over the food, and as they began eating, Kathy said, "Mr. Turley, I'm going to write a letter to Craig this evening. Even though he won't get it till November or December, I want it to go to him right away. Will you post it from your office tomorrow?"

"I'll be glad to, Kathy."

Maddie's face brightened. "Then I'll write a letter to Craig this evening, too! You'll mail it for me tomorrow, won't you, Papa?"

"Of course, sweetheart."

When the meal was finished, Wallace said, "Maddie, I need to have a private talk with Kathy in the parlor. You go ahead upstairs to your room and play with your dolls."

Maddie grinned. "I won't play with my dolls till after I write my letter to Craig, Papa."

"Oh, yes, the letter. I forgot about that. Well, you go ahead. Kathy will join you later."

Maddie left the dining room, hurried down the hall, and bounded up the spiral staircase.

As Kathy walked beside Wallace toward the parlor, fear clutched her heart. *What in the world does he want to talk to me about? Have I done something wrong? Is he going to fire me?*

They entered the parlor, where Harold was adding logs to the fire. He smiled, saying the room would be comfortable for the rest of the evening, and left the room.

Wallace and Kathy sat down on the sofa that faced the fireplace. Kathy nervously entwined her hands together as they lay in her lap to try to stop them from trembling.

Wallace saw her trembling hands and the look of consternation on her face. He laid a steady hand over her own hands. "Kathy, dear, I didn't mean to worry you or upset you. There's nothing wrong. I just want to have a little chat with you about Craig."

Kathy's hand went to her mouth. "Oh. I—I was so afraid I had done something wrong or disappointed you in some way." She sighed deeply and relaxed against the back of the sofa. "What is it we need to discuss about Craig?" she asked, a bit of anxiety still noticeable in her soft voice.

Wallace looked into her eyes. "Kathy, I have felt for some time that you are in love with Craig. Am I right?"

Kathy nodded. "Yes, sir, I am. I know that Craig thinks a lot of me, and I have sensed lately that he might be on the verge of falling in love with me."

Wallace smiled. "I think I've seen it, too."

"Mr. Turley, even if Craig fell in love with me by the time he comes home, as much as I love him, there are two things that would keep me from marrying him."

"I know that one of them is because you couldn't marry him according to Scripture unless he becomes a Christian. What is the other?"

Kathy bit her lips and said hesitantly, "Well, sir, you—you probably want Craig to marry on his social level…you know, some young woman from a wealthy family. I'm only a governess."

Wallace shook his head. "You're wrong about that. I have long hoped that you and Craig would fall in love. I would be proud and pleased to have you for my daughter-in-law. I'm not concerned with social status."

Kathy blinked at the moisture that had welled up in her eyes. "Oh, thank you. Thank you."

"Tell you what. When I have my daily prayer time, I'm going to be praying that the Lord will bring Craig home as a child of God so you and he can marry." He patted her arm and said with a quaver in his voice, "You're a wonderful girl, Kathy, and you will make my son an excellent wife."

Kathy felt the tears begin to spill down her cheeks. They dripped off her chin, splashing on her folded hands. After a brief moment, she gained a measure of control. She palmed tears from her face and looked at him through the mist that remained in her eyes. "Mr. Turley, I am greatly honored that you want me to be your daughter-in-law. It means more than I can express that you want me as a member of your precious family. Knowing this will make the wait for Craig's return so much easier. Thank you, sir. I will do my best to see that you are never sorry that you feel this way toward me."

"I'm sure I'll never be sorry, dear. Now, let's keep this little conversation just between the two of us, okay? There's no need to involve Maddie at this point."

"Of course. I understand." A bright smile of hope and confidence lit up her face.

Wallace stood up. "Thank you for talking to me. I'll let you go to Maddie, now."

She arose from the sofa, looked up into Wallace's eyes, and threw her arms around him. She held onto him for a long moment, then eased back and said, "I'll look in on Maddie, but I'm going to my room to write that letter to Craig."

Maddie was still composing the letter to her brother when Kathy looked in on her. Kathy told the child that she was going to write her letter to Craig now, and went next door to her room.

In her letter, Kathy told Craig how much she loved him, how much she missed him, and that she was praying for him. When she finished it, she went to Maddie's room. They prayed together, then Kathy tucked her in, kissed her goodnight, and put out the room's two lanterns.

A short time later, as Kathy lay in her bed in the dark, she prayed for Craig. She asked the Lord to keep His protective hand on the man she loved and to bring about the circumstances that would make him seriously consider eternity without Jesus and draw him to Himself. She also prayed that the Lord would bring Craig back home to her safely and soon.

Then she cried herself to sleep.

Just before midnight on Tuesday, February 27, the Ashlock ship, *Bristol,* entered the harbor at Sydney, Australia, with the ship's captain, Henry Briggs, at the wheel. The other four crewmen stood with Colin Ashlock just outside the door of the pilot's cabin, observing the harbor lights as they cast erratic ribbons of radiance on the dark waters, zigzagging among the shadowed silhouettes of more than a dozen ships at anchor.

When Henry Briggs saw an open space between two ships, he eased back the throttle and turned the wheel. As they glided up toward the dock, they saw that passengers were just getting off the ship to their right. A few minutes later, Briggs had the *Bristol* in place, and two of the crewmen dropped anchor.

Colin's line of sight went to the adjacent ship, and just coming down the gangplank was his attorney and friend, Graham Middleton, Sydney's most prominent lawyer.

Colin hurried to the side of the deck and called out, "Hey, Graham!"

The attorney stepped off the gangplank onto the dock, whirled, and waved with a smile. "Hello, Colin! Glad to see you're back!"

Colin's crewmen were letting down the *Bristol's* gangplank.

"Wait up! I'll be right down!" Colin hollered.

Moments later, the two friends were shaking hands on the dock.

"So where've you been?" Colin asked.

"London. I hired another attorney to come and join my firm. His father and I went to law school together. He'll be coming in about a month." He paused, then asked, "So how did it go in Borneo?"

"Swell! As I told you, I went there to establish a new ship building company. Well, the Ashlock Ship Builders, Incorporated, in Borneo is now in business. I left it in the hands of two men you know well."

"Really? Who?"

"Fred Cotten and Alex Ramsey."

Middleton's mouth fell open. "You took Fred and Alex to Borneo with you?"

"Sure did."

"How?"

"Well, I had no doubt I could establish Ashlock Shipbuilders in Borneo, so I convinced them to leave Monument Shipbuilders to help me establish the new company with better pay. They sent for their families and are doing well."

Middleton nodded. "I'm glad it's in good hands. And I'm glad for you, Colin. Well, I've got to get home. See you later."

Colin and his crew went to the stable where they had left the ranch wagon and team, and headed through the business section toward the ranch.

The next morning, Colin rode his favorite stallion into Sydney to make a deposit at the bank. As he moved among the heavy downtown traffic, he noticed on a street corner a newsboy holding up the latest edition of the *Sydney Courier* and shouting out the news that the California gold rush was making people very rich, and fortune seekers were going there from all over the world.

Colin guided his horse over to the boardwalk and pulled rein. News had come to Sydney a few months previously about the California gold strike, but according to an article in the *Courier,* it was only a pipe dream. Swinging from his saddle, Colin told himself that what the newsboy was shouting out sounded like more than a pipe dream.

Colin purchased a copy of the newspaper, then stood next to his horse and read the entire front-page article. It stated that there was a very rich gold strike in California several miles inland from San Francisco at the city of Sacramento on the American River, and along tributary creeks in the Sierra Nevada Mountains. Thousands of people from China, Japan, Australia, all over Europe, and many parts of South America were flocking to California in hopes of finding instant riches.

In the United States and Territories, they were traveling on foot, in wagons, and on horseback across the American plains and over the towering peaks of the Rocky Mountains and, hundreds of miles later, over the lofty peaks of the Sierras.

Colin smacked his lips and said to himself in a low tone, "So our Aussie brethren are sailing for California. Well, Colin Ashlock, you and your ship crew are sailing for San Francisco Bay as soon as we can get ready! Gold! Riches! More riches!"

NINETEEN

On Monday, March 5, in Iowa City, Iowa, Luke and Sandra Daniels alighted from their wagon in front of the Main Street Bank. The sky was cloudy, and a cold wind whipped along the street.

When they entered the lobby, they found Ed and Dora Garberson waiting for them. The Garbersons were just a few years older than the Danielses, and were also members of the same church. The newspaper articles that had been in the *Iowa City Press* the past several weeks about how people were making their fortunes in gold around Sacramento had convinced Luke and Sandra after much prayer that the Lord wanted them to take their boys and go to California. They were selling their farm to the Garbersons, and the bank was going to finance the purchase for them.

The two couples made their way to the conference room where bank president Vance Edwards was expecting them. When everyone was seated, Luke took papers from a large brown envelope and handed them to the bank president. "Here are the legal documents our attorney drew up for the sale of the property, Mr.

Edwards. You may keep one set for your records."

Edwards thanked him, then carefully read over the papers.
When he was satisfied that everything was in order, he opened a
folder and produced the papers Luke and Sandra were to sign that
would legally release them from their mortgage loan, which would
be taken over by the Garbersons. When the Garbersons had signed
the mortgage note, Edwards would then issue a check to the
Danielses to cover their equity in the transaction.

"Mr. and Mrs. Daniels, are you going to be traveling alone to
California?" Edwards asked.

"No, sir," Luke said. "We know the trail that passes by Iowa
City is one Joseph Ware suggests in his *Emigrant's Guide to
California*. We're also going to follow his strong suggestion to join
a wagon train and not attempt to make the trip alone. Fortunately,
the trail the wagon trains follow is adjacent to our farm property.
The Garbersons have been kind enough to let us stay in the farmhouse until we can flag down the next wagon train that comes
through and head west."

Edwards smiled at the Garbersons, then said to Luke, "Are you
ready for the trip?"

"Yes, sir. We're packed and ready to go. We bought a new covered wagon last week, and we already have a good team of horses.
A new wagon train passes by once or twice a week."

The bank president spread the papers out before him and slid
an ink bottle and pen toward the two couples. A cold chill slid
down Sandra's spine that had nothing to do with the frigid tem-
perature outside. Although she had gone along with Luke in
making plans to go to California, she was having an inward battle
about leaving their home.

Are we really doing the right thing? she asked herself. I know
Luke and the boys are so excited about this adventure, and that's

exactly what it is to them—an adventure. Luke wouldn't do this, though, unless he had perfect peace. I must do everything I can to help him and encourage him.

Sandra felt a hand on her arm. "Okay, honey," said Luke, dipping the pen into the ink bottle and handing it to her, "it's your turn to sign."

With a slight trembling in her hand, Sandra quickly signed the papers beneath where her husband had signed. When she finished, she exhaled her pent-up breath.

"Well, folks," said Vance Edwards, touching a blotter to Sandra's signature as he had done with the others, "that takes care of everything." He then slid the equity check to Luke. "You can cash this at a teller's cage on the way out."

Moments later, the two couples stepped outside into the cold air and pulled up their coat collars. Luke helped Sandra into the wagon, and as she settled on the seat, she felt a sharp pain in her left side. She put her hand on the spot, then moved it quickly so Luke wouldn't detect it as he climbed up onto the seat.

Luke took the reins in hand and put the team in motion. The pain spread across Sandra's abdomen as it usually did, and she did her best not to show the agony she was feeling. She told herself that she was just having stomach trouble because of all the upheaval the family had known the past several months.

By the time they reached the west edge of town, the pain was easing, but Sandra's face was slightly pinched.

Luke glanced at her and asked, "Honey, is something wrong? You look like something's troubling you."

Sandra forced a weak smile. "Not really wrong, sweetheart. It's just—well, it's difficult for a woman to pull up her roots and move. Especially when the move is so far away."

"I can understand how you feel, but we have to look ahead.

There's nothing left here for us. We have the responsibility of our two sons, and we must go where we can make a living. Just wait. When we get to California, I know you'll really enjoy the warmth and sunshine. No more subzero winters. Won't that feel good?"

She made a smile. "Yes. You're right. It will feel good. I'll be fine, Luke. It's just hard to pull up my roots."

As the wagon bumped along the road toward the farm, Sandra thought about the abdominal pains she had been experiencing for several months. The nearest medical doctor was nearly a hundred miles away, so she hadn't told Luke about the pains. She feared if she let on to him now, he might not want to make the trip, and she couldn't allow that to happen.

On Sunday, March 11, after the morning service at the church in Sacramento, Doug Dyson approached Rena Powell. As he was coming toward her, she thought about the fact that he hadn't asked her for a date in several weeks.

She smiled at him. "Some sermon Pastor Skiver preached this morning, wasn't it, Doug?"

"Really good. Ah...Rena, could I talk to you?"

"Of course. What is it?"

"Well, I want to tell you that I have relished being one of your boyfriends and have enjoyed dating you over the past couple of years."

"Why, thank you, Doug. I've enjoyed our dates, too."

A serious look captured his face. "Rena, you know that I've dated other young ladies, too. Just like you've dated other young men."

"Uh-huh."

"And you know that I've dated Wanda Price a lot."

"Yes. She's a good Christian and one of my best friends."

Rena caught sight of Wanda standing several feet away, looking on as Doug talked to her.

Doug cleared his throat gently. "Well, Rena, in the past couple of months I have found that I was falling in love with Wanda. She feels the same way about me. After much prayer together and separately, we both feel that the Lord has chosen us for each other. Last night I asked her to marry me. I felt since you and I have been good friends, I should tell you."

Rena smiled warmly. "Well, that's wonderful, Doug. I'm glad for both of you. I'm sure you'll be very happy together." She smiled at Wanda and walked over to her and gave her a hug.

Then Rena joined the rest of her family and told them about Doug and Wanda being engaged. "I'm so glad for them," she said.

Carrie took hold of her daughter's hand. "Well, honey, you still have Layne, Tom, and Carl."

"Yeah, sis," Randy said. "You sure aren't anywhere near out of boyfriends."

Darin smiled. "And you won't ever be, sis, as pretty as you are."

Rena blushed. "You're so kind, both of you. But I want you and Mama to know I've been praying that the Lord will soon reveal the one He has chosen for me to marry. After all, I'm twenty years old."

As she spoke, Bruce Follmer, Marshal Cade Ryer's newest deputy, drew alongside them and said, "Howdy, Powell family. Great sermon this morning, wasn't it?"

All four answered in the affirmative as Bruce walked past them toward his horse, which was tied among other saddle horses at a hitching post. He mounted up and spoke to them once again as he trotted past toward the business district.

Rena kept her eyes on Bruce until he passed from view.

"Have you noticed how many people are on the streets anymore, even on Sundays?" Randy said.

"The gold seekers are coming to the area by the thousands," Carrie said.

"And lots of them are eating at our café," said Rena. "We're already putting more money in the bank than I ever dreamed."

Carrie smiled. "Yes, and praise the Lord for that."

The next day, a group of nearly a hundred gold seekers arrived in Sacramento, ready to stake their claims. They had been in a wagon train together that started in Texas. Others had joined the train along the way. The wagons were parked in a circle just outside of town to the southeast, where their wives and children waited for them to return.

The group headed down the boardwalk on Main Street, looking for the government office where they could make application. They came upon a silver-haired man who was standing on the boardwalk watching them, and one of the gold seekers stopped and asked him where they could make application to stake claims. The man pointed out two men a short distance down the boardwalk, at the corner.

"Those fellers right there are officials with the Miners' Association. Just tell them what you want, and they'll help you."

The eager would-be gold miners approached the two men, and one of them explained that they had just arrived from Texas and wanted to stake claims.

The Miners' Association officials introduced themselves as George Beavers and Lester Atkins. As they guided the group down the street, Atkins said, "The Miners' Association is headed up by an ex-army colonel, Clark Fletcher. He's the association president."

"So who're we gonna talk to?" asked one of the group.

"Mr. Fletcher, himself."

"Oh, good," said another one. "Might as well start right at the top."

Beavers laughed. "You can't get no higher than Clark Fletcher!"

When they arrived at the Association office, the group took note that it was in the same building as the Gold Assaying office.

Moments later, Clark Fletcher stood before the group, where he had led them to gather at the side of the building. He explained that the function of the Association was to keep the law among the miners, and was backed by the federal government, the territory of California, and the town marshal's office of Sacramento.

Fletcher handed out to each man a printed copy of the rules for staking claims and explained that the Association had some fifty "law officers" who patrolled the American River, the mining camps, and the mountain creeks where gold was being mined. He said these officers wore badges and revolvers and were the keepers of the law for the protection of all miners in the area. They would prosecute anyone who broke the law, which included not only stealing another man's gold or encroaching on his legal claim site, but stealing his tools or other personal property.

Fletcher added that Sacramento's Marshal Cade Ryer and his deputies would assist the Association's officers if needed. He told them that already lawbreakers in the gold fields were behind bars, and two men who had committed murders had been hanged.

Fletcher then explained that each man who staked a claim must pay $30 a month dues to the Association in order to keep it functioning for their protection and security. Officers would be appointed to help each man properly mark off his claim with wooden stakes so all was legal.

Fletcher said that all the gold regions on the banks of the mountain creeks and the banks of the American River were public land, held in common by the people of the United States and Territories. A claim was valid only when approved by the Miners' Association.

After Clark Fletcher answered a few questions, the men each signed up to join the Association and paid the first month's membership dues. Officers were assigned to the group, and they accompanied them as they drove their covered wagons toward the mountains to stake their claims.

Late on Thursday afternoon, March 22, the Iowa sky was clear and a cold breeze was blowing as Craig Turley guided his covered wagon into Iowa City, leading the other wagons.

Shortly after leaving the Ohio River, the other people in the wagon train had noted how well Craig had studied the trail on Joseph Ware's map and asked him to make his the lead wagon in the train. Richard Dawson made sure the wagon he was traveling in was just behind the lead wagon. He often rode with Craig, just to keep him company.

Craig was on the seat alone, however, as he led the wagons to a wooded spot just outside of town to the west, then had them form a circle. They would all go into town and buy needed supplies so they would be ready to pull out at sunrise in the morning.

Luke Daniels was just about to leave Ganton's Feed and Supply after a hard day's work when he saw four strangers coming into the store. Bob Ganton and his full-time man, Bill Duxbury, always stayed until closing time, but Bob allowed Luke to leave early each day because he had cows to milk at home on the farm.

Before Luke went out the door, he heard the strangers tell Bob and Bill they were in a wagon train on their way to the gold fields in the Sacramento area and needed to buy grain for their horses.

Luke's heart leaped in his chest. As the travelers were making their purchases and talking, Luke learned that their wagon train was camped for the night just outside of town and that they would pull out at sunrise.

Sandra and the boys were in the kitchen where she was just beginning to prepare the evening meal when they looked out the window and saw Luke ride up to the back porch. They could see the bright look in his eyes as he dismounted and dashed up the steps.

Paul opened the door and said, "You look excited, Papa! What's happening?"

"There's a California-bound wagon train camped just outside of town. I saw it on my way home! Some of the men came into the store to buy grain for their horses just as I was getting ready to leave. I heard them say they'll pull out at sunrise."

The boys jumped up and down with excitement as their mother moved up to their father and said, "Well, we'll have to do our last-minute packing right after supper so we'll be ready to meet up with the wagon train when they're about to pass the farm."

The cows were milked, then after a quick supper, the Daniels family finished packing the last of their belongings and loaded them into the new covered wagon.

When the boys were asleep in their room, and Luke was asleep beside her, Sandra lay quietly beside him, her eyes focused on the moonlight that filled the room with a soft, silver glow. Tears fell in a silent path down Sandra's pale cheeks. She sniffed. *This house is where Luke brought me after our wedding. It's been my home for so many years. I know every inch of this house and property. Will I ever feel at home somewhere else? My babies were born in this very room. I have watched them grow up on this farm day by day.*

The pain in her abdomen that had been plaguing her struck again. She gripped her left side and stifled a gasp with her other hand. A terrible sense of foreboding claimed her heart.

She quickly sought her heavenly Father in silent prayer, asking for healing of whatever was wrong and for God's grace.

Moments passed that seemed like hours, but the pain began to subside, and God's ever sufficient grace entered her heart with a calming effect. She gently slipped her hand into Luke's hand, and even though he was fast asleep, he squeezed it.

Long before daylight, the family was up and ready to go. Sandra fixed a hearty breakfast to sustain her eager husband and sons, and helped them load the last things into the wagon. Putting on a happy face, she did not let on about her sleepless night.

The Iowa sun was just peeking its rim over the eastern horizon as Craig Turley put his team in motion and led the other wagons onto the trail that would take them west. Richard Dawson rode on the seat beside him. The air was quite cold, and little vapor clouds escaped their lips and noses as they breathed.

The creaking wagons had been out of Iowa City for only a few minutes when Craig saw a covered wagon coming toward the road from a nearby farmhouse. The driver was waving his hat to get the attention of the people in the wagon train.

"Richard, I think we may have some folks that want to join up with us," Craig said.

"I think you're right."

As the covered wagon was about to meet the train, Craig stood up, looked back, and called out, "Hey, everybody! We need to stop!" As he pulled rein, the others came to a halt also. Men got out of the wagons and walked to the front.

Craig and Richard climbed down from the wagon seat and stepped up to meet the oncoming wagon as the driver was drawing it to a stop. In addition to the man and woman on the driver's seat, they could see two boys looking out from inside the wagon.

"Good morning," said the driver. "We understand that this wagon train is bound for the California gold fields."

Craig smiled. "Yes, it is. We're going straight to Sacramento."

The other men were drawing up, and as they joined Craig and Richard, the driver said, "My name is Luke Daniels, gentlemen. This is my wife, Sandra, and these two boys are our sons Paul and Silas. We just sold our farm so we could go to Sacramento, too. Would we be able to join your wagon train?"

"If everyone in the train is in agreement, you certainly may, Mr. Daniels. My name's Craig Turley. I sort of got elected to drive the lead wagon. We'll have all the occupants gather around so they can meet you."

Moments later, the occupants of the seven wagons were collected in a semicircle. Craig introduced the Daniels family to them and explained that they wanted to go with them to Sacramento. Luke explained their situation in brief, and when Craig put it to a vote, it was unanimous to welcome the Daniels family into the wagon train.

Luke thanked them and then explained that they would have to hurry into Iowa City and let some people know they had joined the wagon train. Craig told him they would wait for them.

The Daniels family hurried into town, where Luke let Bob Ganton know that they were joining the wagon train, and the

Garbersons were also advised that they could now occupy their newly acquired farm.

Just over half an hour had passed when the Daniels family returned. The people of the wagon train were still standing around, talking. As they headed for their wagons, one couple stopped at the Danielses' wagon. The man said, "Howdy, folks. My name is Clint Crandall, and this is my wife, Stacy. We're from Maryland. We were both pleased when we heard that your boys' names are Paul and Silas. Did you take their names from the two close friends in the Bible?"

"We sure did," Luke said.

"Sounds to me like you must be born-again Christians."

Luke grinned. "All four of us. Born-again, blood-washed children of God."

Clint stuck out his hand. "Well, put 'er there, brother!"

As the two men shook hands, Clint said, "Stacy and I were both saved when we were teenagers. It's wonderful to have you with us!"

The Daniels wagon was placed in line just ahead of the Crandall wagon, and Craig Turley put the train in motion, heading west.

In the Daniels wagon, Sandra made sure her sons were settled and warm under the canvas cover behind Luke and herself. She then turned and looked back toward the farm. She watched as her home grew smaller and finally vanished from view.

Tears threatened to flow, but Sandra was determined to keep them from falling. In her heart of hearts, she told her home goodbye, then straightened around on the wagon seat and pulled her coat collar up around her neck. She blinked at the excess moisture in her eyes, then reached over to touch her husband's hand as it held the reins. She found Luke looking at her.

TWENTY

In the last moments of sunset on Monday evening, March 26, in Australia, Colin Ashlock and his five-man crew boarded the *Bristol* in Sydney Harbor. The ship's bow was already pointing toward the open sea.

Captain Henry Briggs sent crewmen Chip Sharpe and Dave Adkinson to the steam room below the deck to build a fire in the boiler. Crewmen Ronald Peters and Wilbur Mayfield went to work to put the sails up while Briggs raised the Australian flag on the main mast. Colin playfully saluted the flag that was now waving in the evening breeze as Briggs moved to where his boss stood. The *Bristol's* deck was scrubbed smooth, and the deckhouses and pilot's cabin glistened with varnish.

"Well, Mr. Ashlock," said Briggs, "as soon as Chip and Dave start up the engines, I'll have Ronald and Wilbur weigh anchor, and we'll be on our way."

Just over forty minutes later, Captain Briggs was in the pilot's cabin, accompanied by his smiling boss. The steam engines were running, and Sharpe and Adkinson stood on deck observing as

Peters and Mayfield hoisted the anchor by turning a large wheel which rolled up the anchor chain.

At the bow, Chip Sharpe lifted the rope that was looped over a post on the dock, coiled it, and dropped it on the deck. He looked up at Briggs in the pilot's cabin and said loudly, "All right, Captain, we're ready to go!"

Briggs waved at him and thrust the throttle forward to about half power. The two powerful steam engines, with pistons that traveled eight feet on each downstroke, spun the underwater propellers at the rear of the ship, and the *Bristol* pulled away from the dock. The ship's bell sounded out, echoing across the harbor, giving notice in the gathering darkness that they were headed out to sea.

Moments later, Captain Briggs thrust the throttle to maximum power. The ship rippled with full muscle, and the propellers left a white wake in its trail. The four crewmen joined the ship's owner and its captain at the pilot's cabin as the *Bristol* cleared the harbor and turned north onto the Tasman Sea.

Early on Tuesday morning, March 27, on the Iowa plains, an icy wind was gusting as the dark-clouded sky began spitting snow. In the wagon train led by Craig Turley, everyone crawled inside the covered wagons, except for the men who were driving. Those with the reins in their hands blinked at the snow striking their faces and followed the lead wagon.

The snow was soon sheeting along on a northwesterly gale. The flakes were small and hard and stung the faces of the drivers. The strong wind made it difficult for the horses to pull the wagons.

In the rear of the Daniels wagon with her two sons, Sandra was having severe abdominal pains, but did not let on. Paul and

Silas huddled together under a blanket as the wind howled and whistled through the canvas that covered the wagon.

On the wagon seat, Luke had his heavy mackinaw pulled tightly up under his chin. His snow-caked Stetson—purchased at the general store in Iowa City a few days before they joined the wagon train—was tilted over his forehead and crammed down against his ears. Still the wind-driven snow seeped in, trailing icy fingers across the back of his neck. He told himself it would be worth it all when they got to California and made their gold strike.

In the lead wagon, Craig Turley held the reins in gloved hands and carefully guided the team over the snow-covered trail. Periodically, he would hold a hand up in front of his eyes, palm outward, to ward off the stinging sleet, raise up, and look behind his wagon to see if the others were all in line. Satisfied that all was well, he would once again settle on the seat and peer into the swirling whiteness ahead of him.

By noon, the ground was completely blanketed with snow some two to four inches deep, and beginning to pile up deeper in drifts along the trail. Craig had a cloth sack on the seat beside him, and began to munch on bread, cookies, and beef jerky as he knew the others in the train were doing.

It was late afternoon as Craig was wiping snow from his eyes that he noticed just ahead a saddled, snow-covered horse standing over a mound in the snow, which appeared to be in the shape of a man.

He stood up, turned toward the rear, and waved at the wagons behind him, shouting his usual call to alert the other drivers that he was stopping. He then pulled rein, hopped down, and headed for the horse.

A voice from behind him called out above the howl of the wind, "What is it, Craig?"

It was Luke Daniels. Others were right behind him, including Richard Dawson.

Craig looked back and said loudly, "I think I've found a man lying in the snow!" He then hurried on.

The wagon train was in a slight curve, and the women and children were peering out at the scene through the canvas openings in the wagons.

The snow-covered horse whinnied when Craig reached the spot, and he bent over and began brushing away snow from the lump. The other men drew up just as he uncovered the man's face.

"He dead?" asked one of the men.

Craig nodded without looking up. "Yes." He then brushed away more snow, inspected the man's chest and abdomen for a bullet wound, then turned the body over and examined his back for the same thing.

"He hasn't been shot," Craig said, rising to his feet, "but for some reason he fell from the saddle. He's frozen stiff. I think we should drape his body over his horse's back, and the next time we see a farm, leave the horse and the body with the farmer. He probably lived somewhere around here."

Bending their heads against the wind and snow, the men agreed. The dead man was hoisted up by two of the men and draped over the saddle. They found a length of rope in one of the saddlebags and tied the body securely. The horse's reins were tied to the tailgate of the last wagon in the train, then Craig led them out against the storm once again.

It was almost dark, and the blizzard was still fierce when Craig spotted lights in the windows of a farmhouse about sixty yards from the trail. There was a large barn, and near it were other out-buildings. He turned into the lane that led to the farmhouse, and the others followed.

∽

In the kitchen of the farmhouse, Larry Whitaker, his wife Amy, and their teenage daughters, Heather and Michelle, were just finishing supper when above the howl of the wind, they heard a knock at the front door. Surprise showed on their faces as Michelle said, "Who would be out on a night like this?"

Larry shoved his chair back and headed toward the hall door, saying over his shoulder, "I don't know, but we're about to find out."

When Larry opened the front door of the house, he saw a snow-caked man by the light of the lantern that burned on a small table behind him. Craig Turley introduced himself, then quickly explained that he was leading a wagon train to California, and they had found a dead man who had fallen from his horse on the road a few miles back. He figured the dead man was probably a local resident, and wanted to know if they could leave the body and the horse with him.

By this time, Amy and her two daughters had joined them. Larry introduced himself and his family to Craig, then said he could bring the body in so they could see if they knew the man.

Moments later, Clint Crandall and Luke Daniels carried the body into the house, with Craig at their side. When Larry saw the face, he said, "Yes, we know him. His name is Archie Betz. He is— he *was*—a neighboring farmer. Archie had a bad heart. He must've had a heart seizure and fell from his horse. We'll put the body in an unheated room at the back of the house, and I'll take the body to his wife and family tomorrow. I'll put his horse in one of the sheds with our horses."

Amy was standing at the window beside the front door, looking out the window at the wagon train by the faint light of day that was left. Heather and Michelle were beside her. She turned to her husband and said, "Larry, that storm is still bad. I know we don't have room for all those folks to come into the house, but could we offer to let them sleep in the barn tonight? At least they'd be out of the weather."

Larry turned to Craig: "Would you like to spend the night in our barn? We have room for your horses, too."

Craig smiled. "I'm sure our people would welcome it."

When the travelers and their animals were safely inside the barn, they made straw beds in the hayloft, using their own blankets for covers. Then with lanterns burning, they sat down on benches and boards on the floor of the barn. Luke Daniels looked at the group and said, "Let's have Clint Crandall lead us in a prayer of thanks for the food."

Clint then led in prayer. When he closed by also thanking God for sending His Son into the world that lost sinners might have a way to be saved, everyone heard Larry Whitaker say, "Amen!"

The group then began to eat the food the farmer's wife and daughters had provided.

While they were eating, Sandra turned to Luke and said, "It'll be wonderful to actually sleep in a building tonight. It's not as cold in here as it is in the covered wagons. And what a feast!"

Amy Whitaker was standing close by. She smiled down at Sandra and said, "It's hardly a feast, Mrs. Daniels, but at least it's nice and hot and should help you thaw out."

"You may not call this a feast, Mrs. Whitaker, but it certainly is to us. Thank you so much for your kind hospitality."

Every member of the group spoke up and expressed their thanks as well.

Amy said, "We just thank the Lord that He's allowing us to help all of you like this."

When the meal was finished, Luke looked around at the weary travelers and said, "I'd like to offer a prayer of thanks to the Lord for providing this shelter from the storm, and for letting us meet fine Christian people like the Whitaker family."

Luke prayed, then the Whitakers told them all to rest well and took the dishes and utensils to the house.

The travelers sat and talked about the storm. Craig Turley was seated close to the Daniels and the Crandalls and heard them talking quite openly about the Lord. Craig thought of his own family back home. Some of the things that were being said by the two couples he had heard many times from his father, Maddie, and Kathy.

Kathy. Craig's heart was stirred as he thought of her and the love she had expressed to him. He missed his father and his little sister, but there was a different feeling as he pondered how much he missed Kathy.

As all conversation in the barn began to dwindle, Craig stood up and said, "Well, folks, this has been quite a day. I don't know about you, but my straw bed up there in the loft sounds mighty inviting."

Murmurs of assent were heard throughout the group. Soon, everyone had crawled beneath warm covers, and only a single lantern was left burning on a bench below the loft.

The wind outside began to subside, which was encouraging to all. What wind was left, however, served to help lull the worn-out bunch to sleep.

By morning, there was no wind at all, and the sun rose into a clear blue sky. After a delicious breakfast provided by the Whitakers, the wagon train pulled out. The sun shone down on a prairie covered with a blanket of snow as the horses trudged through the white depth, pulling the wagons, and the hopeful travelers continued their journey westward.

In Manhattan, New York, on Monday evening, April 2, Pastor Charles Finney and his wife enjoyed a delicious meal at the Turley mansion, prepared by Elizabeth Loysen. Maddie and her governess enjoyed the Finneys, whom they had come to love and admire very much.

The conversation at the table during the meal centered on Craig and his venture westward. Wallace told the Finneys that the wagon train Craig had joined was probably in Iowa by now, nearing the Nebraska border.

"I just hope Craig is all right," Kathy Ross said. "If there was only some way of having contact with him."

Charles Finney smiled at her. "The only contact we have with him is through the Lord, Kathy. He knows where Craig is, and because of our prayers for that young man, I believe the Lord has His hand on him."

"That's the only thing we can cling to, Pastor," Wallace said. "We've got to keep praying for that son of mine."

They were just finishing the meal, and Pastor Finney said, "Well, let's pray for him right now."

With heads bowed and eyes closed, Finney asked the Lord to protect Craig and to bring Christians into his life who would witness to him, watering the seed that had already been sown…and that He would bring about circumstances that would cause Craig to turn to Him for salvation.

When the amen was said, Kathy was wiping tears.

Mrs. Finney took hold of her hand across the corner of the

table and said, "Don't ever give up, honey. Keep on praying earnestly for Craig. In Psalm 77, the psalmist said, 'I cried unto God with my voice, even unto God with my voice; and he gave ear unto me.'"

Kathy dabbed at her tears with her napkin. "Yes, Mrs. Finney. I won't give up. I believe my God will give ear to me."

That night, Kathy sat up in her bed, resting against a pair of pillows, reading her Bible by the soft glow of the lantern on the small table next to her.

After almost an hour, she laid her Bible on the table and blew out the flame. She lay down, closed her eyes, and said, "Dear Lord, I'm asking again that You keep Craig safe. As You well know, he isn't ready to die. He needs to be saved. Please, Lord, work in his heart and mind, and bring Him to Your saving grace. Help me to be faithful to You, and to be a faithful witness to him in every letter I write."

She choked up, then went on. "And…and dear Lord, after You have saved Craig, please bring us together."

Tears were flowing again, but peace filled Kathy's heart, and soon she was asleep, dreaming of the man she loved.

The *Bristol* moved across the rippling waters of the South Pacific Ocean on April 3. After a smooth, easy run eastward for the past eight days, they sighted the islands called the Three Kings off the northern tip of New Zealand's North Island.

Captain Henry Briggs kept steering east, which made his boss and the other crewmen wonder why he wasn't heading north toward the United States and Territories. They gathered at the door of the pilot's cabin, and Colin asked him about it. Henry told him he was staying on an eastern course in order to gain as much seaway as possible before turning north into the trade winds, which would try to push them back west. Colin told Henry he was glad his captain knew what he was doing.

Two days later, Briggs turned the ship northward. On the next night, with the ship heading due north, Wilbur Mayfield was at the wheel in the pilot's cabin, taking the captain's place while he and the others were sleeping in their quarters.

The wind was picking up, the sea was getting rough, and Wilbur was having a struggle keeping the ship on course. He glanced at the compass in front of him repeatedly, doing his best to hold the ship on its proper path.

Suddenly a fierce squall slammed the side of the ship. The wheel spun in Wilbur's hands, and the *Bristol* listed dangerously to one side. Wilbur licked his lips and gripped the wheel as the ship bounced up and down on the raging waves.

In their berths, the rest of the crew awakened as the ship rocked back and forth. They could hear the roar of the wind, punctuated with the rattling sounds in the sail rigging. Quickly they left their cots and staggered toward the pilot's cabin on the wet, bounding deck. When they finally stumbled into the cabin, Wilbur said, "I'm sure glad to see you, Captain! Please take the wheel!"

Henry Briggs grasped it, and Wilbur carefully made his way to the others, who were holding on to anything they could.

By daylight, the squall had passed, and the *Bristol* continued across the choppy waters.

Several days later, they spotted Pitcairn Island, where they had planned to dock so they could purchase fresh fruits and vegetables.

Henry was at the wheel, guiding the ship toward the island.

Colin and the other four men stood on deck at the bow, holding onto the rail, as they kept their eyes on the island.

"You boys remember the historical event that took place at Pitcairn Island?" Colin said.

Chip Sharpe chuckled. "Mr. Ashlock, every English schoolboy knows about that strange, stirring tale."

"Pitcairn Island was the last refuge of the mutineers of the *HMS Bounty,*" said Dave Adkinson, "who seized the ship from its commander, Captain William Bligh, in 1789."

"We all know that story, Mr. Ashlock," Ronald Peters said.

They made their stop, purchased the fruits and vegetables, and resumed their journey northward on the blue South Pacific.

Weeks passed, and finally the *Bristol* arrived in San Francisco Bay on Thursday, June 21. Colin arranged with the dock authorities to keep his ship docked in the bay, then purchased a wagon and team. They headed immediately for Sacramento.

As the Australians drove into Sacramento with Dave Adkinson at the reins, they stopped on Main Street and asked a small group of men on the boardwalk where they might find the Miners' Association office. They were directed to two officers of the Association who were coming down the boardwalk. The officers guided them to the Association Office, where they sat down with Clark Fletcher.

"Mr. Fletcher, I own a large cattle and sheep ranch in southern Australia," Colin said, first off. "These men are employed by me and are here to help me make a gold strike. We'll only need to stake one claim."

The Association president smiled and said, "All right, sir. Let me go over the rules with you."

Fletcher went over the rules and gave Colin a printed copy. Then Colin paid the $30 dues for the first month and joined the Association.

Fletcher then gave Colin a map of the area and pointed out the places on the American River that still had not been claimed, and also the many creeks in the hills and mountains where claims could be staked. He marked each spot with a pencil, then said, "You can tell a claimed site because it will have a wooden sign nailed to a stake with the legal owner's name on it. You and your men can go wherever you want, check out the unclaimed sites, and pick out the one you like best. Then come back here, and I'll send an officer of the Association there with you to mark the claim as yours."

"I appreciate your help in this, Mr. Fletcher," Colin said. "Since it's almost noon, we'll grab lunch somewhere, and go take a look at the available sites. Where's a good place to eat in this town?"

"I'll tell you the *best* place. It's called Carrie's Café. Just head on down the street that way, and you can't miss it. It's at Third and Main, right on the corner, directly across the street from the Sacramento Bank and Trust Company."

Colin and his men left the Association office, sat down on a bench on the boardwalk, and looked the map over. When they had examined each area where claims were available, Colin said, "Gentlemen, I'd like to try one of the creeks in the nearby hills." He placed his forefinger on a creek on the map and said, "According to the mileage scale, that spot is about twelve miles from where we sit."

"Looks good to me," said Chip Sharpe.

The others agreed. Then they proceeded down the street to Carrie's Café.

When they finished their meal and stepped out of the café, Wilbur Mayfield was the first to notice a crowd gathering on the street a half-block away, in front of the county courthouse.

"What do you suppose that's all about, boss?" Wilbur said.

Colin frowned as he focused on the scene. "Well, it's got to be a hanging. A rope was just tossed over a limb of that big cottonwood tree, and it's got a hangman's noose on one end."

The five men hurried down the street, and as they joined the crowd, they saw a saddled horse standing just beneath the noose that swayed in the breeze. Two men who wore badges that identified them as deputy marshals of Sacramento stood there, looking down the street toward the marshal's office and jail.

Colin turned to a middle-aged man in the crowd and said, "What's going on? Looks like somebody's going to be hanged."

"He sure is, mister," said the man. "One of the gold miners. He got into an argument about two hours ago with another miner whose claim was next to his on the American River, and killed him. Other miners saw it, and they tied him up good and dragged him to Marshal Ryer's office." He pointed down the street, where a man with a badge on his chest was leading a man whose hands were cuffed behind his back toward the big cottonwood tree. Other men wearing badges were with them. "Here comes the marshal with him, right now."

Colin raised his eyebrows. "You say this happened two hours ago?"

"Yep."

"They could hold a trial that quickly?"

"Oh, no. When it's the gold seekers around here, there ain't no trial. That guy was caught red-handed. The Miners' Association sentenced him to death in less than a minute. Sacramento's marshal and his deputies actually have the authority to carry out the execution. Those other men with badges on their chests are Association officers."

The crowd was growing rapidly, and the condemned man was now being hoisted into the saddle by two of the Association officers. The man pointed out as Marshal Ryer looped the noose over the killer's head and cinched it up tight around his neck.

Dave Adkinson leaned toward the man who had told them what was going on. "Sir, doesn't this town have a gallows?"

"Nope. Not yet. But I think they'll be a-buildin' one soon. This is the sixth man they've had to hang since the gold rush started."

At that moment, a leather belt slapped the rump of the horse under the cottonwood tree. The horse bolted, and the convicted killer swung by his neck.

TWENTY-ONE

At the Wallace Turley home in Manhattan on Monday evening, June 25, Horace Greeley and his wife, Genevieve, were enjoying a delicious meal with Wallace and Maddie, and Kathy Ross. The subject at the dinner table was Wallace's son, Craig, and his venture to the gold fields of California.

Horace looked across the table at Wallace. "Do you have any idea where Craig might be by now?"

"Well, if all has gone well, he's somewhere in mid-Wyoming right now. He said he would write us along the way, but so far, we haven't had a letter. I realize postal service is especially slow the farther west you go, so if he has remembered to write us, it may take many months for a letter to get here."

Horace took a sip of hot coffee and set the cup back in its saucer. "I'll tell you this much. More and more people are getting rich in the gold rush. I receive reports two and three times a week from the newspaper owners in both Sacramento and San Francisco. It's a real bonanza out there."

"I read your article a few weeks ago about the Miners'

Association in Sacramento," Wallace said. "Sounded like they and the local law have their hands full."

Horace nodded. "For sure. The Association is there to make sure all those gold seekers do right by each other and by the laws of the territory of California. They rule with a rod of iron. There's strict discipline on troublemakers and lawbreakers. Last report I received from Sacramento a few days ago was that so far, six men guilty of murder have been hanged. Many others—thieves, claim jumpers, crooked men who have unlawfully staked claims, and troublemakers in general—have been flogged and sent away from the gold fields. Some have been flogged and put behind bars."

Maddie looked at her father. "Papa, I sure hope Craig won't be hurt by any of those bad men out there in California."

"Me too, sweetheart. We must continue to pray that the Lord will take care of him."

Tears misted Kathy's eyes. As she dabbed at her eyes with her napkin, she prayed silently for God's protection on the man she loved.

On July 18, Craig Turley and the people in the seven wagons behind him pulled into Salt Lake City, Utah, to stock up on supplies. They formed a circle with the wagons in a large lot just off the main thoroughfare, then went together to the general store just over a block away. It was midafternoon, and the hot sun blazed down from the yellow sky without mercy.

When they were in the store, the owner told them to be sure and fill up their water barrels and canteens before they started across the Great Salt Lake Desert. He explained that water was scarce in the fifty-mile stretch from the beginning of the desert all the way to the town of Wendover, on the Utah-Nevada border.

When everyone had returned to the wagons, Craig gathered them together in the shade of some nearby cottonwood trees and said, "I think we all got the message that we need to be very careful not to waste water. In the *Emigrant's Guide,* Joseph Ware warned of the lack of water in the desert ahead of us. He said it can be found, but not in abundance. And sometimes when we come upon water, it will be brackish and not fit to drink. So we must all be very careful with our water."

"Especially now, Craig," said one of the men who rode in the same wagon as Richard Dawson. "It's midsummer, and what we thought was hot back there in western Nebraska and Wyoming will seem cool compared to the heat we'll face out there on that desert."

"Yeah, we'll be wishing we were back there in that blizzard in Iowa!" Dawson said.

They all had a good laugh, then Craig said, "Mr. Ware said in his book that we should rest the horses and ourselves in the hottest part of the day and start out before dawn to make up for the lost travel time. It's already hot enough right now that I think we should rest during the hottest part of the day even while we're covering the seventy miles from here to the eastern edge of the desert."

Everyone agreed as they mopped perspiration from their brows with handkerchiefs and bandannas.

The next few days passed slowly. The vast, rolling land glowed in each rosy sunrise, glared in the white noon hours, and burned at sunset; a foreshadowing of what was to come on the desert, only to a much greater degree.

On the sixth day, when they reached the edge of the desert, Sandra Daniels's pains were getting worse. Hardly a day had gone by without some pain, but on that day, she was suffering severely. She kept telling herself that it was just the stress of the trip, along with the heat. She would get better once they got to California and the traveling was over.

Craig Turley had Richard Dawson riding with him, and Richard got excited when he saw a small creek about a half-mile ahead. Soon those behind them had spotted it also, and were calling out for Craig to stop at the creek.

The wagons formed their usual circle, and they made camp for the night beside the creek. The men jumped out of their wagons, holding tin cups, and when they tasted the water, a series of happy whoops filled the air. They watered the horses and filled all barrels and canteens.

Soon the sun set over the western horizon, and meals were cooked over small fires. In the deepening red twilight, when the heat rolled away on a slow-dying wind, everyone felt relief. But as they pillowed their heads, they felt the dread of the heat they would face on the actual desert.

Morning came with the blazing ball of fire rising in the east. As the wagon train moved out toward the west, the travelers saw their long shadows moving before them. The sun soared hot into the sky. The heated air from the burning sand lifted, and incoming currents from the east swept low and hard over the barren, cactus-ridden earth.

From noon until three o'clock, the wagon train remained in a circle while the horses rested and everyone lay in the shade of their wagons. Then they were back in motion once again until suppertime. When the meal was over, everyone prepared to bed down for the night. Craig had already announced that they would start out the next day two hours before dawn.

It had been a long and difficult day. The children were fussy and restless, and the younger ones cried incessantly. Nerves were on edge, and even some of the adults bickered and quarreled with each other.

While Luke Daniels was watering his horses, Sandra tucked Paul and Silas in their beds in the front part of the wagon bed, then sat on the seat of the wagon and brushed her hair. The pain in her abdomen was stabbing her.

It won't be long till sunrise and another scorching day, she thought as she was braiding her hair. *Oh, how I would love a bath and to be able to wash the dirt out of my hair. Brushing helps, but clean, clear water would be such a blessing.*

A little later, when Sandra and Luke were getting ready to lie down at the rear of the wagon bed, a pain suddenly pierced her lower abdomen. Luke was about to blow out the lantern when he saw her clutch her midsection and heard her eject a sharp cry. The boys stirred, but did not awaken.

Luke took hold of Sandra's shoulders and looked into her eyes. "Sweetheart, what's wrong?"

Sandra looked away without answering, and Luke sat her down on the bedding and knelt in front of her, holding one shaky hand while she pressed against her midsection with the other hand. "Honey, what is it? What's hurting?"

Sandra winced, then said, "I'm not sure what it is."

"Have you had these pains before?"

She met his gaze, then looked down. "Yes. Many times. But I think this is the worst."

"How long has this been going on?"

"Ah—well, several months." She looked up at him once more. "I kept thinking the problem would go away, so I didn't say anything to you or the boys. They started out quite mild, and I only had them once in a while."

"Have you had them recently?"

"Yes."

"Why didn't you tell me?"

She bit her lower lip. "I didn't want anything to stand in the way of our going to California. I know how important it is to you."

"But honey, *you* are much more important to me!"

"I know that, but I'll probably be fine once we're settled in California and get our lives back to normal."

Luke was quiet for a few seconds, then said, "Well, I want you to take it as easy as possible. The boys and I will help you with your chores around the wagon. And the first town we come to where there's a doctor, I'll take you to him."

Sandra tried to smile. "All right, darling. I'll do as you say. The pain is easing off now, so I believe I'll be able to get some sleep."

Moments later, after praying together, they lay down on the soft blankets, and holding hands, drifted off to sleep.

The wagon train was in motion two hours before dawn. The grand arch of the heavens was filled with twinkling stars, and a thin crescent moon was visible to the west. With the dread of another hot day in the minds of the travelers, the time seemed to pass quickly. Soon the first faint gleam of gray light appeared over the eastern horizon. It quickly brightened and the wan stars faded. The gray light turned pink and yellow, and the shadows lifted from the desert.

Soon the blazing-hot sun bore down on them again. They continually drank water, though in small amounts, and made sure their horses had plenty. As the day slowly passed, the children cried from the heat and the animals showed it was taking its toll on them, in spite of getting to rest in the hottest part of the day. They saw two fresh graves beside the trail.

Late that evening, after they had stopped for the night, Luke Daniels brought up the two graves they had seen and talked to the group about being ready to face God in eternity.

No one commented. They all went to their beds, enjoying the relatively cool air.

Luke's words echoed in Craig's mind as he lay in the back of his wagon, trying to go to sleep. Finally, he was able to shake them off and slip into slumber.

One hot day dragged into another as the wagon train made its way slowly across the burning desert. Travel time was lost periodically when they had to stop to let the fatigued horses rest. In the lead wagon, Craig squinted against the glare of the sun and its reflection off the white sand, searching for a stream. They needed to find more water soon.

On Monday afternoon, July 23, Craig spotted a small creek that was lined with cedar trees. The water proved to be cool and sweet, and the wagon train made camp beside it, enjoying the shade of the cedars. The water barrels were all filled, as well as the canteens.

After breakfast some two hours before dawn the next morning, the travelers were preparing to pull out. They were watering the horses and filling canteens once again.

Paul and Silas Daniels were in their usual places in the rear of the wagon. Luke was about to help Sandra onto the wagon seat when suddenly she gasped, clutched her abdomen, and let out a painful wail. Her knees gave way, but Luke caught her before she fell. She gritted her teeth in agony as he carried her to the rear of the wagon.

Paul and Silas had heard their mother's wail. They were about to climb over the tailgate when Luke told them to let it down. The boys let the tailgate down and jumped out as their father laid their mother on the floor at the rear of the wagon. Eyes wide, he said, "Boys, go tell Mrs. Crandall we need her immediately."

As Paul and Silas dashed away, Luke used his bandanna to wipe Sandra's face as she moaned in excruciating pain. Luke unfastened the top button of her dress's high collar and fanned her with an old newspaper.

Some of the travelers had heard the commotion and were gathering close to the rear of the wagon. One of them was Craig Turley, who asked what was wrong. Luke quickly explained the situation to Craig, and at that moment, Stacy Crandall drew up with the boys at her heels.

She looked at Luke. "Paul and Silas told me Sandra's been having pains in her midsection."

"Yes."

Stacy stepped past him and laid a hand on Sandra's brow. Looking back over her shoulder, she said, "Craig, get me some water, quick. She's burning up with fever. I've got to get some water in her, and I've got to bathe her face in it. Luke, do you have some washcloths?"

"Yes." He turned to Paul. "Son, climb into the wagon up front and bring Mrs. Crandall a couple of washcloths."

As Paul darted toward the front of the wagon, Luke leaned close to Sandra and rubbed her arm. "Craig's bringing some water, sweetheart. Stacy's going to get you cooled down." He looked at Stacy, brow furrowed. "She's so pale."

Stacy nodded silently.

Sandra opened her eyes weakly. She worked her jaws and made a grunting sound, but couldn't seem to speak. She began to moan again. Luke bit his lips and stared down at her. His shoulders twitched with an involuntary shiver.

Paul returned with the washcloths and handed them to Stacy just as Craig rushed up carrying a cooking pot full of water. He also had a tin cup in his hand, which was about two-thirds full of water.

Stacy thanked him and dribbled water into Sandra's mouth a few drops at a time, then dipped a cloth into the cool water and began to bathe Sandra's sweaty face. Sandra writhed in pain, her moans becoming louder.

Luke's whole body stiffened.

Clint Crandall noted the frightened look in the eyes of Paul and Silas, who were pressing up close, trying to see their mother's face. He stepped up between them, put an arm around each boy's shoulder and took them a few steps away. "Let's wait here, boys, and give Mrs. Crandall room to work." He tried to smile reassuringly at them, but it did not remove the fear etched on their young faces.

While Stacy tenderly bathed Sandra's face, Luke held her hand and said softly, "Hold on, honey. It'll be all right. The pains will go away just like they have before."

Sandra suddenly stiffened, clutched her abdomen, and wailed. Her eyes were squeezed shut against the overpowering pain. She moaned, then opened her pain-dimmed eyes with obvious effort and looked up at her husband. Raising a trembling arm, she ran her hand over his cheek. Luke took hold of the hand, kissed the palm, and held it close against his face.

Her lips quivered as she said, "Take care of our boys, darling, and always remember how very much I love you..." Her voice trailed off, her eyes closed, and her hand went limp in his.

Blood thrummed thick in Luke's ears and tears furrowed down his cheeks as he felt Stacy's hand on his arm. He looked at her through his tears. "She's gone, Stacy. My precious Sandra is gone."

Paul and Silas wrapped their arms around their father and sobbed. Clint put a hand on his friend's shoulder and squeezed it tightly.

Stacy was blinking at her own tears as she said, "I'm sorry, Luke. I think it was a ruptured ovary. I didn't know what else to do for her."

"You did all you could, Stacy. She's been hiding these painful episodes from the boys and me for months. She finally told me about it just a few days ago. If—if I had known, I would've taken her to a doctor. We certainly wouldn't have come on this trip."

Stacy patted his arm and said with a tear-clogged voice, "Luke, Sandra wanted to make this trip with you. She wanted you to realize your dream. Now you must go on with your boys and do this for her."

Luke blinked at his tears. "Thank you, Stacy. I'll do my best...for her."

The men dug a grave in the hot, barren soil, and Luke asked Clint Crandall to read some Scriptures over the grave. Clint read from the Bible with the travelers standing in a circle around the grave, then said that because of Sandra's faith in the Lord Jesus Christ, she was now in heaven.

Craig Turley thought about how Pastor Charles Finney had told him that the reason God sent His only begotten Son into the world to die on the cross was to provide the one and only way of salvation. He also thought of how his father, Maddie, and Kathy had repeatedly shown their desire to see him saved. Craig's throat constricted as he told himself if he had died today, he would now be in hell, according to God's Word.

The travelers agreed to wait until tomorrow to travel on.

Some two hours before dawn the next morning, Luke and his sons wept as their wagon pulled away from Sandra's grave.

Two days later, the wagon train pulled off the desert, purchased food and supplies at Wendover, and filled up their water barrels and canteens. Craig Turley posted a letter to his father, Maddie, and Kathy, telling them he was sorry he hadn't written before, and that they had just crossed the Great Salt Lake Desert in Utah. The owner of the general store, who was also the postmaster, told Craig it would take quite some time for the letter to get to New York.

The next morning, the California-bound travelers pulled away from Wendover and began their long trek across Nevada.

One evening in the first week of August at Sacramento, Rena Powell was carrying a tray of food to a table when she saw a stranger enter Carrie's Café and take a seat at one of the few empty tables. She took an order from a miner and his wife, turned it in to her mother at the kitchen, and headed for the stranger, who was reading the menu. She estimated him to be in his late twenties.

She smiled as she approached the table and said, "Good evening, sir. You must be new in town."

The stranger noted the name tag on her apron. "That's right, Rena. What's your last name?"

"Powell, sir. My mother, Carrie Powell, owns the café. Those two boys over there busing tables are my brothers. And what might your name be?"

"My name's Blade Cultus. I came here to make my fortune just like so many other people are doing. I just staked a claim this morning on the American River a few miles upriver. I'm from a small town in East Texas called Kildare Junction."

Rena thought Blade Cultus appeared to be a loner, and he had an odd look in his eyes. But he was friendly, and she would be friendly, too. Smiling warmly, she took his order and headed for the kitchen to give it to her mother.

Blade Cultus watched Rena walk toward the kitchen and told himself she was the most beautiful girl he had ever seen…and she seemed to like him. He observed her as she waited on other customers, and told himself that beyond her good looks, she had such a sweet and pleasant way about her.

When Rena brought Blade his meal, she smiled again and told him she hoped he enjoyed the food.

Blade felt a tingle in his heart and whispered to himself, "Blade, ol' boy, that girl really does like you."

In the week that followed, Blade Cultus made it to the café every evening for his supper. Rena was friendly as usual, and by the end of the week, when Blade pillowed his head in his miner's shack on the bank of the American River, he decided he had fallen in love with her…and she with him.

While at work on his claim the next day, Blade daydreamed about the two of them holding hands as they walked together along the bank of the river. That evening, his heart banged his ribs when Rena came to take his order. He ate slowly, just wanting to be near her as long as he could.

When it was almost closing time, Randy Powell was working the cash register while his brother Darin cleaned up tables. Rena was in the kitchen with her mother when Carrie looked into the eating area and said, "Oh, honey, Carl just came in. I'm so glad you and he have been dating more often lately."

"Me too, Mama. He's such a sweet person, and he's so dedicated to the Lord."

The last two customers, except for Blade Cultus, were about to leave. They stepped up to Carl, and one of the men introduced

Carl to his friend. At his table, Blade Cultus heard it.

Blade was almost finished when he saw the man named Carl Wagner move toward the kitchen. Blade scowled when he saw Rena greet Carl warmly, then take his arm as they walked out of the café together. He quickly ate the last bite of his food, paid Randy for the meal, and hurried toward the door.

Carl and Rena—who had made a date to take a moonlight ride together—were just driving away in Carl's buggy when Blade moved out onto the boardwalk.

He watched the buggy until it vanished from his sight. Breathing heatedly, he moved a short distance down the boardwalk and hid in the shadows until he saw Carrie and her two sons come out of the café. As they walked toward their home, Blade followed, keeping himself in the shadows.

When Carrie, Randy, and Darin reached their house and went inside, Blade Cultus remained in the dark gloom across the street and waited.

An hour and a half later, Carl and Rena pulled up in front of the Powell house. Carl walked around the rear of the buggy, helped Rena out, and walked her to the door.

Blade was seething. This Carl Wagner had no right to be with Rena. She was in love with *him*!

Carl and Rena embraced, then Rena went into the house. As Carl drove away, Blade whispered, "Rena is *my* girl, Carl Wagner! You'll pay for this!"

Two days later, Carl Wagner was working alone at Sacramento's blacksmith shop. His boss, Dale Haswell, had gone to the bank to make a deposit.

Carl was forming a set of horseshoes at the fire pit, pounding them into shape with a hammer, when he thought he saw movement in the shadows of the shop's interior. He stopped hammering and turned around to see a stranger with a hunting knife in his hand.

But it was too late.

Blade Cultus plunged the knife into Carl's heart.

Some thirty minutes later, Dale returned from the bank. When he stepped into the office of the shop, he noted that the place seemed unusually quiet.

He looked toward the open door that led to the rear of the shop. "Carl! I'm back!"

Silence.

"Hey, Carl!" he said, moving through the doorway. "You back here?"

Dead silence.

Dale ran his gaze to the fire pit, which was still smoking. Suddenly, he caught sight of a form lying on the floor just past the pit. He dashed to the spot and stood frozen in horror as he saw Carl lying faceup with a knife in his chest, buried to the hilt.

Dale uttered a choked cry and dropped to his knees beside the still form. "Oh, Carl! Carl! Who did this awful thing to you?"

Dale made his way to his feet and hurried through the office to the boardwalk. A man he knew well was walking his direction, and saw the look on the blacksmith's pale features. He dashed up to him and said, "Dale, what's wrong?"

"Wally, Carl has been murdered! Will you go tell Marshal Ryer for me?"

✑

Moments later, Marshal Cade Ryer and Deputies Jarrod Benson and Bruce Follmer were on the scene. The knife was removed from Carl Wagner's chest, but it was not familiar to any of the lawmen nor to the blacksmith.

None of them had a clue as to who had done the horrible deed.

Sacramento's undertaker was called, and the news of Carl's murder traveled fast through the town. When it reached Carrie's Café, Rena broke down and sobbed with customers watching, and her mother and brothers were quickly at her side.

Two days later, after Pastor Richard Skiver had preached the funeral sermon at the church, the entire crowd of mourners went to the cemetery for the graveside service.

Standing unnoticed behind a tree several yards away, Blade Cultus observed Rena weeping heavily while family and friends attempted to comfort her.

Blade whispered, "It's all right, darling. I'll be around to make you feel better. He was only a boyfriend, but I'm the man who really loves you. And I know you love me. We were meant for each other."

That evening, Rena was at the cash register, taking money from customers, when she saw Blade Cultus come into the café barely a half hour before closing time. He paused, looked past the man and woman she was taking care of, and said, "Good evening, Rena."

She smiled at him and said, "You're running a little late, aren't you, Blade?"

"Well, I guess I am. I made a big strike on my claim today, and it took me quite a while to dig up all that gold."

Blade sat at a nearby table and picked up a menu from the small metal holder. Less than a minute later, he looked up to see the girl he loved step up to the table. Blade gave her his order, and she returned with his food a short time later. She set his plate on the table and said, "I'm sure glad to hear about your big strike. You'll have to tell me more about it sometime."

His eyes flashed. "I'd love to."

As Rena hurried away to take care of more customers at the cash register, Blade smiled to himself. *She loves me, all right. It's in her eyes and her voice.*

Blade was the last to finish his food, and as he headed for the cash register, Randy and Darin hurried from the kitchen to clean up his table.

Rena was placing currency in a metal box to go into the safe at the back of the café when Blade stepped up, money in hand, and said, "Maybe we should set a time to be together when you're not working so I can tell you more about my gold strike."

She smiled as she took his money and said, "We'll talk about it one of these nights when you're in here for supper."

When Blade stepped out onto the boardwalk and headed for the river, he fantasized even more about the romance he and Rena would soon enjoy together.

TWENTY-TWO

In early September, the wagon train that followed Craig Turley's lead wagon was making its way over the Sierra Nevada Mountains in northern California. All about them lay sunken gorges, rushing rivers and creeks, and towering mountain peaks. In the daytime, the higher peaks—above eleven thousand feet—showed jagged, gleaming walls of rock in the California sunshine. Below those peaks were rugged, timber-clad mountains and valleys with the restful green of pine and fir.

Above the Sierras in the vast blue sky were great masses of cumulus, piled to majestic heights. The crests of the clouds were glorious with sunlight.

At night, the travelers made camp in beautiful forested places and enjoyed the cool, sweet wind, the luminous, twinkling stars, and a haunting silver moon.

The westward trek was now lonely for Luke Daniels and his sons. Every night, Paul and Silas cried for their mother, and Luke did his best to comfort them. At times, when the Crandalls heard the boys crying, they went to the Danielses' wagon and did their best to console them.

One starlit night, after the boys were asleep, Luke lay in his own bedding in the back of the wagon and shed silent tears. Wiping the tears away with his blankets, he looked out the opening of the canvas and focused on the twinkling stars and a soft half-moon.

"Lord," he said, "I know You don't make mistakes. You had a reason beyond my understanding for taking my precious wife home to heaven when she was still so young. I just ask You to help Paul and Silas cope with the loss of their mother, and give them peace and comfort about her home-going. And Lord…I need that peace and comfort, too. We can't go back to Iowa. There's nothing in Iowa for us, now. We must go on to California and find whatever You have for us there."

Upon awakening the next morning, Luke felt a deep, abiding peace within his heart, and he immediately thanked God for it. When he awakened Paul and Silas, they crawled sleepily from under their covers into his open arms. Luke hugged them, ruffled their hair, and said, "Time for breakfast at the Crandall wagon, boys."

While Luke and his sons ate breakfast with Clint and Stacy Crandall, the boys talked excitedly about the remainder of the trip and how much they were looking forward to helping their father make a fortune in gold.

Later that morning, Craig Turley led the wagon train out, and they made their way slowly westward, winding through the Sierras.

During the day, though Paul and Silas talked of their mother, not once did they break down and cry.

That night under a canopy of twinkling stars, Luke lay in his bedroll and while his sons slept close by, he whispered, "Thank You for helping my boys as I asked You to do, Lord. They did a whole lot better today. Tonight was the first night since You took Sandra home that Paul and Silas haven't cried themselves to sleep. And thank You for the peace You've put in my heart. Please help the boys and me to be a good testimony to others of Your marvelous grace, and use us for Your glory."

Having crossed the high mountain passes and streams of the Sierra Nevada Range, Craig Turley's wagon train rolled into Sacramento at midmorning on Wednesday, September 12. Craig found a large vacant lot in the business district, and after they had made their usual circle, they were greeted by several people on the street and welcomed to Sacramento.

Richard Dawson asked two middle-aged men where they might find the Miners' Association office. By this time, Craig was at Richard's side, and the two men introduced themselves as Wiley Stout and Edgar Mullins. Wiley pointed down Main Street, showing them the Association office, then said, "Gentlemen, you've been on the trail a long time. Have you heard how well us gold seekers have been doing here in the new El Dorado?"

"We've picked up a little along the way," Craig said. "So you two are miners, eh?"

"Not anymore," Mullins said. "We came here together just over six months ago from Kansas, and struck it rich. We've made enough money to easily live on for the rest of our lives. We turned our claim site over to someone else. We sent for our wives, and we're having two mansions built out on the north edge of town. From now on, Sacramento is home to us."

By this time, all the travelers had gathered around, listening to what Mullins was saying. He could see that he had their rapt attention, and he began telling them about a southerner who brought his slave with him from Alabama. They staked a claim on a creek in the mountains where another miner had been. The miner had built a small cabin on the claim, and having done well in a short time, took his gold and returned to his home in Wyoming. The man from Alabama was assigned the claim site by the Miners' Association and was happy to have it…especially since there was already a cabin on it.

As the southerner and his slave worked the creek, they found very little gold and were quite discouraged. To add to their discouragement, one day when they were in Sacramento to buy groceries with what little gold they had, the cabin caught fire and burned to the ground. When they were digging in the ashes, trying to salvage some of their possessions, the slave's shovel pierced the dirt beneath where the floor had been, and he saw something shiny. It was gold! Eventually, the southerner and his slave dug up over $20,000 in gold from beneath the ashes of the cabin.

Wiley Stout then told them of a man right there in town who recently found $3,000 in gold under his doorstep.

Edgar Mullins told them of three Frenchmen who uprooted a tree stump next to their shack on a creek in the nearby hills and found $25,000 worth of gold in the hole.

The wagon train people talked excitedly among themselves as Mullins added that on another creek, a gold seeker sitting on the trunk of a fallen tree, discouraged because he had found nothing along the creek bank of his claim, kicked a rock in anger. The rock rolled over, revealing a huge nugget of shining gold.

While the crowd laughed, Wiley Stout told them that in one of the mining camps along the American River, a little girl found a strangely colored rock on the ground and took it to her mother. The mother washed the dirt off it and saw that it was a seven-pound nugget.

When he realized they had heard the final story from the two men, Craig Turley said, "All right, folks, did these stories encourage you?"

The answer was affirmative, and Clint Crandall spoke for everyone when he thanked Stout and Mullins for passing the stories along.

The men of the wagon train then went to the Miners' Association office, and when they came out an hour later, all but Craig Turley and Luke Daniels were set to go into the mountains to seek gold. Six Association officers were in the office, preparing to lead them and the others in the wagon train into the mountains and help them establish their claims. Two others would accompany Craig and Luke to where they wanted to go.

While the men were standing in front of the building, waiting for the officers, Clint Crandall looked quizzically at Luke. "How come you're not coming into the mountains with us?"

Luke smiled at him. "Well, Clint, I've decided to try it a few miles further upstream on the American River."

Richard Dawson looked at Craig. "And what're you gonna do, my friend?"

"I'm going to stake my claim on the American River where those two brothers made that huge discovery of gold only a few weeks ago, then headed back home to Indiana."

Richard frowned. "But Craig, that claim has no doubt been emptied of its gold."

Craig shook his head. "Not necessarily. There just might be a whole lot more there. I'm going to find out."

"Well, I hope it turns out that way for you."

Together, all the men walked back to the wagons with the eight Association officers accompanying them on horseback. As the women and children climbed into the wagons, the men thanked Craig for driving the lead wagon on the trip. Richard shook Craig's hand, saying he hoped they would run into each other sometime. Craig said he hoped so, too.

The wagons pulled out with all but two of the officers accompanying them. Luke and his boys left in their wagon with Officer Doke Slater riding his horse alongside. And Craig drove his wagon, with Officer Chuck Tracy accompanying him on horseback, along the bank of the American River. Soon Tracy told Craig to stop. He dismounted and said, "This is it, Mr. Turley."

Craig smiled when he saw the small shack on the claim site where the former miners had lived. He climbed down from the driver's seat and walked over the site with Chuck Tracy guiding him. When they returned to the wagon, Tracy entered the shack and came back, carrying a wooden stake and a 14-by-6-inch board. He then took a small can of black paint and a paintbrush from a canvas bag on his saddle and painted Craig's name on the board. He attached it to the stake and drove it into the ground with a fist-sized rock.

He then produced papers from one of his saddlebags for Craig to sign, making him the legal owner of the claim. After Tracy rode away along the riverbank, Craig carried his belongings into the shack from the wagon. Then he watered his team and unhitched them from the covered wagon.

Craig noticed a man panning gold on the riverbank just south of his claim site. The man glanced at him and gave him a crooked smile. Craig walked to where the man was kneeling on the bank and said, "Hello, I'm your new neighbor—Craig Turley from New York City."

The man stood up, and when Craig looked into his eyes, a strange feeling came over him.

"My name's Blade Cultus. I'm from a small town in East Texas called Kildare Junction. I'm relatively new here, too. I staked this claim as you staked yours—after someone else had worked it. I hit it big last month, though, and I'm still doing well."

Craig grinned. "You say you hit it big. Do you mind telling me how much?"

"Well...uh...I guess not. So far I've taken fifty thousand dollars' worth of gold out of this claim. Most of it was in the ground."

"Hey, that's great! I hope I can do that well on mine."

That evening, Craig walked into town, looking for someplace to eat. He asked a man and woman on the boardwalk where he could get a good meal, and they directed him to Carrie's Café at Third and Main.

When he reached Carrie's, he found there was a waiting line. While he stood with others who were waiting for a table, he noted the friendliness of the waitress, who wore a name tag identifying her as Rena.

After nearly an hour's wait, Craig was given a table, and again was impressed with Rena's friendliness when she waited on him.

He was almost finished with his meal when he looked up to see his neighbor, Blade Cultus, come in. Blade spoke to him with a smile, then took a table nearby.

Craig noticed how Blade's face brightened when Rena moved up to his table to take his order. He heard Blade ask when they were going to get together so he could tell her all about his big gold strike, adding that it had been weeks since he first told her about it. Craig heard her say she just hadn't had time, yet.

When Rena headed for the kitchen, Craig noticed that Blade's eyes followed her. As she disappeared through the kitchen door, Craig saw Blade glance his direction. He smiled and said, "You kind of like her, don't you, Blade?"

Blade rose from his chair, stepped up to Craig's table, and said, "Rena Powell is the most wonderful girl in the world. I more than like her. I'm in love with her. And she's in love with me, too. But don't you dare tell her I told you."

"Oh, I won't breathe a word," Craig said.

Blade went back to his table, and Craig finished his meal. He rose from his chair, told Blade he would see him in the morning, and headed for the cash register where a teenage boy was working.

When Craig left the café, Blade looked up to see a young man come in and walk right up to Rena. She smiled at him and said, "I'll be ready to go in just a few minutes, Layne."

Blade noticed that it was closing time. He gulped down the last of his food, paid Randy at the cash register, and hurried outside. There, he waited in the shadows to watch for Rena and the young man she called Layne. They came out moments later, and Blade watched the man help Rena into his buggy. She was laughing at something he had just said, and patted his cheek.

"Layne Adams, I love your sense of humor!"

Blade Cultus clenched his teeth. Wrath rose up in him toward Layne Adams as he drove away with Rena.

Two days later, at the Powell home, Randy and Darin were ready to leave for school when there was a knock at the front door.

Randy said, "I'll get it, Mama," and hurried to the door. When he opened it, he found Pastor Richard Skiver there with Marshal Cade Ryer and his deputies, Jarrod Benson and Bruce Follmer. The look on their faces told him something was wrong.

"Randy, we need to talk to Rena," Pastor Skiver said.

"Sure, Pastor. Come in."

As the pastor and the lawmen stepped inside, Carrie, Rena,

and Darin were coming toward them, puzzlement showing on their features.

Marshal Ryer said in a broken voice, "Rena, Layne's landlord found him dead this morning in his room at the boardinghouse. Just like Carl, he had a hunting knife in his chest."

Carrie gasped, and Rena burst into tears. Pastor Skiver put an arm around Rena's shoulders and talked to her in soothing tones. They all sat down together in the parlor, and as Carrie and her sons held onto Rena, she stammered, "This is the second man I've dated who has…who has been murdered! Why is this happening?"

"I'm sure it's just a coincidence, Rena," the marshal said. "This certainly is not your fault."

Rena started to fall apart. Pastor Skiver knelt in front of her and did all he could to assure her that in no way was she at fault.

At the graveside service the next day, the mourners stood in a half-circle near the coffin, still in shock over what had happened to Layne Adams. Carrie Powell and her sons, as well as Rosie Skiver, were holding onto Rena, whose face was shiny with tears.

Hiding behind a tree several yards away, Blade Cultus observed the scene. When the pastor had finished his prayer, Blade noticed a young man step up to Rena. He took both her hands in his and spent several minutes talking to her.

When Rena wrapped her arms around him, clinging to him, Blade trembled with rage. When the young man stepped aside, allowing the pastor to talk to Rena, Blade heard someone call him Tom.

"Well, Tom," Blade said, "you'll never hug her again."

When the service was over and the crowd broke up, Blade followed Tom Hixson back into town, where he returned to his job at the wagon and farm implement repair shop. Blade waited across the street from the shop, gripping the handle of the hunting knife he held in his hand.

After a while, he crossed the street and entered the alley behind the shop. Peering inside from the alley, Blade waited until he saw that Tom was alone, then entered through the back door.

That night, when Carrie Powell, Rena, and the boys arrived home from the café in the bright moonlight, they were surprised to see Marshal Cade Ryer, his deputies, and Pastor Richard Skiver waiting for them on the porch.

Rena gasped. "Oh, no. What now?"

As they mounted the porch steps, the pastor said, "Rena, we have more bad news."

Carrie took hold of her daughter's hand as Marshal Ryer told the Powells about Tom Hixson being murdered at the repair shop. A customer had entered the shop and found Tom lying dead on the floor with a hunting knife in his chest.

Rena's whole body trembled as she sobbed, "It's all my fault! Carl, Layne, and Tom were murdered because they dated me! Oh, it's my fault that they're dead!"

Pastor Skiver laid a hand on her shoulder and looked into her tear-filled eyes. "Rena, you can't blame yourself."

"That's right," the marshal said. "With so many miners in Sacramento, it could be anybody. Whoever he is, he obviously doesn't want any other man in your life."

Deputy Bruce Follmer said, "Marshal, we've got to make this maniac think there's another man interested in Rena. I'm volunteering to be that man. If we make it appear that Rena and I are dating, the killer will come after me."

"Oh, no, Bruce!" Rena said. "I don't want you in any danger!"

"But the man must be caught, Rena. If we don't, he may just start murdering people at random. We've got to stop him."

"It *is* dangerous, but Bruce is right," the marshal said. "We must set a trap for this bloody killer. Jarrod and I will be watching Bruce closely, I promise you."

Rena put a shaky hand to her cheek. "Promise?"

Ryer grinned. "Promise."

In the days that followed, Bruce spent time with Rena, dropping into the café quite often and chatting with her in a friendly manner between her customers.

One evening, Blade Cultus was eating supper at the café when he saw the young deputy talking to Rena, and even flirting with her. Seething as he walked back to his shack on the American River, Blade decided to bring the whole thing to an end. He would take Rena and leave Sacramento with her.

Midafternoon the next day Rena was cleaning tables by herself. Lunchtime was over, and she was getting ready for business that evening. She heard the door open and turned to see an angry Blade Cultus stomping toward her. Before she could make a move, Blade grabbed her and growled, "You're mine, Rena, and I'm taking you away with me! Those men weren't good enough for you, anyway."

Blade dragged her out the door and was forcing her toward his wagon as she screamed for help when Deputy Bruce Follmer came out of a nearby store with Carrie Powell. While Carrie looked on in terror, Bruce dashed toward the scene. When Blade saw him coming, he forced Rena up to the wagon and grabbed a revolver. He locked Rena in the crook of his arm and put the muzzle to her head.

"Hold it right there, lawman!" Blade bellowed. "If I can't have her, nobody else can, either! Not even *you*! Back off, or I'll kill her!"

People were collecting in small groups along the street and looking on wide-eyed.

The deputy already had his gun in hand and cocked when he skidded to a stop. He saw quickly that Blade had forgotten to cock his revolver and that he was more than a head taller than Rena. Bruce aimed his Colt .45 at Cultus's face and said, "Let her go or I'll put a hole in your head!"

The killer looked at the lawman over the top of Rena's head and guffawed. "Don't try to kid me, tin star! You won't fire that gun! You might hit Rena!"

The Colt .45 in Bruce's steady hand roared, and Blade Cultus dropped in his tracks, taking Rena to the ground with him.

Bruce dashed to Rena, picked her up, and said, "It's all right, Rena. It's all over. He's dead."

That evening, Deputy Bruce Follmer entered Carrie's Café, wanting to see Rena more than he wanted to eat. He sat at an empty table by the front window and picked up the menu. He looked around the crowded room until his line of sight fell on Rena. A happy grin spread over his face as he watched her move from one table to another, order pad and pencil in hand.

Rena saw him, and moments later, she drew up to Bruce's table, smiling engagingly. "Hello, Deputy Marshal Bruce Follmer."

"Hello, yourself, Miss Rena Powell."

She giggled. "What would you like for supper?"

"I'll just have the blue-plate special, coffee, and a piece of apple pie."

"All right. Blue-plate special coming up."

Bruce's eyes followed her as she headed for the kitchen. She came back a short time later and set his food in front of him.

"There you are, sir."

"Thank you, honey."

Rena met his gaze. "Do you call all the girls 'honey'?"

Bruce's brow furrowed. "Absolutely not."

"I was just wondering."

He smiled. "Well, ah…it just came out. I guess because I really do like you."

Her eyebrows raised. "You guess?"

"Okay. I called you 'honey' because I really do like you."

This time, Rena was speechless.

"Rena, would you…would you consider going out with me after closing time some night soon?" Bruce asked.

"Of course. After all, you're my hero. You saved my life today!"

"Well, in that case, how about Saturday night? I'm off duty then. Do you like music?"

"I love it."

"Do you know about the outdoor concert in the park this Saturday night?"

"Yes."

"Well, I know you close the café at nine. The concert starts at eight, so we'd still get in on about an hour and a half of music. How does that sound?"

"Sounds wonderful to me."

"Good. I'll be here for supper at eight, then we can go to the concert as soon as the café closes."

On Saturday night, Bruce and Rena thoroughly enjoyed the concert in Sacramento's City Park.

When Bruce walked her home, they paused on the front porch, and he said, "Rena, could I spend tomorrow afternoon with you? I mean…if you don't have other plans."

Rena smiled. "No other plans. How about coming home with us after church? You could have dinner with us and stay the afternoon."

"You sure I won't be imposing?"

"Absolutely not! After what you did for me today? Don't you remember how my mother hugged you for saving my life?"

"Well, yes, but—"

"But *nothing*! Mama would love to have you for Sunday dinner, and so would my brothers. You ought to hear how they talk about you! Will you come?"

"I sure will."

Rena's face lit up with an inner glow. "Great! Then I'll see you at church in the morning."

"Thank you for such an enjoyable evening, Rena. I'll look forward to spending tomorrow afternoon with you."

Bruce took hold of her right hand, did a bow, and planted a kiss on it. He turned and started toward the street, then called over his shoulder, "See you at church in the morning, *honey*."

Rena's heart pounded as she gave him a wave and went inside.

From that night on, Bruce and Rena knew the Lord had chosen them for each other.

TWENTY-THREE

As Craig Turley worked his claim on the American River, he panned gold from the river some days, and others he spent digging in the dirt of the small piece of land.

One day in late September, Craig was kneeling on the bank of the river, panning for gold, when his thoughts went to Kathy Ross at the Turley mansion in New York. He found that he was missing her more every day.

He paused in his work, looked eastward, and a yearning look captured his eyes. Kathy was three thousand miles away. He wished he could see her and hold her in his arms.

After a moment, Craig shook himself and said, "Craig, ol' boy, now is not the time for daydreaming. You've got work to do."

On Tuesday afternoon, October 9, a smiling Craig Turley entered the United States Mint building that had been recently established in Sacramento. In each hand, he carried a heavily loaded canvas bag, which contained gold nuggets, and draped over his shoulder was a canvas bag loaded with gold dust.

A middle-aged man stood behind the counter, talking to two miners who had just brought in gold. Craig could see three other Mint employees at the rear of the room, working over coin minting machines.

The man behind the counter smiled at Craig. "I'll be with you in a few minutes, sir."

Craig nodded. "Fine. Thank you."

Nearly half an hour had passed when the two happy miners walked out with bags of gold coins.

The man behind the counter looked at Craig. "All right, sir. I can help you now."

Craig laid the heavy bags on the counter. "My name is Craig Turley, sir. I have a claim on the American River, and I just hit pay dirt! I was told that you could convert this gold dust and these nuggets into coins for me."

"Sure can, Mr. Turley," the man said. "I'm Ken Addleman, the manager. Have you seen the gold coins we produce?"

Craig shook his head. "No."

"Well, my men will melt down your gold for you, and with our machines, they'll stamp out gold coins in denominations called eagles."

Craig's eyebrows arched. "Eagles?"

"Yes sir. The largest we make is the twenty-dollar double eagle. We also make the ten-dollar eagle, the five-dollar half eagle, the three-dollar gold piece eagle, and the two-dollar-and-fifty-cent quarter eagle. You can choose what you want of each, once we weigh out the gold."

"All right. Weigh it, and I'll tell you how I want it."

Moments later, the gold had been weighed, and Craig was pleasantly surprised to learn that the gold he had carried in was worth fifty-two thousand dollars.

As his gold was being minted into eagles, Craig couldn't help but think of Proverbs 23:5, which his father had pointed out to him: *Riches certainly make themselves wings; they fly away as an eagle toward heaven.* He steeled himself against the thought that the gold he had just found could ever be taken from him.

In the days that followed, Craig found more gold, and each time it was being minted into eagles, he thought of Proverbs 23:5. To make sure his gold was safe, he made a small trap door in the floor of his shack underneath the new sofa he had recently purchased, then dug a hole in the dirt and hid the cold coins in a strong metal case. Each time he put more coins in the case, closed the trap door, and moved the sofa back over it, he told himself his gold was *not* going to fly away as an eagle.

One day while having more gold minted, Craig saw a man come in, carrying heavy canvas bags. Behind the counter, Ken Addleman looked past Craig and said, "Well, Mr. Ashlock, are you back again so soon?"

Craig noted the man's British accent as he said, "Yes, sir, Mr. Addleman! And my men are digging up more as we speak." With that, he stepped past Craig and placed the heavy bags on the counter.

"Well, good!" Addleman said. "Ah…Colin Ashlock, I'd like you meet another successful young man, Craig Turley from New York. Craig, Mr. Ashlock is from Australia."

Craig shook Colin's hand and said, "Glad to meet you, Mr. Ashlock. Sounds like you're doing all right."

Colin laughed. "You might say that. My hired men and I landed here in late June. As of yesterday, we've taken almost two million dollars' worth of gold out of our claim. I figure these bags have about fifty to sixty thousand worth, so it should put us well over two million."

"Wow! You're *really* doing all right!"

"So how long have you been here, Turley?"

"Almost a month."

"And how much have you made so far?"

"Well, I've done quite well, I think. With the gold I brought in today, my total is just under a hundred thousand dollars."

"Well, good. I hope you keep doing well. We're going to dig out another few thousand, then sail back to Australia."

Periodically, Craig Turley and Luke Daniels ran into each other at the mint, or some other place in town. Both were happy because of the gold they were finding.

On Saturday afternoon, October 13, Craig was panning gold on his claim when he looked up to see Luke walking toward him along the riverbank. They greeted each other as Luke drew up, and Craig asked, "To what do I owe this most welcome visit?"

"Well, I just wanted to come by and see if you would go to church with us tomorrow morning," Luke said. "You've told me several times that one of these Sundays you would go with the boys and me. How about tomorrow? I've told you before…you'll like Pastor Skiver's preaching."

Craig thought about how lonely he was. He smiled and nodded. "Okay, Luke. I'll do it."

The next morning, Craig sat in the preaching service with Luke and his sons. He found Pastor Richard Skiver's style of preaching captivating, though at times he felt an uneasiness as the preacher talked about sin and man's need of salvation.

Some things Skiver said reminded Craig of what his father, Maddie, and Kathy had told him...and of what Pastor Charles Finney had said to him. Once again, he heard the gospel plain and clear. When the sermon was finished and the invitation was given, several people walked the aisle to open their hearts to Jesus. But Craig Turley gripped the pew and steeled himself against it.

On Tuesday morning, October 16, Colin Ashlock and his crew headed to San Francisco with their gold coins in boxes. The five crewmen were jubilant over the amount of gold coins Colin had given them for helping him mine the gold. They knew that their boss still had well over a million and a half dollars for himself.

That evening, the *Bristol* sailed from San Francisco Bay onto the vast Pacific Ocean.

In Manhattan, New York, on Wednesday, October 17, Kathy Ross was in the front yard of the Turley mansion, standing beside the rose garden and holding a single long-stemmed rose in her hands. It was an unusually warm day, and even though the roses had faded some, she found that they were still beautiful and fragrant.

As she looked at the rose in her hands, she thought of Craig and said, "Craig, I miss you so very much." She took a deep breath and looked toward heaven. "Dear Lord, You've put this love in my heart for Craig, and I just know You will bring him home to me as a born-again child of Yours, and we will be able to enjoy the rest of our lives together."

Kathy saw the postman coming from the mansion next door. As he drew near the Turley yard, he smiled, lifted up several envelopes, and waved them at her. "Hello, Miss Kathy. Here's the mail."

Kathy moved toward him, took the mail in hand, and headed toward the front porch.

When she entered the house, her eyes were bright. Maddie was standing in the hallway and saw her smiling as she held the long-stemmed rose and several envelopes in one hand, but was looking at a single envelope in the other hand.

Maddie dashed to her. "Kathy, is that something special that came in the mail?"

"It sure is! It's a letter from your big brother postmarked in Wendover, Utah, on July 26."

"Who's it addressed to?"

"You, your father, and me. Do you suppose it's all right if we open it?"

"Sure! Papa won't care, since it's from Craig!"

Kathy laid the rose and the other mail on a table in the foyer and quickly ripped open the envelope. She handed it to Maddie. "Here, honey, you read it to me."

Craig's letter was dated July 26, 1849, and he first told Maddie and his father that he missed them, then said he missed Kathy, also. He apologized that he hadn't written before, but told them he was doing fine so far. He told them that because he had studied Joseph Ware's *Emigrant's Guide to California* and knew the route so well, the people of the wagon train had elected him to drive the lead wagon. He said they had just crossed the Great Salt Lake Desert and were about to enter Nevada. Closing it off, Craig told all three that he loved them, and that when he had made his fortune, he would come home and see them.

Both Kathy and Maddie wept and agreed that they must continue to pray hard for Craig. He had said nothing in the letter about receiving Jesus as his Saviour.

❧

On Sunday morning, October 28, the *Bristol* was sailing across the smooth, sapphire-blue south Pacific Ocean. Wilbur Mayfield was at the ship's wheel giving Captain Henry Briggs a break. Colin Ashlock, Briggs, and the other three crewmen were sitting on deck chairs, talking about the great fortune they had amassed in California.

Dave Adkinson smiled at his boss and said, "Now that you have the money from the gold, along with the ranch and your ship building company in Borneo, are you going to settle back and just enjoy life?"

Colin grinned and shook his head. "If you mean am I not going to seek more riches, the answer is *I am going to seek more riches*. I still want more."

Dave shrugged his shoulders, smiled, and looked out across the deep-blue sea.

As the hours passed, a stiff wind came up, and dark clouds blotted out the sun overhead. Captain Henry Briggs was back at the wheel, and steering the ship into waves that were rising almost as high as the ship's deck.

Because of the stiff wind, Colin had ordered his other four men to pull down the sails, and now he was standing with them on the tossing deck, holding onto the handrails. They watched the black smoke swirling as it came out of the smokestack, then disappeared quickly against the ever-darkening clouds above.

Chip turned to his boss. "Looks like we might have a heavy storm to battle."

Colin nodded. "Could be. We'd best go to the pilot's cabin."

In the next half hour, the wind stiffened, and the blue Pacific turned lead gray. Colin and the others stood behind Henry Briggs, watching the waves grow higher, spraying the cabin's windshield. The wind continued to grow stronger, and the rising waves lifted the *Bristol's* bow higher and higher, before dropping her into the angry, roiling sea.

Soon the storm was raging, and the foamy waters of the Pacific and the dark sky seemed to be crashing together. The waves broke over the bow, sprayed across the deck, and splashed against doors and walls, as well as the elevated pilot's cabin.

Soon, heavy rain joined the waves to pelt the ship, and Captain Briggs announced that the winds were now over sixty knots and growing stronger. The *Bristol* pitched and rolled in waves whitened by the wind, and was pummeled by the driving rain.

In the pilot's cabin, Briggs gripped the wheel to keep from being tossed about, and the others hung on to whatever they could.

The wind blew with greater fury. The boiling sea rose higher until the waves now towered above the ship, then exploded high into the air, salt spray mixing with rain. The wind drove it all with a furious whistle through the bare rigging.

Fighting the wheel, Captain Briggs looked back over his shoulder at his boss. Colin saw the fearful look and the pallor of terror on his face as he shouted above the roaring wind and waves, "Sir, we're in trouble! This ship can't take this battering much longer. I can tell by the sounds I'm hearing that it's coming apart!"

Colin's eyes bulged. "What? Coming apart?"

Suddenly there was a deep-throated ripping sound, and through the water-covered windshield, they saw a portion of the deck disappear at the bow. Just as suddenly, the wheel in the captain's hands began to spin freely.

Briggs's voice came with a strangled cry, "I no longer have any control over the ship!"

The ship abruptly lurched sideways, went down deep into the raging sea, and with an earsplitting sound, the entire deck just ahead of the pilot's cabin ripped apart.

The pilot's cabin suddenly tore free of its foundation and swirled about, tilting sharply, and tossing the men through its open door as it sailed downward into the ocean.

Colin Ashlock found himself being tossed about in the churning waters, and caught a glimpse of Briggs and Mayfield as they went beneath the surface, just as a broken piece of the ship appeared before him. He grabbed onto it and looked for the others, but they had already disappeared in the deep.

Colin gasped as water splashed in his face, filling his mouth. He spit it out repeatedly as the wooden piece whirled and bobbed. It took everything he had to hang on.

Moments passed, and Colin soon realized that his strength was playing out. He shook with terror, and his mind flashed back to the night that Charles Wesson tried to reason with him from the Scriptures.

Luke 12:20 echoed in his head: "Thou fool, this night thy soul shall be required of thee…"

With those words reverberating in his mind, Colin lost his grip, let out a wild cry, and went down into a watery grave.

By the last week in November, Craig Turley had amassed a genuine fortune. He had now minted eagle coins in the amount of nearly a million and a half dollars. He decided to keep working until he had doubled that amount, then see if he could leave the gold coins with Luke Daniels for safekeeping and make a trip home. He wanted to see his father and Maddie, but even more, he wanted to see Kathy. The love he felt for her filled his heart.

Craig knew that Kathy would not marry him unless he became a Christian. He convinced himself, however, that he could talk her into marrying him anyway.

On Thursday, November 29, Craig was busy panning gold at his claim site when he looked up to see Luke Daniels coming toward him along the riverbank. When Luke drew up, Craig laid down the pan and rose to his feet. "Hello, Luke. What brings you out here? I figured you'd be digging gold right now."

"Well, I was just at the post office to see if any mail had come from our friends in Iowa, and the postal clerk asked me to tell you that there's a letter addressed to you from Manhattan, New York. He couldn't give it to me to take to you, otherwise I would have. I thought since you've been going to the post office periodically the past couple of weeks to see if you had any mail, you'd want to know."

"Hey, my friend, I appreciate that. I'll finish filling this pan, then I'll head into town. Thanks for letting me know."

Craig worked another half hour, then took the pan of gold into the shack. When he came back out, he put the padlock in place on the front door and hurried into town.

At the post office, the clerk handed Craig the envelope. He saw that it was from Maddie Turley and Kathy Ross. The postmark showed that it had been mailed in February, shortly after he had left home.

Craig stepped outside, opened the envelope, and found two letters—one from Maddie and the other from Kathy. He decided to read Maddie's letter first. Tears filled his eyes as he read her kind, loving words. It made him miss his little sister even more than he had already.

He then read Kathy's letter, which brought even more tears. He was deeply touched by her words of love and her assurance that she was praying for him. "Oh, Kathy I miss you terribly," he said.

He hurried back to the riverbank and hastened toward his claim site. When he moved up to the shack, he froze in his tracks. His mouth went dry when he saw the broken padlock lying on the wooden floor of the small porch and the door swaying in the breeze.

With his heart pounding, he dashed inside. The kitchen cupboards had been rifled, and furniture was turned over and scattered about.

His eyes were drawn to the trap door, which had been covered by the sofa. It was open. "Oh, no!" he gasped. He dashed to it, fell on his knees, and looked into the hole for the four metal cases he had filled with gold coins. They were gone.

Craig clenched his fists and blinked back the tears that sprang to his eyes and burned like the bile that was pushing into his throat.

When he regained control of himself, he went into town to the marshal's office to report the theft. Marshal Cade Ryer and his deputies went with him to the shack. After examining the broken padlock and the shack's interior, Marshal Ryer told Craig no clues had been left that could help identify the guilty person or persons. Craig went with the lawmen to question other miners on claim sites nearby, but no one had seen the thief or thieves at his shack.

Craig stood at the door and watched the lawmen ride away until they were out of view, then devastated at his loss, he straightened up the shack, put everything in place, and sat down on the sofa.

His mind went to the passage in Proverbs his father had pointed out to him: "Labour not to be rich: cease from thine own wisdom. Wilt thou set thine eyes upon that which is not? for riches certainly make themselves wings; they fly away as an eagle toward heaven."

All of his gold eagles had made themselves wings and flown away.

Pastor Richard Skiver opened the door of his study in response to the knock. When he saw who it was, he smiled. "Well, hello, Craig. Come in."

Craig stepped into the office, his face drawn and pale.

"Something's wrong, Craig. What is it?"

Craig quickly told the man of God how all of his gold coins had been stolen, and how Marshal Cade Ryer and his deputies could find no evidence of who did it.

Skiver laid a compassionate hand on his shoulder. "Craig, I'm so sorry."

"I know why God allowed this to happen, Pastor."

"You do?"

"Yes. I've been fighting Him for a long time, and now I'm through. Pastor, I want to be saved. I need Jesus to be my Saviour."

A smile spread over the pastor's face. "Well, praise the Lord! Sit down here on the sofa."

With a Bible between them, Richard Skiver reviewed with Craig a number of passages that talked about the gospel and repentance and faith in the Lord Jesus. Then he said, "Craig, are you willing to call on Jesus in repentance of your sin, receive Him into your heart, trusting Him and *only* Him to save your soul, wash your sins away in His blood, make you a child of God by the new birth, and take you to heaven when you die?"

Tears were now spilling down Craig's cheeks. "Yes, sir. I am."

"Then let's bow before Jesus right now, and you call on Him."

After Craig had called on Jesus for salvation, Pastor Skiver asked the Lord to bless him and use him for His glory.

Wiping tears, Craig told Skiver about Pastor Charles Finney likening him to the prodigal son, and how right he was. "I still have enough money in my pocket to travel home. This prodigal son is going home to his father and ask his forgiveness."

Pastor Skiver said, "Craig, I know a way for you to travel between San Francisco and New York that takes only four or five months."

"Really?"

"Mm-hmm. You can sail from San Francisco to Panama, then cross the isthmus of Panama by river and by land, board another ship at Panama City, and make it to New York by mid-April."

"Sounds wonderful to me, Pastor. I'll leave as soon as I can let the Miners' Association know that I'm vacating the claim site."

The next day, Craig Turley was in San Francisco Bay aboard a ship that was sailing to Panama. Standing at the rail alone, he looked out on the blue horizon. "What a fool I've been," he said quietly. "I had everything I needed right there in New York. Thank You, Lord, for waking this fool up. I can hardly wait to see Kathy, Dad, and Maddie, and tell them of my new birth."

He took a deep breath as the ship glided its way toward home...*and toward Kathy.*

TWENTY-FOUR

New Year's Day 1850 came, and soon winter was past.

In Manhattan on Thursday morning, April 18, there was a knock at the door of the Turley mansion. Housekeeper Adelle Brown was dusting in the parlor, and she left the feather duster on the mantel, hurried into the foyer, and opened the door. She smiled. "Oh, hello, Charlotte. Please come in."

Charlotte McClain's features showed that she was upset about something. As she stepped in, she said, "Adelle, I need to talk to Mr. Turley. Is he feeling well enough to see me?"

"I'm sure he is. Right now, he's in the library with Maddie and Kathy. Come on. I'll take you in."

As they walked down the hall, Adelle said, "You seem upset, Charlotte. Is something wrong at the office?"

"Yes. Very much wrong. Mr. Turley can tell you if he pleases, after I advise him of what's happened."

The library door was open as they approached it. Adelle stepped ahead of Charlotte and said, "Mr. Turley, your secretary is here to see you."

Wallace was sitting in his favorite overstuffed chair, with

Maddie and Kathy on the sofa, facing him. He was wrapped in a blanket. All three turned to look that way. Wallace, whose features were a pasty white, smiled and nodded.

Kathy rose to her feet. "Please come in, Charlotte."

Adelle closed the door and headed back to the parlor. Kathy guided Charlotte to an overstuffed chair next to the sofa, then sat down once again beside Maddie.

Wallace's brow furrowed as he saw the strained look on his secretary's face. His voice was weak as he asked, "What is it, Charlotte?"

"Sir, I have just learned that Dirk Reyes is trying to take over the corporation."

Wallace licked his lips, the left corner of his mouth twitching. "What? Are you sure?"

"Yes, sir. I have found positive evidence of it. He has been working at it ever since you had your stroke in October. He has stolen large sums of money from the corporation, too. I have proof."

"You mean you can prove all of this from corporate records?"

"Yes, sir. When we bring in the law, they'll see it. It will stand up in court, sir. The evidence will convince any judge and jury."

Wallace stammered in his weak voice, "In spite of my...condition, I must...I must handle this matter."

Charlotte shook her head. "Mr. Turley, I'm afraid what it might do to you to handle it yourself. If you confront Dirk, there will undoubtedly be a heated argument, and it would just be too much for you. I want to see someone else with authority handle it. One of your other vice presidents, such as—"

There was a knock at the library door.

Kathy hurried to the door and found the housekeeper there, her eyes bright and dancing. "What is it, Adelle?"

In a hushed voice, Adelle said, "Can you and Maddie come out? There's someone here who wants to see you. It's very important, believe me."

Kathy turned and said, "Mr. Turley, Adelle says there's someone here to see Maddie and me, and it's very important. Will you excuse us?"

"Of course."

Maddie slid off the sofa, a puzzled look on her face, and hurried to the door. Adelle backed away, and Kathy took Maddie's hand.

"Who's here to see us?" Maddie asked.

Kathy shook her head. "I don't know. Who is it, Adelle?"

"Come and see. He's in the parlor. Hurry!"

As Kathy and Maddie walked beside the housekeeper down the long hall, Maddie said, "Can't you tell us who it is before we go in the parlor?"

Adelle shook her head. "I'll open the door, and you two can go in without me."

When they reached the door, Adelle motioned for them to stand back a ways, stuck her head in and smiled. She then turned to Maddie and Kathy. "All right. You can go in now."

Maddie and her governess stepped into the parlor.

"Craig!" Maddie squealed, and threw herself into his open arms.

Kathy moved closer, hardly able to believe her eyes.

"Oh, Craig!" Maddie said excitedly, "I'm so glad to see you! Are you all right? Why are you back so soon? Oh, I'm so very, very glad you're home!"

"I'm fine, honey," said Craig, looking over his little sister's head at Kathy.

Kathy stood smiling at him, her dark brown eyes sparkling.

Craig kissed the top of Maddie's head, squeezed her again, and said, "I'll explain later why I'm back so soon. All right if I give Kathy a hug?"

Maddie looked up at him and giggled. "Of course."

Kathy and Craig rushed toward each other and embraced.

When they let go and eased back, Craig looked into Kathy's eyes and said, "I've missed you. I mean, I've *really* missed you."

"I've missed you, too," she said softly.

Maddie moved up, and Craig put an arm around her. He ran his gaze between them. "Adelle told me about Dad's stroke, so I wouldn't be shocked when I see him. It was in October, she said."

Kathy nodded. "October seventeenth. Did she tell you he's doing much better now?"

"Yes. I'm so glad to know that."

"There's something else you need to know, Craig. Your father put Dirk Reyes in charge of the corporation shortly after he had the stroke. Charlotte McClain is here right now. She just discovered that Dirk is trying to take over the corporation behind your father's back, and she has proof that he has embezzled a large amount of money. Your father wants to handle the matter, but Charlotte is trying to talk him into letting someone else in the corporation handle it. She knows your father is in no condition to do it."

Craig nodded and bit his lower lip. "How about I go see him now?"

Kathy smiled. "Of course."

When they stepped into the library, Wallace wept with joy to see his son. After they embraced, Craig greeted Charlotte and asked her about Dirk Reyes. Charlotte told him what proof she had of Dirk's skullduggery.

Craig looked at his father, then back at Charlotte. "I'm home to stay, which I'll explain later. And I want you to know I'll take care of having Dirk arrested and prosecuted for his deeds."

"Oh, son, I'm so glad you're home," Wallace said. "I know you'll handle Dirk appropriately."

After Charlotte was gone, Craig sat down on the sofa in front of his father while Maddie and Kathy looked on, and said, "Dad, the prodigal son has come home—just like the one in the Bible. Broke."

Kathy and Maddie sat down on either side of Craig as he explained how he lost his entire fortune. He added quickly that he knew it was the Lord who allowed it to happen. He referred to Proverbs 23:4–5 and said, "Dad, just as it says, my golden eagles sprouted wings and flew away."

Craig told them how the Lord had been dealing with him ever since he left home, of the many Christians who witnessed to him, and how Pastor Richard Skiver had led him to the Lord.

Maddie squealed and wrapped her arms around her big brother. "Oh, Craig, this is so wonderful! You're going to be in heaven with us!"

Kathy hugged him, weeping for joy. Wallace lifted shaky arms, and Craig rose from the sofa. They wept together as Wallace praised the Lord over and over for answered prayer.

When their emotions had settled down some, Wallace said, "Son, since you're home to stay, I want you to take over the corporation as president. I'll double the salary you were getting as first vice president before you left."

Tears filled Craig's eyes. "Thank you, Dad. I'll be honored to be your new president. And as I said, I'll handle this Dirk Reyes problem personally. Reyes will go to prison."

"You don't know how glad I am that you're here to take care of this," Wallace said.

Craig wiped tears and said, "Now, Dad...Maddie...if you will excuse us, I need to talk to Kathy alone for a few minutes."

"Of course."

Moments later, Craig and Kathy entered the parlor. Craig guided her to the sofa, sat her down, then sat down beside her.

He looked into her eyes. "Kathy, is there some other young man in your life?"

She smiled. "No."

He took both of her hands in his. "Kathy, I've been such a fool. Everything I've ever needed is right here. I knew before I ever left that you were very special to me, but I didn't realize *how* special until time and miles separated us. I've been in love with you since long before I left home, but I didn't realize it until I was away from you. I've missed you terribly. I should never have gone away."

Tears misted Kathy's eyes.

Craig squeezed her hands. "Kathy, I was wrong, but God has forgiven me for my stubborn foolishness. Will you please forgive me as well?"

The tears started down Kathy's cheeks. She looked down at their entwined hands, then up at him again. In a voice barely above a whisper, she said, "Of course, Craig."

Craig swallowed hard. "Now, I need to ask you another question. Do you still love me like you said in your letter?"

Kathy smiled through her tears. "Yes, darling. I just love you more since I wrote that letter over a year ago. And—and I love you even more since I know you're now a child of God."

Craig smiled. "Kathy, you are my everything. I love you more than words could ever tell." He slipped from the sofa and went to his knees, still clutching her hands. "Kathy, will you marry me?"

"I thought you'd never ask. Yes, darling, I will marry you!"

They returned to Wallace and Maddie, and when the engagement was announced, both father and little sister rejoiced.

"Of course, this means Maddie will have to have another governess," Craig said.

Maddie looked up into her brother's eyes, and a huge grin spread from ear to ear. "That's all right. I'd rather have Kathy be my sister-in-law than my governess."

Kathy hugged Maddie, and they praised the Lord together for all His blessings.

In the days that followed, Dirk Reyes was arrested, and in court was convicted of his embezzlement. The judge sentenced him to ten years in prison.

On Saturday, June 8, 1850, Craig and Kathy were married by Pastor Charles Finney in a beautiful ceremony at their church. After the reception in the fellowship hall, Craig and Kathy made their way to their new horse and buggy in a shower of rice and words of congratulations from their friends, and the groom took his bride to the new home he had bought in the Central Park West section.

Kathy sat on the seat in her beautiful white wedding dress, smiling while her groom hopped out of the buggy, rounded it, and stepped up to her with open arms.

"Mrs. Turley," he said, his own smile glistening, "may I carry you over the threshold of our new house?"

"Yes, you may."

He took her in his arms and carried her up the steps of the front porch. Pausing at the door, he said, "Kathy, after all that searching for gold, then losing it all, I've finally realized just where *true* riches are."

"Where, darling?"

"Right here in my arms!"

She kissed him soundly. His heart pounding, Craig opened the door and carried his bride over the threshold.

EPILOGUE

Although our story ends in June of 1850, the gold rush in California went on until the late 1850s. Many people rushed to the Sacramento area to seek gold in 1848, but the big rush came in 1849, which served to tag even those who came before and after the Forty-niners.

California became the thirty-first state of this country on September 9, 1850.

The peak of the gold rush, in terms of gold output and mining population, was in 1852. By that time, 100,000 miners and would-be miners swarmed through the central valleys of the newly admitted state and up the western slopes of the Sierra Nevada Mountains.

Whether they arrived in 1848, 1849, or in the 1850s—distinctions that those who participated might make among themselves—to the rest of the world they were, and are still today, the Forty-niners.

The Orphan Train Trilogy

THE LITTLE SPARROWS, Book #1

Kearney, Cheyenne, Rawlins. Reno, Sacramento, San Francisco. At each train station, a few lucky orphans from the crowded streets of New York City receive the fulfillment of their dreams: a home and family. This orphan train is the vision of Charles Loring Brace, founder of the Children's Aid Society, who cannot bear to see innocent children abandoned in the overpopulated cities of the mid–nineteenth century. Yet it is not just the orphans whose lives need mending—follow the train along and watch God's hand restore love and laughter to the right family at the right time!

ISBN 1-59052-063-7

ALL MY TOMOROWS, Book #2

When sixty-two orphans and abandoned children leave New York City on a train headed out West, they have no idea what to expect. Will they get separated from their friends and siblings? Will their new families love them? Will a family even pick them at all? Future events are wilder than any of them could imagine—ranging from kidnappings and whippings to stowing away on wagon trains, from starting orphanages of their own to serving as missionaries to the Apache. No matter what, their paths are being watched by Someone who cares about and carefully plans all their tomorrows.

ISBN 1-59052-130-7

WHISPERS IN THE WIND, Book #3

Young Dane Weston's dream is to become a doctor. But it will take more than just determination to realize his goal, once his family is murdered and he ends up in a colony of street waifs begging for food. Then he ends up mistaken for a murderer himself and sentenced to life in prison. Now what will become of his friendship with the pretty orphan girl Tharyn, who wanted to enter the medical profession herself? Does she feel he is anything more than a big brother to her? And will she ever write him again?

ISBN 1-59052-169-2

Mail Order Bride Series

Desperate men who settled the West resorted to unconventional measures in their quest for companionship, advertising for and marrying women they'd never even met! Read about a unique and adventurous period in the history of romance.

Shadow of Liberty Series

Let Freedom Ring
Book One

It is January 1886 in Russia. Vladimir Petrovna, a Christian husband and father of three, faces bankruptcy, persecution for his beliefs, and despair. The solutions lie across a perilous sea.

ISBN 1-57673-756-X

The Secret Place
Book Two

Popular authors Al and JoAnna Lacy offer a compelling question: As two young people cope with love's longings on opposite shores, can they find the serenity of God's covering in *The Secret Place*?

ISBN 1-57673-800-0

A Prince Among Them
Book Three

A bitter enemy of Queen Victoria kidnaps her favorite great-grandson. Emigrants Jeremy and Cecelia Barlow book passage on the same ship to America, facing a complex dilemma that only all-knowing God can set right.

ISBN 1-57673-880-9

Undying Love
Book Four

Nineteen-year-old Stephan Varda flees his own guilt and his father's rage in Hungary, finding undying love from his heavenly Father—and a beautiful girl—across the ocean in America.

ISBN 1-57673-930-9